NIGHT OF THE ANGELS

by

William Kerr

For Marsha,
A good friend or
lovely, lovely lady.
Enjoy the read

William Kerr
(Bill)

Night of the Angels is a work of fiction.
Names, characters, Places (other than governmental
or other such locations open to public access)
and incidents are the products of the author's
imagination or are
used fictitiously. Any resemblance to actual events,
locales or persons, living or dead, is entirely
coincidental.

ISBN: 9781095554425

Cover Art by RAK

Other Novels by William Kerr

Dragon Path
(Path of the Golden Dragon)

The Red Hand

The Collector

Death's Bright Angel

Judgment Call

Mark of the Devil

Night Scream

Deadly Logic

Tears of the Gods

DEDICATION

To the members of the
Ponte Vedra (Florida) Writers Group
for their thoughtful critique of my work.
More importantly,
the warm friendship shared by all.

ACKNOWLEDGMENTS

My deep appreciation to both the Central Intelligence Agency, the British Foreign Office and the London Metropolitan Police (New Scotland Yard) for providing much of the research material for this book. Also, the Staff of the Imperial War Museum and Churchill's wartime underground headquarters, the Cabinet War Rooms. Finally, my thanks to the National Trust and the hospitality shown my wife and myself during our visit to Sir Winston Churchill's beloved Chartwell.

NIGHT OF THE ANGELS

by
William Kerr

Chapter 1

Guernsey, British Channel Islands
October 2007

Roberts finned his way some twenty feet beneath the night-darkened surface of the Gulf. Only the greenish glow of the compass face mounted inside the air and depth gauge console broke the suffocating blackness of surrounding water. Twice since leaving the relative safety of the small inflatable he had felt a nudge against his legs from some invisible creature. Twice, icy tentacles of fear had swept the length of his spinal column. But Roberts refused to give way to something he could neither see nor defend against. Too much at stake, and from the elapsed time on his watch, he knew he was almost there.

Maintaining the lubber line on the compass between 350° and due north, Roberts angled his body upward until his head broke the surface. A grunt of satisfaction formed in the lower reaches of his throat. More than a quarter mile of underwater navigation by compass, and now he was less than fifty yards from shore. Only a single line of surf separated him from what he knew to be a narrow white
sand and pebble beach.

With his head and the tip of the torpedo-shaped air tank on his back barely above surface, he allowed the tide to carry him toward the shore. At the same time, long since accustomed to the darkness and now aided by a partial moon nodding in and out of the clouds, Roberts surveyed the beach and as far beyond as the night would allow.

Just inland at the entrance to a narrow valley, Roberts could see the outline of a tall, circular stone tower, a dark, deserted sentinel from the time of Napoleon. It had been built to protect the valley and its surrounding hills from an invader's seaward approach.

As he worked his way closer, he could almost feel the haunting gaze of the tower's sentry ports. Black openings placed in stair-step fashion from the structure's lowest level, one port, then another, moving up, round and round to the tower's highest point. A concrete sea wall he estimated to be approximately four to five feet in height stretched across the width of the beach. Like a bulkhead to hold back the constantly eroding surf from the base of the tower. A two-foot-high guardrail ran across the top of the wall.

On either side of the beach were sharply angled slopes covered with vast growths of bracken and prickly gorse. Shadowy hills rose steeply from the valley and its lonely tower until they abruptly peaked in cliff-like promontories, leaning out over the northern waters of the Gulf of St. Malo. With the exception of a clearing, which offered a spectacular view of the Gulf, he knew from earlier reconnaissance that a line of trees stood near the top of the westernmost hill. Their thickness shielded the ancient village of St. Cyril de la Bot. And there lay his target.

The surf, as minimal as it was, rolled him once,

and then his fins scuffed against the sand bottom. With the water now only chest deep, he stood and, with the fins on his feet restricting movement, shuffled sideways toward the beach.

* * *

From within the tower, hidden by stonewalls and darkness, a man named Brendan pushed back the monk's cowl from his head and moved closer to the sentry port. Very slowly he scanned the length of beach. Back and forth, not once allowing his eyes to remain on any particular spot. But the fatigue of boredom had taken its toll several hours earlier. He longed for the tiny cot and roll of blankets in the room below, but Damien had said...

Suddenly, movement! The faint light of the moon revealed the silhouette of a man slowly emerging from the waters of the Gulf. The man's body, all in black, was slightly bent from something heavy, presumably an air tank, strapped across his back. The moon reflected momentarily off the mirror-like lens of a dive mask.

Brendan picked up the telephone, listened for a click at the distant end, and whispered nervously, "Tell Damien he's here. What should I do?"

At an adjacent sentry port, another eye, cold, calculating and without feeling, moved with the intermittent image of the diver as the man worked himself free of the heavy graphite fins on his feet, then made his way farther up the beach. The wet suit, its outer layer of neoprene rubber chilled by the dark waters, created confusion for the heat-sensing eye until the broken image disappeared below the top of the sea wall.

Unlike Brendan, the eye waited, patiently, its "brain" programmed to know about things that moved in the night, about living creatures and the warmth of their bodies.

* * *

Moving close against the base of the sea wall, Roberts removed the facemask, the buoyancy jacket holding the air tank, the weight belt and finally, the wet suit. Around his waist was a waterproof pouch held snug against his body by an overlapping Velcro strap.

After slaking the dampness from his body with the edges of his hands, Roberts removed and opened the pouch, quickly dressing himself in a dark nylon warm-up jacket, jogging pants and soft neoprene slip-on shoes. This was followed by a black balaclava, which he pulled over his head, leaving only eyes, nose and mouth exposed to the night.

Next, a small Colt Mustang .380 semiautomatic pistol and two extra ammunition magazines which he tucked inside the jacket. The only things remaining in the pouch were a one and a half-kilo cake of Semtex with its pencil-shaped, radio-activated detonator wrapped in plastic.

Strapping the pouch again around his waist, the weight of the Semtex resting against the small of his back, Roberts paused and looked toward the sky. He waited for a large, rounded puff of clouds to race across the hills and slip beneath the moon.

As light faded and darkness settled even deeper, he pulled himself to the top of the wall. He crouched for a moment, looking first one way, then another, listening, alert to the sounds of the night. Finally satisfied, he eased one leg over the metal railing, then stopped, quickly reaching for the pistol. Something was wrong. He couldn't identify the source, but he knew he was being watched.

* * *

High in the tower, the eye sensed the heat of living prey, the clear image of a man on top of the sea wall. The man's image transferred immediately to the software in its "brain" and onto a small, target-data display screen.

With hands trembling from excitement, Brendan reached to the command module and pushed the button marked SELF FIRE MODE.

* * *

A narrow shaft of light penetrated the night, a pencil-thin laser beam from one of the sentry ports near the top of the stone tower. Roberts saw it for only a millisecond. Like a surgeon's scalpel, dissecting with white-hot precision, the beam cut deep into his chest. His cry, more of surprise than pain, turned into a deep-throated gurgle as organs exploded inside his rib cage, torrents of steaming blood erupting from both mouth and nose.

Body spread-eagled in midair, he toppled backwards to the rocks and sand below. Though a reddish glow emanated from the crumpled heap, there was no further movement, no call for help, no cry of pain. Only silence at the foot of the wall and the sound of tidal water sucking at the beach.

* * *

Two men, both dressed in monk's robes and hoods to protect against the chill, made their way across the sand toward the base of the sea wall. Even before they could kneel beside the lifeless figure, the acrid stench of burned flesh penetrated their nostrils; the faint sizzle of internal body fluids still boiling created a barely audible fizzing sound in their ears.

Tugging the blood-soaked balaclava from the dead man's head, Damien, the larger of the two robed men, switched on a small flashlight. Despite the smear of blood coagulated around the man's lips and chin, the youngish face that stared back seemed almost placid; the surprise and anguish sounded in its earlier cry gone forever.

Damien guided the light down along the body. Where the chest had been, a gaping cavity yawned wide. Nylon jacket, melted; skin, flesh and bone, charred beyond recognition; arteries and vessels cauterized as if seared by some gigantic soldering iron. Wisps of steam still rose from the burn-encrusted opening.

Brendan, standing just behind Damian's shoulder, gagged at both sight and odor, but held his gaze. "Is this the one?"

"Yes," Damien answered as he pushed to his feet and turned toward the Gulf. A swath of moonlight stretched like a broad path across the waters. To Damien, it symbolized access by both the wanted and the unwanted.

"And he'll not be the last," Damien warned. "As long as we've the secret to guard, there's sure to be more to come."

Chapter 2

One Week Later

Langley, Virginia

The leased automobile sat idling in the gray, rain-soaked afternoon while an overly officious guard checked Royce Hawkins' identification. It had been at least two years, maybe longer, he couldn't remember, since he'd visited CIA headquarters. To be honest, so far as he was concerned, he could have gone the rest of his career without ever coming back.

In an attempt to delay the inevitable and provide a few extra minutes to himself, he had taken the long way around: the Dulles Access Road to the Beltway and then north to the George Washington Memorial Parkway. Only today, the rain had done little more than accentuate his dreariness after the long, mostly uncomfortable flight from London.

A sharp tap against the glass brought him back to the moment. The guard's voice grew in volume as the window slid down into the door and Hawkins' identification card was handed back to him. "A temporary parking space has been reserved in your name in front of the auditorium near the main entrance. Mr. Samuelson's expecting you."

After parking the car, Hawkins made his way into the central lobby and ran the gauntlet of security checks designed, not only to establish identity, but to insure he carried no undeclared weapons or explosives hidden within his clothing. There were times that, yes, he would like the place to simply disappear for all the good it did.

At least all those bureaucrats like Herb Samuelson. The ones who more often than not crawled back into their ass-saving shells when hard, life-and-death decisions had to be made.

A smirk crossed his face as he passed the words etched into the south wall of the lobby:

And ye shall know the truth and the truth shall make you free.
John VIII-XXXII

"Bullshit!" he muttered under his breath.
After a silent, unaccompanied elevator ride, the tiled, fifth floor corridor, otherwise deserted, echoed with his footsteps until he stopped. The door, large and stained the color of rich mahogany, supported a single laminated plate which read:

DEPUTY DIRECTOR, OPERATIONS.

He fingered a button at the side of the door, heard the electronic buzz from somewhere inside, and pushed his way in.

Entering a small outer office, he moved past an unoccupied secretary's desk toward an open door.

"Hawk," a familiar voice called out. "Ruppert and I were just talking about you. Glad you could make it."

"As if I had a choice," Hawkins answered, a layer of sarcasm thick on his voice.

Herb Samuelson, CIA Deputy Director for Operations, stood and extended a chubby, well-manicured hand as Hawkins walked across the heavily carpeted floor. Large, rain-splattered windows overlooking the wooded suburbs of Northern Virginia served as a backdrop for the cherubic-faced, overweight Deputy Director.

Hawkins knew Herb Samuelson well, almost too well. Just past fifty years of age, Samuelson had moved rapidly up the ladder to head the largest of four major CIA departments. Headquarters and foreign assignments in espionage and counterespionage as well as tours with the plans and covert action staffs had marked his phenomenal rise.

Hawkins, Samuelson's senior in age by a good ten years, had once been his field supervisor, but now their positions were reversed. That reversal had been the beginning of the end of their relationship.

Samuelson quickly became a micromanaging midget in Hawkins' eyes, while he, Hawkins, had never taken well to someone constantly supervising his every move. Especially a desk jockey who always erred on the side of caution, politically speaking.

"Give me the mission," Hawkins would say, "and I'll get it done. Just stay out of my hair." He had fought with Samuelson over policy decisions for the past five years and he'd be damned if he was going to change.

After a quick, obligatory handshake, Hawkins turned to Ruppert Bailey. The memory of their past friendship brought a smile to his face.

"How the hell are you, Roop? Still with the gadget and gun brigade? Pumping out new toys for all the double O-Seven wannabes?"

Bailey, a handsome, gray-around-the-edges black man in his middle sixties, one of the agency's whiz kids in what Hawkins considered the "good old days," shook hands and laughed. "No way. Graduated to Science and Technology a couple of years back.

"Besides, gadgets and guns are out! With DOD,

Homeland Security, Justice and FBI getting all the funding after we took blame for the screw-ups before Nine-Eleven and Iraq, we're at the bottom of the money tree.   All we can issue nowadays are smiles and handshakes."

"So why are you here?" Hawkins asked.   "Now? This meeting?"

"Because of the subject matter," Bailey answered, "and…"   Bailey paused a moment before saying, "And to act as referee between you two."

With one eyelid raised in question, Hawkins stared at Bailey.   "What the hell does that mean?"

"C'mon Hawk.   You know as well as I do, you and Herb have been operating on different wave lengths for years."

Knowing exactly what Bailey meant, Hawkins shrugged his shoulders, then turned back to Samuelson. "Okay, Herb," he drawled in a broad Texas accent he'd managed to retain over the years, "so much for the glad hand.   What the hell's so important you had to call me in from London 'stead of usin' the scrambler phone?   These six-and-seven-hour flights and half-a-dozen time zones beat hell out of an old guy like me."

"You're here because I wanted you here.   That's reason enough for now."

Refusing to take the bait, Hawkins flopped his slim, six foot three, still well-proportioned frame into a vacant chair in front of Samuelson's desk.   He sighed as he loosened his tie and ran his hands through a field of steel-gray, crew-cut hair.

"Anyway, too bad your flight was so lousy," Samuelson answered.   At the same time, he turned slightly in his swivel chair and watched rivulets of rain stretch down the windows.

"Regardless of our current problems, we go back a long way, don't we, Hawk? You and Susan and me in Tel Aviv, weekends in Beirut before it got ripped apart, covert ops in the Middle East. Hell of a time, wasn't it? Everybody, even the Arabs, called you Dirty Harry 'cause you looked so much like the Eastwood guy in those detective movies."

"Uh-huh." A seedling of suspicion was already taking root in Hawkins' mind.

"And then you and Susan on the rocks, the divorce. Me finding you in that roach-infested taverna in Athens, sucking on a bottle of ouzo, so screwed up you didn't know the Acropolis from a hole in the ground. I took care of you, didn't I?"

Hawkins, suddenly alert, pulled in his legs and sat straight in the chair. "What the fuck are you talkin' about, Herb?"

Still staring out the window, Samuelson went on. "Dried you out, and nobody knew the difference. You were clean so far as the Company was concerned, and you still are because I've busted my ass to keep it that way."

Pushing rapidly to his feet and punching the center of his chest with his thumb, Hawkins growled, "And you drag my ass all the way from London just to rehash crap I don't even wanna remember?" Hawkins spun on his heels and started toward the door. "I'm not believin' this shit!"

Ruppert Bailey moved quickly from his chair to head Hawkins off before he could leave. "For chrissake, Hawk, cool it a minute. What Herb's trying to say is he's been there when you needed help, and now he needs yours. How about it?"

With Bailey's hand guiding him by the arm,

Hawkins returned to his chair. A frustrated sigh accompanied his words. "Awright, Herb, I'll ask again. What the fuck's the problem?"

The chair squeaked as Samuelson twisted back around to face the two men. "Nikolai Pachenko. KGB colonel. Defected in eighty-seven."

"He died six years ago. So what?"

"Something he told us. A set of plans for a weapon system smuggled out of Germany in late nineteen forty-four by a Nazi scientist named Gustav, uh..."

"Schiller," Bailey reminded. "Gustav Schiller."

"Right." Samuelson nodded his thanks. "The Reds figured they were delivered to Churchill during the Yalta Conference in February forty-five, and Churchill sneaked them out of the country in a painting. An icon Stalin presented to him as a sign of friendship during the conference."

"Wait a minute, Herb. How did Pachenko know all this?"

"Pachenko was a junior officer in the NKGB. Assigned to Churchill's Yalta quarters as security for the Prime Minister and his staff."

"What kinda weapon system we talkin' about? Nineteen forty-five's ancient history. Fuckin' prehistoric, in fact."

Bailey fielded the question. "A laser weapon for use with refocusing mirrors on hilltops to hit distant targets. The Germans were apparently fifteen to twenty years ahead of us in laser development. Their concept was, in fact, surprisingly similar to certain elements of Ronald Reagan's Strategic Defense Initiative. The Star Wars thing."

"The Germans ever use it?"

"Against tank columns on the Russian front near

the end of the war. A prototype, but it was destroyed to keep the Russians from getting it."

Samuelson again grabbed the lead. "Schiller brought the plans into Russia when he escaped from Peenemünde, a military research and development installation in the north of Germany. Our man Pachenko was the one who eventually led Schiller to Churchill."

"But why would a young, supposedly gung-ho NKGB officer like Pachenko do somethin' like that?"

"Some kind of deal," Samuelson explained. "One of Churchill's aides, a Royal Marine colonel, promised to get both men out of the Soviet Union following the war. Within a month, however, Schiller was caught, tortured and hanged. Without the scientist, Pachenko's value dropped below the line. He never heard from Churchill or the colonel again."

"How come, all of a sudden, these plans are such a hot item?"

Samuelson stood and began pacing in the area between the windows and the back of his desk. "The icon disappeared after Churchill returned from Yalta. Finally turned up in ninety-five and was stolen in ninety-six. Since we know England never developed the weapon, worst case says the plans were still hidden inside the icon when it was stolen. Since then, nobody's seen or heard of the damn thing until last month."

"DEA," Bailey added. "One of their guys working with the French National Police on a drug bust in the south of France stumbled onto something that sounded like the icon."

Hawkins held up his hand. "Whoa up, you two. Since I don't work the froggy side of the Channel, sounds to me like you oughta be talkin' to our man in Paris, not me."

Samuelson shook his head. "From what we've determined, the icon, if that's what it really is, is somewhere in England. That's why I sent Roberts to London, to see if –"

"Roberts?" Hawkins jerked forward in his chair, flush with anger. "Who the hell is Roberts? I'm Chief of London Station, sittin' over there playin' dumb-ass games dreamed up by half the dick heads in Washington, and you don't tell me you're —"

"Goddamn it, Hawk!" Samuelson kicked the back of his chair, sending it crashing into the desk. "Don't give me that holier-than-thou shit. So far as I knew, he was unknown in Europe. I pulled him out of Southeast Asia so there'd be no connection if the Brits started asking questions." Samuelson looked at Ruppert Bailey, but found no support, only an impassive face.

Shaking his head in disbelief, Hawkins leaned forward in his chair and allowed his eyes to focus on raised patterns in the carpet at his feet. Said more to himself than to the other two men, the causticness of his, "Fucking great," cut like acid across the momentary silence that had suddenly enveloped the room.

Finally, he looked up and said, "I probably shouldn't give a damn, but what's his cover?"

"Insurance investigator. To my knowledge, his only contact was a Scotland Yard detective named Stuart. On the case when the icon was stolen."

Ignoring the THANK YOU FOR NOT SMOKING placard on Samuelson's desk, Hawkins lit a cigarette and drew deeply, blowing the smoke in Samuelson's direction. "Where's he now?"

"That's my problem. He's been missing for almost a week."

Hawkins couldn't help himself. Seeing the

20

suddenly pathetic, I-fucked-up-and-I-need-somebody-to-bail-me-out-look on Samuelson's face, an involuntary chuckle escaped his lips along with an equally involuntary, "No shit."

Ignoring, not only the interruption, but the obvious ridicule from a man now his subordinate, Samuelson continued, "He vanished, and I've got the Director and the President and even the SIG-I people –"

"SIG who? Who the hell's that? Another buncha Potomac pontificators?" Hawkins took a drag on his cigarette, exhaled smoke from deep in his lungs and shook his head in disgust.

"If you'd read the monthly Washington news-grams I send out to all station chiefs, you'd know who they are. SIG-I was set up by the President as a watchdog over the entire intelligence community. Even though he won't admit it, to make sure we give him what he wants to hear and nothing else."

"Kinda like you do me and all the other stations chiefs. My way or the highway.   So, what and who is it?"

"Senior Interagency Group – Intelligence.   White House, CIA, NSA, Defense, JCS, Attorney General, FBI, you name it. People like that, all after my ass wanting information. To put it bluntly, I'm screwed if I don't come up with something and fast."

Hawkins watched as Samuelson, his shoulders sinking lower with each word, shambled back to his desk, straightened the chair and lowered his too-broad posterior between its leather-padded arms. Though the rain had stopped, the clouds seemed thicker as darkness, almost night-like, had settled over the office.

Through the windows, the pink glare of lights from Washington and Arlington could be seen reflecting off the high, fast moving clouds in the distance. Samuelson turned on the small desk lamp, its glow only serving to illuminate the desperation etched across his face.

For the first time since arriving, Hawkins felt relaxed, actually enjoying himself at Samuelson's expense, as he flicked ashes on the carpet before snubbing out the glow of the cigarette on the bottom of his shoe. Tossing the butt into the wastebasket at the side of Samuelson's desk, he wondered aloud, "I don't know, man. A set of what? Sixty, sixty-five-year-old plans for a laser weapon? That's shovelin' it pretty deep. They didn't even have butane lighters in those days, let alone some kinda death ray."

"You're right," Bailey responded. "The plans more than likely have no relevance to current U. S. laser programs, but the President is concerned about countries like Iran and North Korea getting hold of them. No matter what North Korea's Kim Jong-il or that still wet-behind-the-ears son of his say about giving up their nukes, if daddy Il had the chance, he'd sacrifice his wife and both testicles to get these plans."

"Worst of all, if al Qaeda or one of their offshoots get their hands on them," Samuelson threw in.

"You know it," Bailey agreed. "So far, we've been able to keep that kind of technology out of their hands, but for how long is anybody's guess. Even something as relatively simple as this, compared to what we have now, could wreak havoc if the wrong people get hold of it. Enough money, the right contacts, sufficient scientific know-how to make the thing work and voilà! Major problem."

"Okay, guys." Yawning and stretching his legs all the way to Samuelson's desk, Hawkins said, "A good night's sleep and tomorrow, you feed me whatever you've got. I'll take it from there."

Samuelson shook his head. "Sorry, Hawk, we talk now. I've got you on an Air Force flight out of Andrews at eleven thirty tonight. If the President thought we weren't doing everything possible to —"

"Awright, Herb. We talk now, but you know what?"

Hawkins said, throwing his hands up in surrender.

"What?"

"Every time I listen to one of your bullshit schemes, I start feelin' like a guy with no hands who just had a grenade shoved up his ass. Fuckin' helpless, just waitin' for somebody to pull the pin."

Chapter 3

London

The fog that blanketed London most of the morning and afternoon had done little to detract from the building's rather ordinary appearance. Ordinary, that is, for that part of London's architectural aristocracy so near the southern exposures of Hyde Park.

Gleaming white stone with tall, black-draped windows that marred its otherwise gentrified façade, the three story, Victorian-style mansion stood in all its imposing stateliness at Number 16 Prince's Gate. A small yet extremely fashionable, L-shaped street, it could be accessed from both traffic-plagued Kensington Road and the relatively quiet and much less traveled Ennismore Gardens.

The embassy building was situated in London's South Kensington district. It was an area sometimes caustically referred to as "The Arab Quarter," or even more irreverently as, "Mohammed's Mecca" because of its numerous Middle Eastern and North African embassies.

A large plaque rested to one side of the bronzed, ten-foot-high, entrance doors, its crest still coated with the damp residue of that day's now dissipated fog. The words *JOMHURI-YE ESLAMI-YE IRAN* were inscribed in Farsi above the plaque. Below in English, EMBASSY OF THE ISLAMIC REPUBLIC OF IRAN.

Jutting out from a small balcony above the entranceway was a flagpole and the Iranian flag with its three horizontal bands of green, white and red symbolizing Islam, peace and courage. In the center of the white band floated a tulip-like, geometrical design of four crescents and a sword signifying the word Allah. Repeated eleven times at the bottom edge of the green band and again at the top edge of the red band were the small yet distinguishable words in Farsi, *ALLAH AKBAR* – God is Great.

While its Consular Section, located separately a mile to the west on Kensington Court, performed primarily public transactions such as issuance of passports, visas and other services related to commercial and industrial activities, the embassy itself often served as a safe house. In many instances, it provided sanctuary for those who were willing to use the freedoms offered by their adopted England but desirous of undermining those same freedoms. As such, in the opinion of many, the designation embassy was a misnomer.

Though minimal, there was also oversight of remaining Iranian interests and assets in the United States, primarily through the Iranian Interests Section in the Pakistani Embassy in Washington. At least for those assets not frozen by the American Government. There were also those properties and resources under United Nations sanction in other countries as well as the procurement of weapons in violation of UN Resolution 1747.

Other interests included front organizations in various countries hiding beneath the cloak of charity. These as well as certain activities if known, would definitely meet with the disapproval of British MI5, MI6 and the CIA.

* * *

Former KGB Major Viktor Mikhailovich Strizhenko was escorted by a slightly built man along the embassy's second floor corridor, slowing as a door was opened and he was motioned to enter. The Major, a man in his late fifties with thinning, gray-on-black hair, was short yet powerfully built with the face of an aging prizefighter who had seen more than his share of time in the ring. As trained to do, when he stepped through the doorway, he took in his surroundings with a single glance, immediately memorizing every detail.

The room was large and sparingly furnished. Walls and windows were covered by a thick, carpet-like material of neutral color. It was an obvious attempt to cloak as much sound as possible from the corridors and rooms beyond as well as listening ears outside the building.

The only colors breaking the severe monotony were several large maps of the Middle East and Europe. They were interspersed with life-size portraits of Ayatollah Ruhollah Khomeini, Supreme Leader following the unceremonious ouster of the Shah in 1979, the current Supreme Leader Sayyed Ali Khamenei and Mahmoud Ahmadi Nejad, the Iraqi president. Each exhibited a mixture of fatherly benevolence and absolute power on his respective face. In contrast to the walls, the floor was covered with rugs rich with intricate patterns and designs.

Strizhenko's gaze settled on three men dressed in western-style suits and seated at a large, rectangular table, each facing in his direction. The man in the center, short, almost delicate in stature, the front and top of his head devoid of hair, sipped tea from a small cup. Lightly dabbing the collected beads of moisture from the lower edge of his mustache with a handkerchief, he placed the cup on the table and said, "Good afternoon, Major Strizhenko. You are early, but so good of you to come."

Strizhenko nodded, accepting the pleasantry for what it was: a goodwill gesture to a paid underling and nothing more.

"Please be seated." The man motioned toward one of two chairs facing the conference table. To the servant who had ushered Strizhenko into the room, he directed, "Tea for the Major."

As the servant went about his duties at a nearby table, the man continued. "I am Ahmad Kazemi." Strizhenko knew the name. General Ahmad al Kazemi, to be precise, Deputy Director of Intelligence, Islamic Revolution's Guards Corps, *Sepah-e-Pasdaran*, more commonly known as the *Pasdaran* or the IRGC.

Nodding to the man on his left, Kazemi went on. "Parviz Akhbari, you already know, and on my right, Hajir Khalili, special envoy from the Supreme Leader, also representing President Ahmadinejad."

Strizhenko thought it interesting that Kazemi had pronounced the president's name as one word, Ahmadinejad instead of its two-word spelling, much the same as spoken in Europe and the United States. Putting that aside, he accepted the cup of tea from the servant and, at the same time, nodded to each of the men as their names were spoken.

Parviz Akhbari, until now Strizhenko's primary contact, was the embassy's newly assigned intelligence officer. He was urbane, extremely handsome with jet-black hair swept back from his forehead, sunglasses shielding his eyes. *So young,* Strizhenko thought. *Still learning, but promising.*

Hajir Khalili, known to most only as Hajir, the name meaning Champion of Iran, was to Strizhenko a very different bowl of borscht. He'd heard much about the man during his own time in Iran. A living legend. A tall, fearsome looking man. His most distinguishing feature was a scar snaking from beneath his left eye and across to the edge of his grotesquely disfigured left ear, a souvenir of the Iran-Iraq war of the eighties.

Hajir's position in the Revolutionary Guards had earned him the name Butcher of Basra following the human wave attacks during Operation Ramadan, an Iranian assault on the city of Basra. Strizhenko also knew Hajir was now second only to the commander of the feared Quds Force, the *Niuri-e-quds* or Special Operations and often reported directly to the Supreme Leader for clandestine missions. He had been the principal go-between with Hezbollah during the 2006 Israeli-Lebanon conflict.

He had also been overseer for the transfer of IED technology and equipment to the Mahdi Army and its Shi'a death squads against the Americans in Iraq. But why was he here? More likely the Supreme Leader's assassin than special envoy, Strizhenko decided.

The only similarity between the three Iranians were their business suits and the heavy black mustache each wore.

"There will be one other to arrive shortly," Ahmad Kazemi stated. Turning to Akhbari, the intelligence officer, he added, "You can vouch for the Major?"

Akhbari cleared his throat before saying. "Major Strizhenko, code named Leopard by the former KGB, was some years ago under contract as an instructor and counselor to our own intelligence apparatus. He was recalled by his government along with most of their contingent immediately following the Americans' sinking of our frigates *Sahand* and *Sabalan* as well as destruction of several of our oil platforms in the Persian Gulf in April of nineteen eighty-eight. They were concerned the United States was about to declare war against Iran and wanted their people out.

"Unfortunately, when the Soviet Committee for the State of Emergency attempted to overthrow the Gorbachev government, the Major was among a number of KGB and Internal Ministry officers sent to the Crimea to eliminate Gorbachev and his family."

Akhbari sipped his tea before once again clearing his throat. Continuing, he said, "The purge of Soviet security personnel following Gorbachev's return and subsequent dismantlement of the Soviet Union led the Major to renew certain past alliances outside his native Russia.

He returned to London and our doorsteps. It has proven most fortuitous that he finds himself at odds with the changed political arrangements in his former country and is willing to carry out certain projects on behalf of the Iranian people."

"But why him?" asked Hajir, the scar across his face stretching slightly with the movements of his mouth. "Why not one of our own, especially in such a sensitive matter?"

"His contacts," Akhbari answered, a hint of irritation in his voice as if he had already explained Strizhenko's involvement. "Established during his time as a KGB operative attached to the Soviet Embassy here in London. And certainly, his familiarity with the background of our quest is unmatched by our own people. It would –"

The sound of a door opening and closing brought immediate silence to the room as Strizhenko shifted to see who had entered. A woman, taller than most, slender, in her early to mid-forties, glided silently across the carpet.

Strizhenko had seen many beautiful Iranian women, but this one was spectacular. His breathing quickened as he inhaled the faint aura of perfume that seemed to surround the woman. Her features were like finely sculptured alabaster and lightly dusted with a hint of cinnamon. Her eyes, deep and sparkling, reminded him of the night sky spread across the desert.

The woman's shoulder-length, raven-colored hair was partially hidden by a *ḥijāb*, a chiffon scarf with gray and olive highlights that seemed to meld with her skin. Her body was covered in a cream-colored tunic and matching pants with precisely spaced embroidered designs adding color and depth to the material. The curve of hips and breasts, barely visible, was enough for Strizhenko to unconsciously lick his lips.

Ahmad Kazemi's voice cut through the silence. "Major Strizhenko, may I present Bājī Leila, the Lady Leila, a senior member of our Ministry of Science and National Development."

The woman nodded and took the remaining chair next to Strizhenko. She disregarded the Russian's extended hand, at the same time, waving away the servant who offered a cup of tea. With a voice tinged with immediate dislike, she asked Strizhenko, "What does a former KGB man do these days without a KGB?"

Disregarding the verbal swipe, Strizhenko offered his most pleasant smile and answered, "Whatever allows one to eat, I suppose. But why, may I ask, would one of such regal bearing be present for a meeting such as this?"

Ahmad Kazemi provided the answer. "Though fluent in several languages, Bājī Leila also holds a doctorate in physics from Russia's elite St. Petersburg State University and its Institute of Nuclear Physics. She places particular emphasis on nuclear and beam technology, disciplines highly useful to development of certain of our programs which –"

"Which," Hajir interrupted loudly, the scar on his face coloring with anger, "have been delayed by the IAEA and meddling of the Americans using their influence within the Security Council of the United Nations. Not to mention the Israeli dogs and their subtle threats to destroy our nuclear facilities. Our president, however, has vowed we will not be intimidated or deterred."

"Now that we are all here, Major," Kazemi went on, ignoring Hajir's outburst, "I must hear what you have learned to determine whether Bājī Leila and I remain in London or return to Tehran." Kazemi nodded for Strizhenko to begin, at the same time motioning for the servant to leave the room.

Strizhenko paused, loosened his tie and collar, and drank the last of his tea before beginning. "Afghanistan," he said flatly. "It was there I first learned of the icon and its secret. Colonel Naliskin, a ranking officer of the KGB, was dying in a hospital of wounds received when his headquarters was bombed by the Mujahedin. It seems Naliskin's father, once a general in our internal security forces during the war, –"

"No, no, no, I know all that," Kazemi cut in, waving the back of his hand for Strizhenko to stop. "We have all been briefed by Akhbari concerning the icon and, more importantly the plans concealed within its covers, but what, after so long, has prompted CIA interest?"

Strizhenko shifted forward on the sofa, the muscles of his face taut, eyes narrowed at the abrupt dismissal of what he'd been prepared to say. Pushing aside what he considered a slight aimed at his importance to the project, he went on, "Because of the defection of a KGB agent, a man once my friend, a man who exposed my identity to my enemies…" Lips tight, past betrayal still burning sour in his memory, he paused for a moment before continuing. "The Central Intelligence Agency has been aware of the Churchill Icon and its secret for some years. Why their renewed interest at this time? I can only speculate."

"Then how did you learn of their man Roberts?" Leila asked.

"A former colleague at the Russian Embassy. Whether I agree or disagree, he is disillusioned by what appears to be the growing authoritarianism by Vladimir Putin and the Kremlin. Regardless, my friend recognized Roberts from Thailand. He advised that the man had arrived in London inquiring after the icon."

"Where is he now, this man Roberts?" Kazemi asked.

A flicker of nervousness crossed Strizhenko's face. "Disappeared. A week ago."

"You lost him?" Hajir questioned in disbelief.

Akhbari quickly cut in. "Could he have known you were following him? Why did you not tell me?"

"I needed more time," Strizhenko tried to explain. "I thought I could –"

"Inexcusable!" Hajir charged. "And what of the Russians? Are they also after the icon and its plans?"

"Not according to my informant."

Leila shook her head and laughed. Strizhenko recognized the scorn in her voice as she said, "Then this is an absurdity. Surely the Americans' own laser technology far surpasses a weapon system devised so many years ago."

Stupid woman! Strizhenko countered with, "No

matter how simple, it would still be more than most countries ever dream of having. A death beam even you do not have."

Hajir leaned across the table in Strizhenko's direction, his movement smooth and flowing like a boa constrictor stretching toward its prey. "Perhaps American involvement is merely to prevent others from obtaining the weapon."

"Since Moscow has shown no interest," Strizhenko responded, "I can think of no other reason. I would agree."

Kazemi turned to Leila. "And if we were to obtain the plans for this death beam as the Major calls it, could it be extended to a system of significant destructive power?"

"Perhaps, with sufficient allocation of funds, but..."

Something in Leila's voice caught Strizhenko's attention, a hesitancy bordering on reluctance to explain further, but why?

"Bājī Leila?" Hajir prompted.

Leila stared hard at the General as though looking for support. "This... this thing is nothing more than a mirage. I thought we agreed –"

"Answer!" Hajir demanded.

Kazemi nodded, his look almost sympathetic or so Strizhenko judged.

With a look and sigh of resignation, she explained, "To develop such a weapon, an infrared laser is required that can convert chemical, nuclear, or electrical energy into highly organized electromagnetic radiation. A chemical —"

"We know how brilliant you are," Hajir interrupted. "A technical dissertation is not required.

Simply answer the General's question."

A more than passing level of contempt, perhaps even jealousy, in his voice or so Strizhenko thought. *Already dissension in the ranks,* he noted as he watched Leila bite her lower lip. He was certain she had swallowed the words – bitter words – she would rather have directed at this man with the scarred face. Studying the woman's stiffened posture and clenched fists, he was certain the pretense of a weak smile that crossed her face was an unsuccessful effort to hide her feelings as she continued.

"Much work has been done in the United States and the former Soviet Union, now Russia, with earthbound laser systems working in combination with refocusing mirrors in space orbit. Fully perfected, they would be ideal as antimissile lasers, a defensive measure with which I might agree. A byproduct of such technology, however, could be..." Leila hesitated.

"Go on," Hajir urged.

"Could be the reflection of beams back to the surface of the earth with sufficient power to destroy specifically designated targets."

Hajir pressed for more. "Examples?"

"Destruction of generating plants for electricity, oil fields, refineries, port facilities, but this is not what the people of Iran need."

"Enough!" Hajir ordered, his voice suddenly impassioned with the prospect of regained power for the Persian Empire. "With such a weapon, every oil producing country in the Middle East would be forced to follow our lead. The world's major oil fields under our control. The economies of Western Europe, the United States and the damned Jews at our mercy."

"It would seem to me," the General said

thoughtfully, "to find those who possess the icon of which you speak would be to find the weapon. If we could only –"

"General," Leila interrupted, "surely you agree we would be wasting precious assets and time on plans and theories this old. With the embargo and increasing threats by the Americans as well as certain European countries making our economic situation even more severe, our people need greater access to food, to medicines, to the staples of life. We are a great country with a profound history, but Iran must find its way without –"

"Without an un-knowing CIA agent to lead us," Kazemi quickly interrupted, at the same time holding up his hand for Leila's silence.

Strizhenko was convinced something was wrong, something Kazemi was withholding as he watched the sudden wariness on the man's face.

"If this icon is in fact the key," Kazemi went on, "what do you suggest, Major?"

"I have a plan, General. If –"

Leila suddenly rose from her chair. "I am sorry. Had I known before coming to London that this had nothing to do with the production of nuclear power for peaceful purposes, that this… this pipedream as they say was our mission, I would not have –"

The palm of General Ahmad Kazemi's hand slammed against the table, the smack, like a gunshot, instantly absorbed by the soundproofed walls. "Sit down, woman! Though I respect your reluctance, the Supreme Leader has directed your involvement. There is no other way."

Strizhenko noted the narrowing of Hajir's eyes, suspicious eyes that shifted rapidly from the General to

Leila and back.

Visibly shaken, Leila took her seat as Kazemi went on, "This plan of yours, Major. It must be something that would mask our involvement. Since it apparently involves an object of art, is there someone experienced in the recovery of stolen art or relics of the past, someone of impeccable credentials, who could be persuaded to search out the Churchill Icon on our behalf?"

"Yes, General," Strizhenko answered. "There is such a man, well known to the British and to many in the art and antiquities world." Nodding in the direction of the embassy's intelligence officer, he added, "Already, sanction by Parviz Akhbari, events have been set in motion."

Chapter 4

Waters off Bermuda

Just under 3500 miles west of London and four time zones earlier, the huge, rust-stained barge, its haze-gray deck littered with air compressors, pumps, dive tanks, portable toilets and assorted pieces of equipment, rested comfortably in a four-point moor. To the southeast, some four miles across the blue-green waters of the Atlantic, a slender tip of Somerset Island, the largest and most westerly of the Bermuda archipelago, was visible as it angled away in a ragged half-moon and disappeared beyond the horizon.

Two banners, strung from the top of a makeshift, canvas-covered work area, stretched almost the full length of both the barge's port and starboard sides. Each banner displayed the words:

PROJECT PEGASUS RECOVERY
SPONSORED BY
BERMUDA MARITIME MUSEUM & NORTH AMERICAN
ARCHAEOLOGICAL RESEARCH AND
PRESERVATION AGENCY (NAARPA)

Already, three of the Maritime Museum's artifact recovery staff were hard at work at cleaning tables laden with recently retrieved objects from the ocean's bottom. Scattered before them were metal plates, tin cups, eating utensils, the broken hilt of an eighteenth-century cutlass, rusted cannon balls, several unrefined, irregularly shaped slabs of gold and an array of silver coins, blackened from over two hundred years of salt water deterioration.

Suddenly, a woman's voice blared from the barge's radio speaker. "Project Pegasus, this is the Bermuda ship-to-shore operator. Call for Matthew Berkeley from Jonathan Maybank. Mr. Maybank declares this call to be flash precedence. Says Mr. Berkeley will know what that means, over."

Ignoring the complaining *skreigh* of sea gulls trying to dive bomb the patch of white canvas providing shade for the cleaning tables as well as the monotonous growl of a diesel-powered generator, Joel Pearman grabbed the radio's microphone and answered, "Project Pegasus. Berkeley's not available at the moment. You can stand by while we bring him up or give me your automatic call-back code."

After receiving the necessary information for a return call, Pearman, a tall, rangy black man whose age was as undeterminable as the source of winds in a winter squall, worked his way around several of the tables and those he called the museum's little troop of worker bees. He moved out from beneath the canvas into the early afternoon sun and lowered himself over the side of the barge. Three steps down a ladder and he was on the deck of the thirty-six-foot dive boat, *Amberjack*, nestled alongside the barge's starboard quarter.

"Hey, Bruce," he called to Bruce Woolridge, standing on the boat's dive platform, a surfer-looking guy with sun-bleached curly hair.

While slipping his arms through the straps of a thickly padded buoyancy jacket and hoisting its 40-pound air tank onto his back, Woolridge swiveled his upper body around in Pearman's direction and answered, "Yo, mon?"

"Ship-to-shore for Matt. From Johnny Maybank at NAARPA HQ in Charleston. Better send him up. Besides, we've been going at this thing since six this morning with no breaks. Everybody's tired and hungry, and that's when accidents happen."

"Gotcha. One lift, the big one, and we'll call it a day. Bottom time for most of the divers is about maxed out anyway." He nodded in the direction of the islands. "Besides, I've got business I need to take care of in Hamilton this afternoon."

* * *

Matt Berkeley took slow, measured breaths through the regulator mouthpiece as he hovered just over thirty feet above the wreck. To remain at the same depth, he periodically adjusted the air pressure in his buoyancy control jacket to maintain his position relative to the bottom and the two-man, one-woman dive team working below. This kept him well above the sediment cloud created by the swirl of sand blown up by the high-pressure, compressor-fed hose designed to unearth what remained of the wreck's intact artifacts.

Using sunlight from above assisted by two large, high efficiency, underwater arc lamps lowered from the barge, he visually followed the divers as they steadily worked their way over what remained of the U. S. Navy's *Pegasus*. She was a frigate lost in 1805 to a stormy sea while attempting to make port.

Securing the blast of air from the hose, the divers followed Matt's hand signals as they moved swiftly over the marine-encrusted, eight-to-nine-foot-long cannon lying exposed in a freshly made trench of sand. Matt watched the divers position a set of lifting cables beneath and around the barrel, one loop near the muzzle, one near the breech, attaching the loops to the twin cargo hooks lowered from the swinging boom on the barge.

He had taken the job only after reviewing a copy of the long-missing documents recently discovered by the Bermuda Maritime Museum, documents which amplified those already held by the U.S. Naval Historical Center in Washington. The newly found information gave the first indication of where the *Pegasus* had actually gone down.

It also provided an estimated value in early nineteenth-century dollars of the gold bullion she'd been carrying from the Mediterranean following a successful encounter with the Barbary pirates. More important to Matt, however, were the centuries-old relics still to be found and the muzzle-loaded 24-pounder that was about to be lifted from the past. Their historic significance excited him as much as all the gold that might be buried beneath the ship's ballast stones and worm-eaten timbers.

Matt felt the presence even before the movement caught his eye. Swinging around, he saw the silhouette of Bruce Woolridge against the slanted rays of sunlight from above. The words written in Woolridge's scribbled handwriting on an underwater tablet gradually came into focus.

Signaling he understood, Matt finned his way upward as the cannon began its journey from the bottom, careful to gauge his own ascent by the rise of air bubbles exhaled through his regulator. When he reached the surface, he spit the mouthpiece from between his lips and pulled himself onto a dive platform rigged at the stern of the barge. He twisted his body around to the point where he was able to sit on the edge of the platform to remove his dive mask, fins and weight belt.

Nearing his fifty-first year and despite the death of two wives, one in childbirth, the other murdered, the latter for which he still blamed himself, Matt Berkeley's looks and the way he carried himself belied the former Navy Commander's age. With only a touch of gray dusting a head of still blond hair and his just under six-foot body in better than average shape for a man his age, he had never considered himself particularly handsome. Clean cut at most.

The life he'd led, one filled with challenge and what many enviously called adventure, had at least kept him young at heart. And yes, there were also those of the fairer sex who considered him still young in various other ways, but his personal relationships were something Matt refused to discuss.

At the moment, however, his concern was getting out of the buoyancy jacket and air tank so he could find out what Maybank wanted. "What's happening?" Matt called over his shoulder to Pearman who had returned to the deck of the barge.

Pearman, working the swinging boom to maneuver the cannon from the water and onto the barge's deck, shouted over the sounds of the winch drum and cables running through hoist blocks. "The radio. Maybank in Charleston. Ship-to-shore operator said use the code one-two-four-BE as in Bravo Echo to automatically dial the Charleston number. She used the term, *flash precedence*, if that means anything to you."

"Yeah, it does and five'll get you ten, it's not good."

Barefoot and still in his cutoff wetsuit, Matt lifted the near-empty air tank up onto the deck of the barge, then hoisted himself up the ladder. At the same time, one of the other divers, the female diver named Debbie, climbed onto the dive platform and started removing her gear.

With air tank in hand to drop off at the air compressor's refill station, Matt started toward the radio. Suddenly, the rifle shot *kapow* of a parting cable and Pearman's shout, "Look out!" reached his ears.

Looking back, two things immediately registered. The female diver partway up the ladder from the dive platform to the deck of the barge, looking upwards, frozen in place; the cannon dangling precariously above her head.

The cries of Pearman's worker bees scrambling out of the way and the clang of the air tank hitting the deck rang in Matt's ears as, without thinking, he dove for the woman, hitting her mid torso. The force of the impact took them airborne, out past the edge of the dive platform and into the water.

Their splash was masked by the crash of the falling, two-thousand-pound cannon. Its breech end slammed into one of the cleaning tables, crushing the aluminum legs and sending plates, cups and coins flying like shrapnel in all directions. Its muzzle end slammed down just past the barge's deck directly over the ladder from the dive platform.

Even underwater it was the sound of the cannon hitting the deck, if only for an instant, that took Matt back to Vietnam. It required a violent shake of his head to force the momentary starburst explosion of gunfire and its accompanying visual back into the dark recesses of the past, a past he tried so desperately never to visit.

As they surfaced, the woman clung to Matt, her body shaking from a delayed bout of fear. "Thank you for saving my life, but I'm so sorry," she said, her voice a weak, tremulous vibrato. "I'm really sorry," she repeated.

Treading water for both of them, his arms around her waist, Matt assured her, "Not your fault. Something happened to the boom."

"Not that," she said, admitting, "I just peed. I couldn't help myself."

Matt fought back a laugh. "It's okay, Debbie, sweetheart. The ocean's a big place and nobody's gonna know but you and me."

The two of them back on the barge with Pearman's help, Matt looked quickly around and called, "Everybody okay?"

With tentative replies of "Yes," and "Think so," from the museum staff personnel, Pearman said for all to hear, "Sorry about that. Vang pendant on the boom parted and everything went to hell. You sure you're okay?" he added to Matt.

Matt laughed, trying to hide the case of nerves sparked by the unwanted memories of Vietnam inside his brain. "I'm sure, but let's find out what the hell happened and get that thing fixed."

Tugging his way out of the wetsuit and slipping on a pair of sweat pants over his swim shorts, Matt worked a towel across deeply tanned arms and shoulders before entering the space beneath the canvas awning. Taking a deep breath to steady himself from the near-fatal accident, he popped the TRANSMIT switch on the face of the radio transceiver to the ON position, punched in the alpha-numeric code Pearman had given him, picked up the handset and placed it to his ear. "Johnny? Matt."

Instead he heard the distant ringing created automatically by the operator code, then a moment of silence before he heard the click of a telephone receiver being picked up.

Again, Matt said, "Johnny?" As usual, whether by undersea cable or satellite link, there was the mandatory three-to-four-second pause before the response from NAARPA's east coast headquarters reached him.

From the loud speaker mounted above the transceiver came, "Hey, Matt, yeah, it's me, Johnny. How's it goin'?"

"At the moment, smashing is probably the best way to describe it."

"If I had the time, I'd ask for a definition of that description, but it looks like I've got somethin' that's gonna take priority. At least so far as you're concerned."

"What do you mean?" Matt asked.

"National office wants you in London by tomorrow. Means tonight's red eye special outta Bermuda."

"London? Since when are we doing business in London?"

"We don't, but looks like you will."

"I don't understand. What the hell are you talking about?"

*   *   *

Johnny Maybank, Deputy Director of NAARPA's Southeast Region operating out of Charleston, South Carolina, was only a few years younger than Matt. He had followed Matt into the NAARPA organization after their time in the Navy. More specifically the Riverine Forces in Vietnam where the PBR he commanded had been shot out from under him; where he thought his time was up before Berkeley risked his own life fishing him out of the Co Chien River under a barrage of withering Viet Cong gunfire.

Hearing the growing irritation in Matt's voice, he turned from the window overlooking Charleston Harbor and directed his words at the speakerphone on the desk. "Some antiquity society's asked for help in locating what they call the Churchill Icon."

* * *

Matt watched as the final two members of his underwater team climbed onto the barge from the dive platform. "I've heard of the Churchill Icon. Damn thing's been missing for I don't know how long."

"I tried to beg off," he heard Maybank say, "but national office wouldn't listen."

"Why not?" Matt asked. "They know the importance of this project. Not only to the museum, but to the Navy Department. And besides, I'm retired, remember? You tell 'em that?

"I came on this gig only because it might help me get my mind off Ashley and the bastards who killed her. And yeah, because you said nobody else in the whole motherfucking world could do it. Your very words, remember? I knew then you were
BSing me, but I did it for you, not some bunch of desk-riding bureaucrats at national."

He could hear the museum workers snickering at his less than genteel vocabulary as they rounded up the various artifacts from the barge's deck.

* * *

Maybank pulled the chair back from his desk and lowered himself onto the seat, took a sip from his coffee cup, frowned at the taste and said, "First, the society's making a three-hundred-thousand-dollar donation to NAARPA and –"

"You're kidding!" Matt's voice burst from the speakerphone. "That's a third of a million bucks? What the hell kind of antiquity society is this?"

"Hey, man, you know national never turns down a donation. Besides, these people are picking up the tab for your salary and expenses, starting today. Second, they asked for you by name. I've got a telegram in the air giving all the particulars."

*   *   *

With the lines on his forehead and the bridge of his nose furrowed with anger, Matt paced back and forth, moving as far in each direction as the cord to the handset would allow. "You told the Bermuda people about this? And the Navy?" Matt asked, unable to hide his growing frustration with NAARPA's national office and their take-him-for-granted attitude.

"The museum curator and the chief archivist for the Navy also asked for me by name to head up the job or so you said. They're gonna be pissed just as much as I am. Maybe more."

"I've told 'em both," Maybank replied, "and you're right, they're pissed, but it can't be helped. We're sending out another diver to take your place. Retired Navy Chief outta the Boston office. Master diver. Salvage. Good as they come."

Matt shook his head, his case of "cannon" nerves forgotten, his anger level on the rise. "I don't give a damn how good he is. We're just starting to make headway on this project. There is no damn way I'm going to London. Not today, not tomorrow, and not tonight. Tell national they can damn well find themselves another boy for this one."

Chapter 5

London

Matt woke with a start, the yellow telegram from Johnny Maybank still crumpled in his hand. The whine of jet engines sang in his ears; warning bells *donged* their familiar monotone signal; FASTEN SEAT BELT signs flashed. As the big Boeing 777 bucked sluggishly through a thick layer of clouds that pressed against the window, he swallowed to clear his ears, for the first time noticing what seemed like a slight angle of descent from the plane's cruising altitude.

"Good morning, ladies and gentlemen." The British accent drifted smoothly over the aircraft's speaker system. "This is your pilot, Captain Cunningham. We've just received clearance to land. Local time is ten minutes after seven. Weather this morning is foggy and cool, but the forecast calls for gradual clearing and a lovely autumn day. Thank you for flying British Airways, and we wish you a most pleasant stay in London."

Still frustrated over having to leave the Bermuda project, Matt shook his head and mouthed, "And the shorter the stay, the better."

* * *

The crowd noise was worse than a London/Liverpool soccer match for the national championship as travelers of every conceivable size, shape, color, language and manner of dress pressed forward into the searching hands of British Customs. And the smell! No matter which way he turned: from salami and sardines to garlic and onions;

from morning breath and slept-in clothes to odor-hiding splashes of body cologne and aftershave lotion. All heavy and pungent, reminders of overnight flights and too little sleep.

Rendering an unqualified thanks-a-helluva-lot to the gods of unfortunate circumstance and shifting his faded navy-blue suit bag from one shoulder to the other, Matt inched a travel-scarred leather Samsonite forward with the toe of his shoe. He had already resigned himself to at least another thirty minutes of growing frustration when he heard, his name paged.

From Heathrow's public address system came the words, "Attention, Mr. Matthew Berkeley, British Airways flight twenty-two thirty-two. Mr. Matthew Berkeley, please report to Customs desk Alpha at the head of Line One. Thank you."

"Maybe they're gonna send me back to Bermuda," Matt muttered under his breath, wishing it was so, as he picked up his suitcase and pushed his way forward. Dispensing "Excuse me's" and "Sorry's" along the way, he held the Samsonite like an extended battle ram as he plowed his way through the fields of arms, legs and oversized waistlines that blocked his path.

Finally, near the head of Line One and a chest-high desk designated with a large A, he saw a youngish man, middle to late thirties or there about. He wore a tweed jacket, regimental tie, dark trousers and was standing behind the metal security barrier at the side of one of several Customs inspectors. The man's chalk-like pallor, accented even more by his thinning red hair and ample supply of freckles, contrasted noticeably with Matt's own deep tan. Creases at the sides of his mouth gave the impression of a perennial smile. Their eyes met, and the man waved and pointed in Matt's direction.

"Mr. Berkeley?" called the "smile" over the noise of the impatient crowd. "Matthew Berkeley from the United States?"

"That's me." Matt fished Johnny's telegram from his jacket pocket and hurriedly rechecked the contact name he'd been given. "You Stuart from New Scotland Yard?"

"Detective Inspector Stuart," the "smile" emphasized. "RCS, Regional Crime Squad." The man, with an accent more Scottish than English, stepped to an electronically controlled turnstile holding back the line of people waiting to pass Customs and flashed an identification card in Matt's direction. "You've already been cleared. If you'll follow me."

"Thank God for little favors."

Several people standing in line grumbled their annoyance as Matt saw the unsmiling Customs officer motion his approval. He pushed through the turnstile and followed the inspector through a maze of crowded passageways, up, then down escalators, through doors and out into the morning fog of the arriving passenger pickup area. The small, dull green Vauxhall, unmarked except for a noticeably large number of rust splotches on its top, hood and trunk – Matt mentally corrected himself; bonnet and boot, if you please – was parked, engine idling, next to the curb as they exited the building. Matt handed his suitcase and suit bag to a waiting police officer who opened a rear door and placed them on the back seat.

Stuart rounded the front of the car to the driver's side, speaking to the officer as he went. "Thank you, Constable. I'll manage from here."

"Very good, sir." The constable gave a short salute, then turned on his heel and disappeared through the doors into the terminal.

Stuart motioned to Matt over the top of the car. "A real pea-souper, this one. One part water and nine parts exhaust from all the bloody cars and busses in London. You'll choke to death if you stand out for long. The door's unlocked."

Matt climbed onto the front passenger seat and quickly slammed the door in a vain attempt to shut out the dampness. Reaching across the seat, he accepted Stuart's hand. "Thanks for meeting me, and by the way, most people call me Matt."

"Matt it is, and I'm Ian." Shifting gears, the inspector pulled away from the curb and across the car park toward the main egress route from Heathrow. "Your Mr. Maybank didn't tell us much when he called, but then again, you're not quite a stranger to the RCS, you know."

"Oh?"

"Your locating the Golden Seal of the Lords Proprietors was an excellent piece of work. And of course, our department read with interest Special Branch's account of your run-in with the IRA's Red Hand and saving our First Sea Lord, Admiral Sir William Douglas, several years back. Rather extraordinary, I must say."

Matt shrugged. "Thanks, but a lady friend of mine was kidnapped by the IRA at the same time they took the Admiral. That's the only reason I got involved." He watched Stuart squinting through the fog as they neared the entrance ramp to the motorway heading east into the sprawling metropolis.

"And of course, there's your naval career," Stuart went on. "Ships. Surface Warfare and Special Warfare, a combination few ever achieve so I'm told. And

Vietnam. Twice. Navy Cross, Bronze and Silver Stars, Legion of Merit, two Purple Hearts, and on and on."

"Most for killing people. Big damn deal," Matt said. The hardness of his voice underscored his attempt to hide from memories that seemed never far away. Hidden behind a word, a sound, or an odor, Vietnam was always there. His own personal ghost for the last twenty-five years.

"Rank of Commander when you left, but said to be a loner. A maverick. Not always a team player."

Matt's eyes narrowed at the obvious lack of privacy in his life. "What about my credit rating? Did you check that, too?"

Stuart laughed again. "Not to worry. I understand its quite good, actually."

Matt stared at the inspector for a moment before his mouth slowly stretched into a grin. "So much for the good old Privacy Act. Guess my life's an open book."

"Not quite. Maybank failed to tell us where you're staying when he called."

Matt pulled the crumpled telegram from his pocket and smoothed it across his thigh. "Jubilee Hotel."

"Ah, yes," Stuart said, a note of recognition in his voice. "St. Martin's Lane. Up from Trafalgar Square near the English National Opera."

"Any port in a storm, but let's talk about the icon," Matt said, wanting to take advantage of the drive into London. "Russian in origin, presented to Churchill at Yalta in forty-five, and stolen from Chartwell, Churchill's home south of London in ninety-six. What then?"

"Truthfully," Stuart began, "we've no idea what happened to the bloody thing."

"Well if you people can't find it, how the hell am

I supposed to?"

"Although we've long suspected someone close to the family or with unquestioned access to Chartwell," Stuart went on, "we've been unable to find the slightest trace. We checked —"

Stuart pounded the horn as a black Mercedes sedan cut in front of the Vauxhall, then slowed, forcing Stuart to swing out and around to avoid a rear-end collision. "And bugger you, too!" Stuart shouted, angrily shaking a fist at the other driver as he passed and pulled back in front of the Mercedes.

Matt laughed. "Close."

"Ruddy bastard! Where was I?" Stuart asked, trying to pick up the string of his conversation.

"You checked something."

"I checked... uh yes, we checked art and antique dealers, their inventories, their receipts, both for purchases and sales. We looked for anything that might resemble the icon or give us a clue to what happened. Absolutely nothing.

"Going a step further, we identified all the major private collectors in England, Scotland, and Ireland, both Northern and the Republic, but to no avail. Interpol was alerted immediately following the loss. Their European connections, you know, but again, nothing.

"Even asked the Russians to assist since it was once theirs, but in those days, a rather definite *nyet* was all we received. In summary, every lead's been dead before we started."

They drove in silence until suddenly, Matt realized they'd left the wide-open speeds of the expressway and were now winding their way through the streets and avenues of London's West End. Whether his imagination or not, its people and architecture seemed to take on the pale-yellow glow of the sun as it slowly embraced the fog and absorbed the blanket of miniature droplets in its warmth.

"Familiar territory," he said, recognizing various landmarks from previous visits. "Kensington Gardens and Hyde Park up ahead."

"Yes." Stuart brought the car to a stop at a red light just up from Royal Albert Hall. "Kensington to the left; South Kensington, Brompton and Belgravia on your right. Quite a grand business and residential area as well as a number of foreign embassies.

"Kathleen and I – that's my wife – often come on Sundays to stroll in the park and watch the embassy people, but..." Stuart's voice tailed off as he kept his eyes on the outside rearview mirror. A frown formed on his face.

"Something wrong?" Matt asked.

"Not certain, but we'll know by the time we get to the hotel, won't we?"

"If you say so."

As the light went green, Stuart eased through the intersection, but Matt could tell the man's eyes were shifting back and forth between the rearview mirror and the road ahead. To warrant that kind of attention, he knew there had to be someone following. Who? And why? Because of me? he asked himself. Or simply a coincidence that he was in the car?

Regardless, he still needed more information. "What you've really been telling me is, nothing's happened with the icon since ninety-six when it went missing. Right?"

"Not quite," Stuart answered, his eyes still darting to the mirror whenever the traffic thinned in front of him. "Though the case is still open, I'd given it little thought until an insurance investigator, an American named Roberts, was here several weeks back and seemed to be onto something."

Matt sat for a moment, mulling over the unexpected disclosure of a man named Roberts. "And now me," he said more to himself than to Stuart, then louder, "If he was who he said he was, he must've had one helluva backlog if he waited until two double-oh seven to get on the case. Kinda stretches the imagination, huh?"

Stuart nodded his understanding of Matt's disbelief. "Said he worked for a company by the name of World Wide Inland Marine Underwriters in New York."

"Worked?"

"Gone. Vanished. Last week, without a word."

"What about his company?"

"I called, but they've neither seen nor heard from him since the day he disappeared. Coincidence, don't you think? Two different Americans, you and this man Roberts? Both suddenly looking for the icon so long after its loss?"

"My very thought."

The Vauxhall moved doggedly through traffic, over dampened streets past Constitution Arch and its winged statue of Peace, its chariot of war and fiery steeds, then onto Piccadilly. Following Stuart's eyes in the rearview mirror, Matt turned and looked back through the rear window. Almost immediately, a red Ford directly behind the Vauxhall turned left, leaving a black Mercedes sedan on their rear bumper.

"Which one?" Matt asked. "The red or the black?"

"The black," Stuart answered. "Same one that passed earlier, then slowed. Getting a good look at who we were… and are, I'll wager."

Stuart went silent, concentrating on his driving as the car wove through Piccadilly Circus, past souvenir stalls, theaters and the bronze-winged Eros precariously balanced on his pedestal above the unheeding traffic. Matt knew what Stuart was doing. Testing the black Mercedes, but he held his voice.

He watched as Stuart hit the accelerator, barely missing two pedestrians, then white-knuckled his way onto Shaftsbury to Charing Cross Road and finally, around Leicester Square. With a final burst of speed, the car swerved onto the relatively narrow St. Martin's Lane, home to the Jubilee Hotel.

As the Vauxhall skidded to a halt, the black Mercedes, still on their bumper, wheeled out and around, slowed momentarily, then quickly shot forward, its tires spinning and squealing against the asphalt. The driver's face was hidden by a chauffeur's cap and dark glasses; the passenger memorable to the extent that a scar straggled down the side of his face.

"That's what I thought," Stuart said, his eyes following the Mercedes until it merged into traffic foraging about Trafalgar Square. "I'd give a gilded quid to know what that was about."

"I don't know what you mean?"

"Russian diplomatic tags. Friends of yours?"

Matt laughed. "Not hardly, but if they're looking for the icon, they can damn well get in line with the rest of us."

* * *

"Stop here," Hajir ordered.

Doubling as chauffeur, Akhbari, the Iranian

Embassy's intelligence officer, eased the Mercedes toward the sidewalk across from the National Portrait Gallery on Trafalgar Square and stopped. Hajir immediately got out and slammed the door shut. Akhbari punched one of the window control buttons, and as the passenger side window lowered, called, "Where are you going?"

Hajir leaned toward the window. "To insure Mr. Berkeley receives the package and is prepared to begin his work."

Chapter 6

Both Matt's and Stuart's backs were turned toward the door as Hajir entered the hotel lobby. They neither saw him pick up a copy of the Times nor take a seat at a small writing table within hearing range of their conversation.

"As your man Maybank requested," Stuart said, "I've arranged an appointment for tomorrow morning, ten o'clock, at the Courtauld Institute. You'll meet Doctor George Cavendish, a retired research scientist and associate professor at the University of London. Strangely enough, he's also an expert on Byzantine and Russian iconology. He can provide you with background and a description of the icon. Afterwards in the afternoon, an appointment at Chartwell."

"Thanks. Chartwell, I understand because that's from where the icon was stolen, but how did Maybank know about this man Cavendish and the Courtauld Institute?

"He didn't. He simply asked where best and with whom you should start. I knew of Doctor Cavendish from my previous inquiries."

Matt shrugged his shoulders. "As good a place as any, but right now, I need to get hold of a man named Lowenstein with the British-European Antiquities Society and set up a meeting. Ever heard of him or the society?"

"Not until I learned you were coming, but then again, we've as many antiquity societies in England and Scotland as we have churches and pubs."

Matt chuckled. "I'm sure you do. I appreciate everything you've done." Looking at his watch, he added, "But I know you've got things to do besides babysitting a jetlagged American."

Stuart nodded. "An ongoing problem concerning a robbery and a rather vicious murder in Bayswater." Stuart pulled a small leather case from inside his coat and handed Matt a business card with the crown emblem of the Metropolitan Police embossed at the top. "Here's my card. Ring me as soon as you finish at Chartwell, and I'll help arrange whatever else you feel necessary."

As Stuart turned and headed toward the exit, Matt gave a thumbs-up and said, "Will do, and thanks."

"Mr. Berkeley!" a voice called.

Matt turned at the sound of his name. "Yes?"

The hotel's desk clerk held up a bulky brown envelope. "Almost forgot. The leased automobile ordered by your people will be delivered by noon tomorrow. And this was left for you earlier this morning. Dreadfully sorry."

Matt turned and took the envelope. "No problem, but you say *my people* ordered a leased car. Do you know who these people were?"

"Again, I apologize." The clerk rummaged through a message box until he found a sheet of paper and handed it to Matt. "The off-going concierge left the package and this note advising of the automobile earlier this morning. Neither indicate the source. I could only assume it was your people from the United States who reserved the room."

After reading the note, Matt said, "I doubt it, but I guess I'll find out sooner or later." With the Samsonite in one hand, suit bag and envelope in the other, Matt started for the elevator. He took only a few steps before abruptly stopping.

The man in the black Mercedes with the scar on his face. The Mercedes with the Russian Embassy plates that followed Stuart and him all the way from the airport. The car that had nearly caused a wreck. Matt saw the man, moving toward the hotel's exit behind two middle-aged women and a hotel porter carrying an armload of luggage. As he approached, Matt said, "I don't know who you are, but I –"

Hajir grabbed the porter by the shoulders and shoved, propelling the man into Matt, knocking both against the check-in counter and sending boxes and suitcases in every direction. The women screamed as Hajir pushed past, elbowing one of the women in the chest as he bolted toward the door.

"Goddamn it!" Matt cursed. He scrambled to his feet and immediately tripped over a cosmetic case and an umbrella in the process. "Stop that man," Matt shouted at two men entering the hotel from the street, but Hajir shouldered his way past startled hands, sending both men to the floor as he burst through the exit.

Getting to his feet and grabbing the umbrella to use as a weapon, Matt ran to the door and onto the sidewalk outside. He looked both ways, but Hajir was gone, disappeared like a magician in a puff of smoke.

"Okay, som'bitch," Matt growled at the scarred face now permanently etched in his memory, promising, "You got away this time, but next time, I owe you one."

* * *

Matt gave a tired sigh of relief as he dropped his suitcase and bag on a fold-out luggage rack and made a brief visual survey of the room. Though small, it was comfortably decorated with the kind of homey furniture one might expect to find in a better than average bed and breakfast in the States.

"Now, let's see what you're all about," he said to the heavy envelope as he ripped off one end and emptied its contents over the bed. "Holy Christ!"

Like a shower of confetti, British ten-, twenty- and fifty- pound notes scattered across the top of the bed, some to the floor. They were followed by a sheet of stationery showing the British-European Antiquities Society letterhead. Blinking away the initial shock and trying without success to put a dollar value to the money, Matt picked up the stationery, walked to the window overlooking St. Martin's Lane and read:

20 October
Mr. Berkeley:
Enclosed are sufficient funds to conduct your investigation. Should you determine who possesses the icon, you are not, I repeat, you are not to attempt retrieval. That is my responsibility alone.

Matt stopped for a moment and watched the traffic passing beneath his window. "That's strange. Wonder why?" he mused, then continued reading.

A member of the Antiquities Society, Miss Howard by name, has been instructed to provide assistance. She will contact you shortly.
Lowenstein

No signature, just the impersonal printed word, *Lowenstein*. A slight? Or a simple lack of courtesy, a trait he had found so often in certain segments of British

Night of the Angels   William Kerr

society. Especially now toward Americans who they blamed for Britain's participation in Iraq.

More worrisome, however, was Matt's mental picture of the historical society's Miss Howard. More than likely, some little old white-haired lady in tennis shoes, tagging along and giving advice on finding the icon.

"Fantastic!" he said, lifting his face and rolling his eyes once more toward the gods of unfortunate circumstance. "Holmes and Watson, I could use, but Miss Howard?" Shaking his head in disbelief, he added, "Who the hell is she?"

61

Chapter 7

Bājī Leila was born in Tehran, the seventh of as many children to a blacksmith and his wife. She had lived with dreams of relative freedom to excel and choose her life's course as those in the West were free to do. While still a young girl, she'd seen many of those dreams crushed with the Islamic Revolution and overthrow of the Shaw.

Only through the influence of an older brother had she been able to further her education. Nine years her senior, his rise in academia, the Revolutionary Guard and later in political circles had opened doors otherwise unavailable to a woman. First at Tehran University of Science and Technology and later receiving her Ph.D. at St. Petersburg State University.

While there had been some improvement in living standards for the Iranian people and relaxation of the strict social edicts of the Iranian Government and ruling Ayatollahs under the former, more liberal and progressive President Mohammad Khatami, everything changed.

During the past two years following Khatami's electoral defeat, Leila had watched with amazement and chagrin the increasing stagnation of the country's economy. She had seen the growing misery of its people and the alienation of Iran in much of the international community due to the new government's increasingly conservative, hardline approach.

And yes, for Iranian women, the disappearance of what freedom members of her sex had gained. Even though she personally still benefited from her brother's influence and name, her every thought and deed had become couched in the belief that things must change. But how? She couldn't bring about that change herself, but with the aid of certain like-thinking people, some of them still in positions of power, there did exist the slimmest of possibilities.

For the woman who would be "Miss Howard," the sixteenth-century, timber-framed Queen's House provided a broad view across Tower Green. Surrounding trees, now gold with autumn, still offered a modicum of shade for those weary of roaming the walled bastion of royal jewels, magnificent crowns, swords and armor.

It seemed at the moment also to be a haven for those impertinent, wing-clipped ravens, which she had learned to despise on earlier visits to London. She also disliked the overly solicitous Yeoman Warders, pointing out each stone and every historical fact relevant to the Tower of London.

A large parasol, its handle resting on Bājī Leila's shoulder, its mushroom cap of black pulled close about her head, provided a semblance of privacy for General Ahmad Kazemi and herself. To Leila, it served both as a brief escape from the swarms of tourists at her back, trooping to and from the Jewel House across the green, and a protective wall against the possibility of prying eyes. As did what she wore. The black, full-length, cloak-like chador, commonly worn by more matronly Moslem women in London, was held together by one hand near the throat. Pulled close about her head, it also served to hide
the real Leila.

"But why this, General?" she asked, her fear betrayed by the slight, involuntary tremor in her voice.

"Already the head of the Central Bank and both Ministers of Oil and Industry have been forced to resign as well as our chief nuclear negotiator with the West. All moderates replaced by extremists. Why give the ayatollahs and the president a weapon that could make them even more powerful?"

"You must be patient. Both the Supreme Leader and the President have ordered it, and we are the logical ones to carry out the mission."

"I don't like it."

"Nor do I," Ahmad Kazemi insisted, "but perhaps it could be put to our own use. Allah willing, you, Bājī Leila, will someday replace the president and with such power, influence the Supreme Leader to accept justice, freedom and equality for the Iranian people. In the meantime, –"

"In the meantime, we play silly games to perpetuate our country's misery and its false sense of defiance and superiority."

"No, Bājī Leila. In the meantime, we must take care when we are with Strizhenko and Hajir. Strizhenko is cunning and would use knowledge of our betrayal to benefit his own cause."

"And Hajir?"

"He would kill us."

* * *

The electronically controlled door descended after the black Mercedes sedan with the Russian diplomatic license tags entered the garage. Leaving Parviz Akhbari behind the wheel, Hajir stepped immediately from the vehicle, walked to the far wall and pushed a button mounted on a small intercom box.

It was Strizhenko's voice that answered. "Yes?"

"He has arrived, Major, driven by the inspector from Scotland Yard as you predicted. Everything appears to be on schedule."

"And the automobile plates?"

"They saw the plates, I am certain. I will have them removed once no longer needed."

"Good. They will suspect Russian interest and not ours, and Hajir?"

"Yes?"

"Constant surveillance must be maintained. Until the icon is found, we cannot afford to lose Mr. Berkeley as we lost Roberts, the CIA man."

Hajir's eyes narrowed and the muscles in his face twitched with annoyance. With words slow and deliberate, he said, "If you recall, Major, you are the one who lost Roberts from CIA, not me. You would best heed your own advice. Such mistakes, I will not make."

As Hajir was about to hang up, he heard, "Hajir, the General and your Bājī Leila. A curious pair, are they not?"

Hajir licked the underside of his mustache in thought before responding, "For once, Major Strizhenko, as the Americans say, you and I sing from the same page of music."

Chapter 8

They watched, three of them, cramped together inside the cab of a lorry. Its bed was covered by a torn, oily looking tarpaulin, its unwashed body scarred with scratches, rust and sideswiped fenders. First the entrance to the Courtauld Institute and the fading outline of Matt Berkeley disappearing through the glass doors. Then the black Mercedes sedan with the Russian Embassy license plates as it parked farther along on the opposite side of the street.

"The same ones as yesterday." the driver said. His long, stringy blond hair left glistening lines of hair gel on the steering wheel as he leaned forward for a better view of the Mercedes.

"Aye," answered a man named Pearly. He was a much older, bearded man sitting on the far-left passenger seat. A crumpled fisherman's cap was pulled down over a mop-like hang of hair, close over eyes permanently narrowed by suspicion of most things and most people.

"You've a good eye for things, 'arry. Tis the same, but Damien says not to bother. If we stop the American, it'll stop 'em all, he says."

The man in the middle, his once white butcher's smock stained with animal blood and tiny bits of dried meat, arched his eyebrows. "And how's that? It's what 'e said about the other one, didn' 'e? That insurance man."

The older man looked down his nose, annoyed at the butcher's impertinence. "'cause Damien says, an' that's good enough fer the likes a you an' me. Now bugger off, Lemmie, an' keep yer mind on what's 'appenin' around ya."

* * *

Matt's knock echoed the length of the corridor. A muffled, high-pitched voice spoke from behind the door. "Come in."

Matt eased the door open and stepped into a world of absolute chaos. Everywhere he looked, clutter. On tables, chairs, desk, floor: research tomes and oversized photographs of paintings and statuary, file folders and notebooks, and pile after pile of loose papers. An endless array of canvases leaned against the walls. Some were blank, some partially completed. Still others were finished works, each color, dabbed and stroked with another into sometimes recognizable forms, at other times, worried, unidentifiable snatches of the artist's imagination.

And the odor! At first stifling, clinging to the air like droplets in an early morning fog. It clung to the membranes of his nostrils and drew tears to the corners of his eyes. Turpentine? Paint thinner? Chemical cleaners? All the same to Matt. It was dizzying at first, then gradually acceptable as his olfactory nerve acclimated itself to the room's pungency. He closed the door behind him, wishing he could leave it open to create a cleansing draft.

"Doctor Cavendish?"

Looking up through a pair of wire-rimmed bifocals, the intense, excruciatingly wizened little man motioned to Matt with a gloved hand. In the other hand he held a large magnifying glass aimed at a canvas spread out before him.

"Mr. Berkeley, I presume? I'm Cavendish." He nodded to the painting that lay on the worktable. "Over here."

67

Although Matt judged the man to be in his seventies, possibly eighties, his hand never wavered. It explored ever so slowly the wash of colors captured beneath the magnifying glass, yet he was visibly upset. "Observe. Hard to fathom how anyone could do such a monstrous thing."

Matt edged closer and studied the canvas. "Van Gogh's self-portrait after he cut off his ear. The original?"

"Yes."

"I don't see the problem."

"Not the work itself, young man. No. Look closer. Take the magnifying glass. Someone besides van Gogh decided they wanted a piece of his ear."

Matt took the glass and examined the painting. "I'll be damned. The bandage over the ear. Looks like a razor cut." Returning the magnifying glass to the doctor, he asked, "Why the hell would anybody want to do something like that?"

"I've never known why any rational person would or could deliberately deface such a priceless masterpiece. One would assume those visiting the Courtauld would be intelligent, thinking people, and not common vandals."

Matt watched as Cavendish placed the magnifying glass on the table and pulled off the white cotton gloves that had protected the van Gogh from the body oils of his skin. Seeing the almost translucent, parchment-like skin stretched across the bones and tendons of the old man's hands, Matt wondered if there really was any oil left in his body to protect the painting or anything else against.

"But come. Our misfortune is not why you're here. Tea?"

"Thank you, no, Doctor."

"Please excuse me if I have a cup. Damned

tedious work slouched over that table at my age." He
motioned with his finger. "Do be seated, Mr. Berkeley."

Matt removed several books from the straight-
back chair at the corner of Cavendish's desk and sat as
the old man dropped a bag of Twinings Earl Grey into
his cup and spooned a snowfall of sugar on top. Wanting
to get directly to the point, Matt said, "As I'm sure
Detective Inspector Stuart explained, the reason I'm here
is because the Courtauld supposedly has the most
complete files available on the Churchill Icon. Especially
the description."

Cavendish poured a stream of water from a small
blue and white kettle kept hot by the heating element of
an electric coffee maker. After waiting a moment for it
to steep, he squeezed the tea bag several times against the
inner curve of a spoon before taking his place behind the
desk.

"Yes, I've spoken with Stuart on several occasions
over the years concerning the matter." Picking up the
phone, he added, "Perhaps I can do somewhat better than
a mere description." He punched out several numbers,
then stirred and sipped his tea as he waited.

Finally, "Cavendish here. Slides of the Churchill
Icon. Have Lottie put them on, will you?" He paused
before acknowledging, "Thank you." He replaced the
handset into its cradle and centered Matt with the probing
gaze of a scientist observing a new biological variation
of the species.

"After the inspector's inquiry on behalf of an
American insurance investigator several weeks back,
I've had copies of my personal slides placed in the
Institute's collection."

"Then you've seen the icon?"

"Oh, yes, shortly after it went on display at

Chartwell. Are you familiar with Chartwell?"

"Winston Churchill's home, or was."

"Near Westerham, Kent, some miles southeast of London. Administered by the National Trust." Looking at the clock on the wall, Cavendish took a final, rather noisy slurp of tea and pushed away from the desk, adding, "But come, Lottie should have the slides ready by now."

Matt followed the frail little man out the door and down the corridor toward a flight of stairs leading to the main galleries, listening and concentrating on Cavendish's continuing tutorial as they went.

"As you may or may not know, Mr. Berkeley, many icons we see today are single paintings, but over the centuries, icons have taken various forms. Some were but mere writing tablets, normally used for inscribing words of the scripture or those of church patriarchs. Others, the majority of what presently exist, are carvings or paintings. Usually of religious subjects."

As they made their way down the stairs and onto the first level of galleries, Matt felt the old man's eyes darting in his direction, exploring his face, still dissecting, still searching for what, he didn't know.

At first, it made him uncomfortable, but he dismissed the feeling as childish nonsense. He attributed Cavendish's apparent interest due to the man's age and long years of experience with recalcitrant students who refused to pay attention to his lectures.

"Without delving into the history of icons to any great extent, let me say that in addition to the single plate of ivory or wood or whatever material used, several construction variations evolved during and after the fifth and sixth centuries."

"The Churchill Icon. It's that old?"

"Oh, no, not by a thousand years or so. Sixteenth century. First came what we call the Diptych, a double tablet hinged together and covered on the inside with wax on which the ancients wrote with a stylus. The two tablets folded together like a book with the outside normally covered with quite intricate designs and embellishments. Gradually, these designs replaced the writing on the inside, leading to some of the greatest religious art known to man. As you'll see, however, the Churchill Icon is even more complex in design."

A uniformed guard nodded to Cavendish and held open the heavy glass door for them to enter the galleries. "Good morning, Doctor."

"Good morning, Jonas," Cavendish said as he led the way through the first room.

Immediately upon entry, Matt found himself immersed in the beauty of Peter Paul Rubens' somber religious scenes, complemented by the meandering colors and oriental designs of a Persian carpet running underfoot.

"This way," Cavendish directed. Taking Matt by the elbow, he led him into a much more modern, spacious, and brightly lighted gallery honoring the likes of Renoir, Manet, Degas, Cezanne, Seurat and many other nineteenth-century impressionists.

Matt pointed to an empty slot in a line of paintings along one wall. A white card was posted conspicuously in the space, its typewritten words explaining, "REMOVED FOR RESTORATION."

"The van Gogh?"

Cavendish nodded. "Sadly, but it will be returned once we've made it whole again. Here we are."

Cavendish's sparrow-like fingers grasped Matt's arm and led him into a small room just off the

Impressionist Gallery. Its normally open viewing windows were covered by heavy black curtains to provide a degree of privacy for its occupants. Cavendish nodded to an attractive young woman standing near a slide projector at the back of the room. "Thank you, Lottie. You may start."

The lights dimmed to almost full darkness as Matt and Cavendish took their seats. The sound of the projector's cooling fan; a shaft of light, spreading stark white against a pull-down screen; a click as the carousel dropped the first slide into position; and the screen turned a burnished copper.

"The Churchill Icon, Mr. Berkeley, or rather its reverse side."

"Interesting, but it doesn't look like any of the icons I've seen before."

Cavendish chuckled, then explained, "This particular icon is in three parts, but here, we see it closed. Like most icons, this one has a protective cover, which is rarely ever seen. In this case, thinly rolled copper, exquisitely hammered into figures of the Christ at different times in his life."

Matt studied the screen. "Amazing," he said aloud, squinting to make certain what he was seeing was real. The shadows of the artist's work gave the illusion of constant motion. Its coppery highlights provided a three-dimensional flow of energy to the Christ as He progressed from Bethlehem to the arms of the cross. Was it his imagination, or the breath of a nearby air vent against the screen, giving life to art? Whatever, he was thankful when Cavendish said, "Next."

Another *click* of the projector, and the near golden brown of polished copper turned to a montage of faces and colors, ochre and cinnabar, dusky purples and blues.

"With the icon in its open position," Cavendish
went on, "we have what is known as a triptych. Three
individual plaques or panels, linear across the bottom, the
central and largest of the panels, arched to a point at the
top.

"As for the side panels, each is shaped exactly like
a wing, an angel's wing, if you will. Each wing is half
the width of the center panel. As you see, they're
attached to the center panel by ivory hinges and capable
of closing like a book. When I saw it at Chartwell, it was
in a standing position as it is in this photograph. Each
wing open and angled outward from the center panel,
thus allowing it to stand without support. Much like an
old fashion, three-piece room divider."

"How large is it?" Matt asked.

"The center panel stands slightly over a meter in
height – slightly over three feet to you Americans – and
approximately, I'd say, two feet wide. With the wings
spread in an open position, the entire width is a little more
than four feet."

"And the paintings?"

"With the exception of the very apex of the arch,
the center panel is almost completely covered with
what's entitled *Transfiguration of Christ the Savior*. A
painting using the medium of tempera, essentially an
emulsion composed of oil usually thickened with a resin,
egg and water."

With the aid of a laser pointer, Cavendish went on,
"If you are a student of art, you know that symbols played
an integral part in the development of Russian
iconography. Referring to the use and interpretation of
fifteenth- and sixteenth-century symbolism, the time
when this icon is believed to have been produced, we
know that the mountain placed against the blue sky in the

arch above the *Transfiguration* represents spiritual ascension."

As though already familiar with a prearranged script, Lottie switched slides to a split screen enlargement of the side panels.

"The two wing panels each contain three separate paintings."

"I recognize the Virgin Mary," Matt interrupted, "but who're the others?"

"As you say, Mary with the baby Jesus on the left wing and by herself on the right. The remaining subjects? The Apostle Paul and John the Baptist immediately below Mary and the babe. With Mary on the right, St. Simeon the Pius and Archangel Michael. Like that above the *Transfiguration*, the symbols separating each figure were those of the times. A candle representing the human soul, a tree for the tree of life, a bowl symbolizing bitter fate and a cup denoting sacrifice."

"And the artist?"

"That is one of the mysteries surrounding the icon. There appears to be no one artist involved. Parts reflect the fifteenth-century poetic style of the Novgorodian school, glittering with brilliant, festive colors. Others mimic Rublev and his contemporaries of the Moscow school dominated by a mixture of such colors you could never imagine. Yet they are tempered by the gentleness and almost unearthly loftiness of Heaven's own touch." The longer Cavendish talked, the more enraptured he became.

"The most astounding of all, however, is the *Transfiguration* of the center panel. The austere, yet passionate and dramatic severity of form, color and expression so characteristic of Theophanes. Those times

I've seen the icon, I've felt as though enveloped in its richness and warmth."

The words seemed to flow from Cavendish's mouth like the surge of a mountain stream, each word feeding on the other, tributaries enlarging the emotional torrent that washed from his soul.

"I thought only God could use such colors, but here, man has done so in an attempt to portray the Deity. Incarnate, embodied in human form, yet, at the same time, surpassing mankind in His dimension, mortal yet immortal. Never, oh never, have I experienced such beauty."

Suddenly, the projector clicked again, interrupting the Doctor's passion. A full view of the open icon appeared on the screen when lights gradually brightened in the room. Cavendish shivered as though abruptly awakened from a deep and wondrous sleep. A single tear traveled over the bony curvature of his left cheek.

"Forgive me, Mr. Berkeley," he said, dabbing at his eye with a handkerchief. "When I see and when I think of the icon's beauty, I... I seem to lose touch with reality."

Matt nodded his understanding. "But beauty is seldom the reason a work of art is stolen. To put it in the most basic of terms, how much was it worth?"

Cavendish was quick to take offense, jumping to his feet as if cold water had been thrown in his face. "Worth? Why it's priceless!"

Matt stood. "I didn't mean to upset you, Doctor, but it's something I need to know."

Removing his glasses, Cavendish placed each lens in his open mouth, exhaled, then wiped each with the handkerchief that had absorbed the tear. "Some years back when it was brought out of the closet, so to speak, several of London's most reputable art dealers were asked to assign a value. To my knowledge, each refrained from making an estimate.

"Even Sotheby's, one of the largest and most successful dealers in all England, refused unless the icon was contracted to them for auction. Only then would they establish a figure for the opening bid, with no assurance it would be anywhere near its true value. In my opinion, its worth as a form of art, its religious significance and its historical association with Churchill and the Yalta Conference make its value virtually inestimable."

Nodding his thanks to the projectionist, Matt followed Cavendish out of the room and back into the Impressionist Gallery. "That raises another point."

Cavendish stopped, his facial expression indicating a sudden dislike of Matt's line of questioning. "Yes?"

"If there was no monetary value placed on the icon, how was it insured?"

Cavendish appeared momentarily disoriented, as if he'd never considered such a thing. "A most interesting thought, most interesting, indeed. Perhaps you should speak with Lord Jeffrey Alanbrooke. Though semi-retired like myself, he continues to function something in the capacity of curator at Chartwell.

"Since Lady Anne, his wife, passed away, his only interest has been preserving Sir Winston's memory. He might also be able to explain more thoroughly the Yalta connection. I could ring for an appointment, if you'd like."

"Detective Inspector Stuart has already arranged for a two o'clock appointment this afternoon, but thanks for the offer."

Suddenly, out of his peripheral vision, Matt saw the man he'd seen in the black sedan with Russian diplomatic plates and chased from the hotel lobby. With his head quickly turning from Matt to Manet's *Bar at the Folies-Bergère*, it was apparent the man was attempting to hide the scar on his face with his hand, but the recognition had already been made.

"Excuse me, Doctor." Matt started toward the man who immediately bolted for the door. "Hey!" Matt shouted, his voice exploding in the whispered silence of the gallery. All eyes turned in his direction, including those of the guard.

The guard chastened, "Here, now, you can't –"

"Sorry 'bout that," Matt called as he darted past the guard. From one room to another, he searched, dodging and sidestepping those who got in his way. Finally, the building's entrance, the closing swish of glass doors and Matt knew he was too late.

Pushing his way through the double doors, Matt shouted to the man already at the curb, "Wait a minute! All I want is –"

The doors at his back burst open and two museum guards grabbed him by the arms. "Bloody Americans! What do you think you're doing?" the guard on his right yelled in his ear.

"This is a museum," the second added. "You can't come over here and ..."

The guards' voices faded into a monotone of blah, blah blahs as Matt watched a now familiar looking black Mercedes sedan slow to a moving halt in front of the museum. His quarry entered through a rear door suddenly swung open. With the squeal of tires echoing on the air, the Mercedes pulled away into the noonday traffic.

"Damn it! He did it again."

Though it was still there, Matt took only passing notice of

the rusted lorry, parked across the street, its bed covered by a torn, oily looking tarpaulin. There was no way for him to know that the lorry's cab sheltered three men prepared to kill for a man named Damien and a hundred pounds sterling.

Chapter 9

"He's turning," Hajir said, pointing to the fire engine red, 4-door Ford Mondeo sedan up ahead and the M25 expressway exit sign which read:

WESTERHAM   5
CHARTWELL   7

Hajir increased the rented Land Rover's speed, shot to the outside lane and hit the exit ramp at a little over ninety-five kilometers or sixty mph. Tires screeched on the curve as the red, easy-to-recognize Ford again came into sight.

Straining against her shoulder strap, Leila cautioned, "Not too close." She watched the green blip representing Matt's car on the dash-mounted tracking monitor.

"We have the transponder under his car. We'll know where he's going."

* * *

Although he hated the god-awful color of the midsize sedan, Matt was thankful to have maneuvered his way without serious mishap through the traffic of London, over the Thames and across the south side of the city. Rather than congratulate himself on his expert driving, he decided everyone that saw him must have recognized him as an American driver constantly muttering to himself, "Keep left, keep left."

He was finally able to relax after turning from the four-lane expressway onto the small, hedgerow-lined, two-lane road designated a single carriageway by the legend on his map. Music drifted from the car's rear speakers. The sweep of symphonic violins and the majesty of brass offered a melodic tone poem to the widening vista of southeastern England.

The landscape unfolded around him like a mural on a never-ending roll of earthen canvas. The myriad shades of that autumn's colors seemed more vivid to Matt than those he'd seen at home over the past several years. On either hand lay cherry orchards, clustered low in the valleys; open fields dotted with rounded haycocks as far as the eye could see; and apple trees, all waiting to be harvested, some bearing red and yellow Galas for juice and cider, others solid red Braeburns for pies, cobblers and what he liked best, the simple pleasure of eating direct from the tree.

Even more captivating to Matt were the acres and acres of ten- to twelve-foot-high wooden poles, all plugged into the soil and crisscrossed at the top with heavy cord. Each "field of sticks" formed an aerial cat's cradle of support for the growth of hop vines.

Nearby stretched a line of oast houses or simply oasts. The half dozen brick structures were round at the base with roofs shaped like up-side-down ice cream cones. The roofs, also of brick, were topped with metal cowls or air vents. Each oast appeared to stand at least forty to fifty feet tall against the distant hills. Matt wondered if inside, hop cones were drying, their essence soon to flavor some of the world's most famous beers.

With hardly any traffic on the road and the confusion of driving on the left having faded since leaving the city, Matt let the little British-made Ford have its head. He finally eased back on the accelerator as the speedometer arm pointed just past the 80 mark and hedgerows on either side of the road became blurs in the periphery of his vision. Rounding a slight bend, he was suddenly confronted with a side road from one of the many orchards and a large, black lorry, waiting to pull onto the road, its bed covered by a torn, oily-looking tarpaulin.

* * *

The two passengers in the cab braced themselves, ready for the impact as Harry shifted gears. The accompanying high-pitched grind cut through the sound of the engine's roar as the lorry shot forward. Harry's massive hands and arms whipped the wheel around, aiming at the driver's side of the fire-engine-red sedan, but the sedan veered away at the last moment.

"Damn!" Harry cursed, swiping away the long stringy hair blowing across his face.

"Bloody fool!" the man named Pearly shouted, "Ya missed 'im!"

* * *

"Goddamn it!" Matt swore. He automatically jerked the steering wheel to the left and braced himself as best he could. The Ford jolted off the pavement and careened into the hedgerow running alongside the road. He fought the wheel, trying to keep the tires from sliding farther into the shrubbery, alternating brake and accelerator pedals to avoid spinning out of control.

He could feel and hear the chalkboard screech of hedge ends scraping the side of the car, until gradually, he brought the sedan to a stop, half on, half off the pavement. In the rearview mirror, he watched the lorry, speeding in the opposite direction, tarpaulin canopy flapping wildly in the wind.

Ignoring the Land Rover with the darkened windows that slowed, then sped up as it passed, Matt shouted at the lorry's diminishing image in the mirror. "Sonofabitch! You did that on purpose."

In his mind's eye, he could still see the long, stringy blond hair and the gaping mouth of the driver. He'd been a giant of a man, almost as large as both of the other two shadowy figures in the lorry's cab. Matt knew damn well, the way the driver leered down on the much smaller automobile, the man had deliberately aimed, not only for the side of the car, but directly at him.

"Bastard!"

* * *

At a distance, Chartwell, its brick walls a dullish red against the afternoon sky, resembled a manor house of the Tudor style, but now, he wasn't sure. Its various wings and four stories of rooms resembled any number of country hotels he'd seen scattered throughout England. Once inhabited by great families, they were now too expensive even for many of England's titled gentry, the once wealthy who still clung to the past.

He parked the car in the shade of a horse chestnut tree cloaked in autumn gold and made his way across the private parking area toward the house, stopping momentarily for an unobstructed view of the grounds. There was little question in Matt's mind why Chartwell had appealed to Churchill.

Across an almost perfectly manicured valley and along a cluster of rolling hills beyond, chestnut, beech and oak grew in profusion while a single cedar of Lebanon stood alone on the highest point. The spread of its branches created a pyramid-like, symmetrical whorl of limbs and needles against the sky.

Stemming a certain amount of envy, Matt turned and walked up the steps to Sir Winston Churchill's Chartwell. The day had warmed significantly under the late October sun. He was glad to feel the soft coolness of the entrance hall.

"Name's Berkeley," he said to the National Trust volunteer collecting entrance fees, a gray-haired lady in her late years, but whose smile had remained young and fresh. "I have an appointment with Lord Alanbrooke."

"Yes, he told me to expect you. If you'll wait a moment, I'll have one of our people take you up. The last tour of the day has just completed, and Lord Alanbrooke thought you might enjoy meeting in Sir Winston's study."

"Thank you, ma'am. How much do I owe?"

"Nothing, sir. You're here on business with Lord Alanbrooke, not for the tour."

"Then consider this a donation." He handed her a 20-pound note.

"Thank you ever so much. Every bit helps. The homes are quite expensive to maintain, and... ah, yes, here's your guide. Jenny, will you take Mr. Berkeley to the study? Lord Alanbrooke is waiting."

The young woman looked at Matt, a twinkle in her eyes as she gave him a quick up-and-down appraisal before smiling her apparent approval. "This way, Mr. Berkeley. It's on the next floor up."

Matt followed, admiring the way Jenny's hips moved under the loosely fitting print dress. His admiration grew even more with the smile on her face as she turned and beckoned toward the lengthy sweep of stairs leading to the upper floors. Involuntarily, his pulse as well as his imagination quickened as he studied the young woman's features: short, light-brown hair, tousled gently by the breeze that whispered through the open doorway; heart-shaped face with skin as white and smooth as cream; eyes that sparkled like sunlight on water.

How much younger was she than him? Twenty years? Thirty? Even so, he wondered if a dinner invitation might be in order. All the while, searching for a wedding ring on her finger. He found none.

She stopped on the first landing before a large door of heavy, dark-stained wood, knocked politely three times, then pushed the door open and stepped barely inside the threshold. "Lord Alanbrooke, Mr. Berkeley's here."

"Good. Have him come in, Jenny m'dear."

Matt stepped through the doorway as Jenny moved back, brushing ever so slightly against his shoulder, her perfume igniting a fire deep inside. "Old lavender?" he asked softly.

Jenny hesitated for a moment, smiled once again as though saying, "We'll meet again, you and I," and then she was gone.

"Come in, Berkeley," Lord Alanbrooke commanded from across the room. "When Inspector Stuart rang, he said you were coming all the way from America to see about the icon. Not sure why, and I don't know how I can help, but I'll try. It's been quite some time since it was stolen, you know."

Jeffrey Chatterton, Earl of Alanbrooke, was a large man, rotund in fact, standing over six feet in height and bald except for a sandy fringe of hair encircling the sides and back of his head. Somewhere in his eighties, even nincties Matt judged, his eyes quickly drawn to the man's nose. It was a large, bulbous red thing with spidery veins showing beneath the skin and pockmarked as though once peppered by a wad of buckshot. The face, however, was the purest complexioned Matt could recall having seen on a man, totally incongruous with its elephantine nasal companion.

"Over here, Berkeley. You on that side of the fireplace, and I'll sit here. Tea and biscuit?"

"Tea only, please. With sugar or sweetener, whichever your have."

Matt glanced quickly about the room as he crossed the tightly woven carpet. The first thing he noted was a desk of the darkest mahogany. It was cluttered with miniature busts of Napoleon and Lord Horatio Nelson and several framed pictures of the Prime Minister's wife, Clementine, and their children.

The fireplace, smaller than most with no mantle, was surmounted by an immense oil painting Matt recognized as Blenheim Palace, Churchill's birthplace. On the walls, photographs of men and women, many of their faces familiar from history books and old black-and-white newsreels. People who, with Churchill, had helped shape the world as Matt now knew it.

Above his head hung a simple, hoop-shaped chandelier
and two large banners representing Churchill's coat of arms and his standard as Knight of the Garter. The banners' crimsons and golds added the only bright note to an otherwise somber and colorless room.

As tea was being poured, Matt took his seat beside the fireplace and looked back, finding it easy to imagine the wily old statesman at the desk. He would be dressed in a gray, pinstripe suit and bow tie with a cigar clenched tightly in the left corner of his mouth. Wire rimmed spectacles would rest midway down the bridge of his nose.

Lord Alanbrooke laughed softly as he handed Matt a cup of tea. "I see you're as caught up in the spell as I, Mr. Berkeley. Many of the decisions that affected the world were made in this room, Sir Winston seated at his father's desk or relaxing during a quiet moment before the fire. The aura of a great man can linger through the years, and that is what you sense."

"Yes, sir," Matt admitted, taking his first sips from the cup. "My father was stationed in England until the Normandy invasion and used to tell stories about Sir Winston. Quite a man, but I know you're busy, so I'll get to the point." Matt took a business card from his jacket, one of the few cards left since his official retirement from NAARPA, and handed it to Lord Alanbrooke.

Alanbrooke studied the card as Matt continued. "My organization's been asked by one of your antiquity societies to locate the icon Sir Winston brought back from the Yalta Conference. Doctor Cavendish at the Courtauld Institute provided an excellent description, but I need to know some of the history. For example, why was the icon presented to Churchill in the first place? And what happened to it between Yalta and its disappearance from Chartwell in nineteen ninety-six? Names, places, events, anything you can remember. Anything you might've thought strange or unusual."

Lord Alanbrooke tucked the card in the breast pocket of his tweed jacket and bit off a small piece of biscuit, washing it down with a generous portion of milk-flavored tea. "From the beginning, eh? Very well, but it started before Yalta. The Tehran Conference, November, nineteen forty-three. Remember it well. Churchill presented The Sword of Honor to Stalin by command of His Majesty, King George. It had been especially wrought and signed to commemorate the glorious defense of Stalingrad."

"You were in Tehran?"

"Oh, yes, young man. I attended the Prime Minister as a special aide throughout most of the war and journeyed with him to numerous meetings, not the least being Cairo, Tehran and Yalta." Lord Alanbrooke finished his biscuit and tea and settled back into the too-small chair, his hands folded loosely and resting on the bulge of his enormous midsection.

"But enough of Tehran. Not one to be outdone, Stalin chose the Yalta occasion to repay the Prime Minister. Representatives of the Big Three were spread along the Black Sea coast. Stalin was in his wartime headquarters in the Yusupov Palace; the Prime Minister and several of his aides, including myself, in the Vorontsov Palace, since renamed the Alupka.

Roosevelt and his staff were quartered in the Livadia Palace, approximately five miles distance. Because of Roosevelt's frail health – he was by that time essentially confined to a wheelchair – all the plenary meetings were conducted in the Livadia. It was there the presentation was made.

At one end of the palace ballroom stood a large conference table, its surface neatly arranged with pitchers of water, numerous bottles of vodka and fruit drinks, glasses and a regiment of note pads and pencils. At the other end of the room, except for Franklin Roosevelt, President of the United States, and his interpreter who knelt next to the wheelchair, uniformed military and Soviet, British and American civilians stood at attention.

As Joseph Stalin neared the end of what had become a tedious and rambling monologue proclaiming the greatness of the Soviet Union, a Russian interpreter spoke softly in Churchill's ear, translating Stalin's words. "And now, it is a great honor to make this gift to our British ally."

Stalin nodded toward two Red Army soldiers who brought an open, three-panel icon forward and placed it on a nearby table. As Stalin continued, Churchill's interpreter translated, "This is one of many great and beautiful paintings removed from the Winter Palace in Leningrad before the German siege of nineteen forty-one. Please accept it as a token of appreciation from the Soviet people to the people of Great Britain."

A round of applause filled the ballroom as Churchill stepped to the table, admired the "gift," and said, "Premier Stalin, on behalf of the British people, I accept this beautiful treasure...."

Matt stood at the window, watching and listening to Lord Alanbrooke while at the same time following out the corner of his eye a cluster of dark clouds building over the line of beech trees on the far hill. "That's all?" he asked. "Nothing to indicate the Russians might want it back someday?"

"No. Why do you ask?"

Turning back from the window, Matt answered, "A man from the Russian Embassy keeps popping up wherever I go. That's why I wondered if anything unusual might've happened in Yalta."

Lord Alanbrooke shifted forward in his chair, took a poker from the hearth and studiously stirred the dead ashes in the bottom of the fireplace, allowing time to further stir the ashes of his memory. "Unusual? Perhaps, though I'm not sure I –"

"Please?"

Alanbrooke replaced the poker and sat back in his chair. "The last night, the thirteenth of February, the meetings had ended, you see. I was with the P.M. in his rooms the night before our departure. In addition to Prime Minister and myself, there was General Sir Edward Mason, then a colonel in the Royal Marines. A rather bleak, austere looking man if I do say so...."

< < > >

At Churchill's direction, Alanbrooke opened the icon and placed it on the table for the Prime Minister to study and admire as Colonel Mason continued discussion of that day's events. "I do feel, Prime Minister," Mason said with some hesitancy, "though President Roosevelt seemed most encouraged, we may regret parts of the agreement once the –"

Several rapid knocks at the door interrupted his words. Churchill was the first to react. "Colonel, if you please."

Mason went to the door and opened it slowly, then turned. "They're here, Prime Minister."

"Let them in, Colonel," Churchill ordered, at the same time blowing a cloud of cigar smoke toward the ceiling.

To Alanbrooke, he said, "The curtains, Jeffrey, and then if you'll leave us. We'll continue our discussions tomorrow."

"Yes, sir," Alanbrooke answered, pulling the curtains across the two windows that opened onto the

palace grounds and the Black Sea beyond. Moving toward the door, he made way for two men who stepped into the room.

One was a uniformed Soviet NKGB officer whose name tag read "PACHENKO." The other, a middle-aged, unshaven civilian in clothes that looked and smelt as though they had been worn and slept in for weeks.

The civilian walked stiffly past Alanbrooke, stopped in front of Churchill, snapped to attention and clicked his heels. With heavy German accent, he said, "Guten Abend, Herr Prime Minister. Ich bin Gustav Schiller."

Chapter 10

Lord Alanbrooke leaned back in his chair and sighed before saying, "'I am Gustav Schiller.' That's the last thing I heard him say and the last I know of the meeting before closing the door behind me. It was also the last I saw of the icon during the trip, which extended through Athens and on to Malta for a final meeting with Roosevelt. We didn't know at the time we'd not see your president again before his death."

"When, after you got back to England, did you see the icon?" Matt asked, finally taking his seat by the darkened fireplace.

"We were preparing for the Christmas season here at Chartwell. Christmas, nineteen ninety-five, to be precise."

"That's fifty years. What the hell happened during all those years?" Matt blurted without thinking. "Where was the icon?"

Alanbrooke grunted a half-laugh. "Well yes, it was a bit of time, wasn't it? Jenny, the young lady who escorted you to the study – and by the way, General Sir Edward Mason's daughter by his second wife..." Alanbrooke laughed softly. "A May-December relationship I must say. Jenny and I were combing the various paintings in Sir Winston's studio. Paintings he had done himself. Looking for something festive to hang inside the house...."

< < > >

Every square centimeter of the studio's walls

91

seemed to be covered with Sir Winston's work, canvases sometimes three and four high, from floor to ceiling. Other than a frequent feather dusting, most were undisturbed since his death. On the easel, an unfinished seascape; brushes and oils on a nearby table; a paint-smeared coverall draped across the back of Sir Winston's chair.

"What do you think?" Lord Alanbrooke asked Jenny.

Jenny turned, her eyes searching from wall to wall, from seaside villages to still life and portraits of faces from Churchill's past. "They're all lovely in their own way, but not very Christmassy." Jenny opened the door to a closet used for storing household cleaning goods. "What might these be?"

"What might what be?"

Jenny pointed to several shelves at the rear of the closet and a number of framed paintings stacked almost tongue-in-groove all the way to the ceiling. "I've known they were here, but never took the time to look."

"Let's find out," Alanbrooke said.

Entering the closet and standing on the toes of her shoes, Jenny stretched upward to remove the top painting, at the same time grasping one of the lower shelves for support. A low crunching sound behind the paintings quickly turned into a loud r-r-i-i-i-p as the shelf she was holding pulled away from the wall. Jenny screamed and stumbled backwards out of the closet, tripping over a broom and wash pail as the shelves, paintings and part of the wall suddenly gave way and fell in an explosion of dust and plaster.

Alanbrooke rushed to Jenny's side and helped her to her feet. "Are you all right, girl?"

Jenny dusted herself off and again pointed toward

the closet. "I think so, but look."

The edge of a large package wrapped in heavy black tarpaper protruded from a hole in the wall where the shelves had been. Quickly moving the fallen shelves and paintings to one side, Jenny pulled the package from the hole and, with Lord Alanbrooke's help, carried it to a worktable beneath one of the windows. Careful not to damage the contents, Jenny tore away the tarpaper and pulled back an inner lining of white linen.

"My God," Alanbrooke breathed. The raised, multiple figures of Christ stared back at him from a sheath of finely burnished copper.

"What is it?" Jenny asked.

"Here child," Lord Alanbrooke said excitedly. "The wing panels. Open them. If it's what I think..."

Jenny laid back the two wing panels to reveal the long-forgotten painting.

"By Jove, it is!" Lord Alanbrooke gasped. "It's the icon from Yalta!"

< < > >

"Good old Winnie," Alanbrooke went on, "he'd taken such tender care of the thing, but why he'd hidden it away like that was beyond me."

"Me, too," Matt agreed thoughtfully.

"As you know, only three short months after we placed it on display, it was gone, stolen by some bloody rotter for his own selfish interests. We immediately closed off the room except for view from the doorway. Of course, Scotland Yard was notified, but they've come no closer to it over the years than they were the first day."

The room had dropped into darkness as storm clouds massed along the western sky.

"There's really nothing more to tell, Mr. Berkeley.

93

I've felt as though I let Sir Winston and Clementine down by being the main contributor to the loss of such a wonderful treasure."

Matt felt sorry for the old aristocrat. "Not your fault it was stolen. You brought it back for the world to see."

"Exactly. Scotland Yard felt it was what you'd call an inside job, but that I cannot accept. I've known our National Trust volunteers for years, like my own family."

"And General Sir Edward Mason. What became of him?"

"Oh yes, Sir Edward. He stayed with the P.M. until the electoral defeat at the hands of Clement Attlee and the Labour Party. Winnie led England through the worst of times only to be turned out by those he loved and served so selflessly.

But to the point, Sir Edward remained in the Royal Marines and was later posted to Egypt where he served as part of the British Staff at Suez. It was there he received his promotion to General rank. Later, stricken with some sort of religious zeal, he returned to England, retired from the service and rejoined Churchill in fifty-two, remaining with him through the second term as Prime Minister and up to the final days. Sir Edward was with the family at Hyde Park Gate when Sir Winston died in sixty-five. Knighthood conferred shortly thereafter."

"Where is he now?"

"Took his own life less than a year after the icon vanished. Terrible thing, certainly for Jenny. She was engaged to be married at the time, but shortly afterwards, broke off the engagement and went away, to the continent, I believe. Only returned two years ago."

The first drops of rain splattered against the

windows. The wind abruptly grew to a howl, and then, just as quickly, died to a low, steady moan as the late afternoon assumed an ominous cast of wintry grey.

Lord Alanbrooke turned in his chair and pointed to a small table against the far wall. "Once had several photographic albums of Sir Winston's war years, some with pictures from Yalta, but they, too, went missing. Meant to have them replaced with copies from the Cabinet War Rooms in London, but never got 'round to it."

From beyond the windows came the mournful sounds of vines and shrubbery clinging to Chartwell's outer walls. They whipped back and forth in the autumn wind and rain. The cry of the wind around the corners of the building seemed to reinforce Matt's misgivings about the icon, both its disappearance and the people linked to its past and present.

"You've been very helpful, Lord Alanbrooke," Matt said, standing in preparation to leave. "One other thing."

"Yes?"

"After you found it, how much was the icon insured for?"

"There was no insurance."

"Then you've never heard of World Wide Inland Marine Underwriters?"

"Neither in relation to the icon nor to anything else at Chartwell."

"Nor a man named Roberts representing that company."

"No."

"Then why would they be involved?" Matt asked, the question meant more for himself than for Lord Alanbrooke.

"Why indeed," Lord Alanbrooke answered as he pushed up from the chair and extended his hand to Matt. "If I think of anything else, where can you be reached?"

Matt shook Alanbrooke's hand as they walked to the door and out onto the landing. "Jubilee Hotel in London. If I'm not there, leave a message, and I'll get back. I appreciate your assistance, and if I learn anything about the icon, I'll let you know."

"Please do," Lord Alanbrooke answered as Matt started down the stairs, "and Mr. Berkeley..."

Matt stopped and looked back.

"Good luck."

"Thank you."

As Lord Alanbrooke returned to the study, Matt made his way down to the entrance, surprised to see the young woman named Jenny standing behind the reception desk, counting the day's receipts.

"My goodness, Mr. Berkeley. You'll catch your death in this weather. Please wait, and I'll find you a brolly."

Though enchanted by her accent, her smile, and in fact, everything about her, Matt shook his head apologetically. "I can't take your umbrella."

"You're staying in London, aren't you?"

"Yes, but –"

"Then return it to me there. I live with my mother near Hyde Park. Here." Almost forcing the umbrella into Matt's hands, she took a sheet of paper from the desk's top drawer and wrote her name, address and telephone number.

"My name's Jenny Mason. If you don't have the time, I'll understand, but if you do, please call. Caroline, that's my mother, would love to meet you, I'm sure, and you could return the brolly. I do have other plans for this evening, but..." She handed the paper to him, pausing ever so slightly as her hand touched his.

Although only a moment in time, Matt's hand lingered against hers for as long as he dared. "I'll take good care of your brolly, Jenny Mason, and yes," Matt looked quickly at the paper before putting it in his pocket, "I'll find the time, I promise."

She smiled as he pushed through the door and struggled to open the umbrella against the wind-lashed rain. Looking back over his shoulder, he saw her standing in the doorway, laughing and waving with one hand while holding her skirt against her legs with the other. The wind molded the cotton print dress against her body, outlining every curve, every detail.

Once to the car, Matt turned as the wind caught the umbrella and whipped it inside out. He waved to the still laughing, deliciously desirable Jenny and said to himself, "Yes, ma'am, Jenny Mason, I will definitely find the time."

Chapter 11

The rain had diminished to a steady drizzle as Matt drove through the village of Westerham on his way back to London, but the gray bleakness of that time somewhere between late afternoon and early evening had settled over the countryside. A fine mist spread across the automobile's windscreen and was intermittently swished away by the rhythmic scrape of the wiper blades. Their back-and-forth motion maintained half cadence with the final movement of Beethoven's Ninth Symphony, its choral brilliance flowing like a river of sound inside the car.

The icon very much on his mind, Matt was startled by a reflection that suddenly materialized in his rearview mirror. It was the image of a large, black lorry rapidly overtaking him. He had long since turned on his headlights and thought it strange the truck's driver had not done the same.

As the lorry drew closer, he could make out a tarpaulin flapping wildly above the top and to the rear of the cab. "Aw, Christ!" The increased pressure of his foot against the accelerator was an automatic reflex to the memory of a similar tarpaulin flying in the wind.

Closing rapidly, the lorry slammed into the rear of Matt's car, causing it to jerk forward and skid as he hit the brakes. The tires slid along the pavement. He knew he had done the wrong thing, but it was too late. He heard and felt the screech of the left fender against the hedgerow as the car left the road. Thrown about like a crash test dummy, Matt fought to keep himself upright in the seat. At the same time, he palmed the steering wheel one way, then the other, trying to find enough tire traction to regain control.

With the car still bumping dangerously along the shoulder, Matt's peripheral vision alerted him to the lorry as it pulled alongside. The scream of metal-against-metal tore at his ears. Feeling the door start to buckle only inches from his body, his immediate reaction was to throw himself to the left, away from the lorry, hoping to get his head and body on the seat below windscreen level, but he moved too quickly. The seat belt and shoulder harness snapped taut and held him captive.

"Goddamn it!" he shouted, throwing hands and arms across his face as the car ripped through the bushes. It spun out over a small stream separating the road from an orchard and crashed on the stream's far bank, the impact directly beneath the driver's seat. The rear of the car dropped downward with a loud splash, leaving the front of the car against the opposite bank pointed skyward while the boot was immersed in mud and water. The engine sputtered and died.

Momentarily stunned, it took only the sound of the lorry's gears being reversed and the slamming of doors on the opposite side of the hedgerow to alert Matt of the danger that still existed. He knew there could be only one thing the man or men in the truck wanted. His life!

Extricating himself from the safety straps and finding his door jammed, Matt crawled across the front seat. He tested the door handle on the passenger side and pushed as hard as he could. The rearward angle at which the vehicle rested seemed to increase fourfold the door's weight. Grudgingly, the door came open, and he dropped headfirst to the rain-soaked bank. Before he could roll away, the door slammed hard against his left ankle.

"Damn!" he swore between clenched teeth, automatically cramming the end of a fist into his mouth and biting down to silence what he knew would be an involuntary cry from the pain.

Tears filled his eyes as he pulled his foot free of the door's crushing weight. Matt grabbed his ankle and willed it not to be broken, but it was the high-pitched shout of orders from the road that refocused his thoughts to the more immediate danger.

"Gi' down there an' find 'im. If 'e ain't dead awready, one way er another, Damien wants him dead. Now move, er I'll kick yer bloomin' heads clear up yer bloomin' arses."

Matt crawled up the side of the bank, using the car to shield himself from anyone approaching from the road, but where to go? He couldn't stay with the car. Off to his right, he saw a ragged clump of willows, and he knew the trees were his only chance.

Bent almost double, pain shooting like barbed arrows from his ankle and up through his knee, he started along the top of the bank toward the willow grove, his movements an awkward half-run, half-limp. Several times, he slipped on the wet grass, his feet sloshing down the side of the bank into the water. Each time it happened, he forced himself back onto the bank as the voice in his
brain ordered, "Move it! Move it! Move it!"

Finally, the trees. Matt flung himself beneath the cascade of willow branches, his breath, ragged and painful. His ribs ached from the impact of the crash and his ankle felt like it was on fire, but again, distant sounds drew his attention.

He watched through the heavy foliage. There was still enough light for him to see three men emerge from the hedgerow and splash their way through the shallow stream to the car. First the driver with the stringy blond hair, a huge man who dwarfed his companions, and a shorter man wearing a white, bloodstained butcher's smock. Last to arrive was an older man with a scraggly beard and greasy hair hanging mop-like from beneath a crumpled fisherman's cap, a sailor's heavy wool pea coat buttoned tight against his chest.

"'E's not 'ere,'" bellowed the man in the sailor's pea coat.

Matt recognized the voice as the one who had already ordered his death. Moving back toward the opening in the hedgerow, he heard the man order, "Spread out en' git 'im. I'll bring the lorry 'round."

The other two, both with revolvers in their hands, responded immediately: "white smock" to the south of the wrecked car, the truck driver toward the willows.

"Aw, shit!" Matt cursed as he watched the driver move in his direction. Ignoring the pain in his ankle and the far-off sounds of the lorry being started, he moved deeper into the grove of willows. Without a weapon, darkness and distance were his only allies.

* * *

Having waited in Westerham during Matt's visit to Chartwell and now following some distance behind, Bājī Leila saw that the green blip on the small tracking screen transmitted from the transponder beneath Matt's car was no longer moving. And then she saw it.

"There," she shouted, pointing to the crushed hedgerow and the fire-engine-red Ford resting against the far bank of a narrow stream, part of the boot in the water.

Hajir brought the Land Rover to a skidding halt on the wet pavement, then quickly backed the vehicle off the side of the road.

As Leila threw open her door, a gunshot rang out from somewhere off to her right. "Hurry, Hajir," she cried, "hurry!"

Chapter 12

A burning sensation penetrated Matt's left upper thigh, accompanied almost immediately by a sticky warmth spreading down his leg. The water-soaked earth felt soft as he slid to his knees. "Not like this," he grunted, violently shaking his head against the shock he knew a bullet could bring and the realization he was going to die if he didn't do something, fast.

"Now, goddamn it, now," he ordered, as though mind and body were two separate beings.

Matt strained to get to his feet. He could feel the swelling in his ankle and the band of red-hot steel beginning to tighten around his thigh, working its way up, past his abdomen and into his chest, his breathing more difficult by the minute. He wanted to vomit, but knew he had to resist.

Blood throbbed against the sides of his temples. The pressure momentarily blotted out his vision, but the fear that surged through his brain prompted movement, demanded action if he was to survive. Shaking the dizziness from his head and rubbing his eyes to bring back sight, he staggered through the thicket, shrugging off low hanging branches as he moved.

Matt paused a moment, and then he saw it. Dead ahead! A clearing populated by weeds and the remains of a hops garden. In the center, a brick oast house like the ones he'd seen earlier in the day. Could he make it? He started, then stopped, clutching his thigh and gasping for breath.

Not only had the rain become heavier, but there

was something else, a movement to his right. The smack of a twig broken underfoot; a sudden flash of light, on for a moment, then off. As he stood in the deepening gloom, his mind's eye visualized the truck driver, the face and the leer that had peered down from the lorry.

Acknowledging how suddenly tired he was and how slow he'd become, he accepted the fact that the driver had somehow gotten in front of him and was waiting for an unobstructed shot once he entered the clearing.

Again, more sounds. Matt reasoned the man had grown impatient, was on the move again, headed in his direction, and ready to kill at first sight.

"Three fucking years in Nam without a scratch and now this?" Matt's pain had increased to the point he could no longer silently consider his alternatives. He had to hear his own voice. Each thought verbalized even if only a whisper. He had to know that he was still rational. "Gotta be a way."

Shivering from a combination of damp, cold and injury shock, Matt waited, silently shifting back into the dripping leaves of the willow trees, praying he wouldn't be seen or heard, but he needed a weapon. What? Grasping one of the lower limbs, he very slowly bent it back until it became a lethal bow, poised to spring forward when released.

At the same time, the suction-like sound of the truck driver's footsteps moving across the waterlogged earth grew closer. Finally. he saw the outline of the man, a faceless shape in the dark, turning one way, then another, searching, listening. Matt tried to control his uneven breathing, but without warning, a cough erupted from his throat.

The driver whirled about. The beam of a flashlight

suddenly exploded in Matt's face. At the same time, the man shouted, "It's 'im!"

The revolver spat flame as Matt released the branch and dropped to the ground. The limb, like a whip's lash, traveled with unexpected force. It struck the man in the throat and drove him into a second limb level with the back of his head. A scream tore the air. The man's feet left the ground, his head caught in a vice between the two branches. Just as quickly, the limbs parted and the driver fell, immediately struggling to get up, trying to
suck air past an Adam's apple jammed against his windpipe.

Moving as fast as his ankle and the pain in his thigh would allow, Matt lunged forward and chopped downward with a single closed fist against the back of the man's neck. Once, twice, three times with lightning speed. With the third strike, the terrible
cr-r-r-rack of bone triggered Matt's memory.

Vietnam! Darkness and the bitter taste of fear. His knee against the perimeter guard's spine. The backwards jerk of the man's head. Neck vertebrae crushed. Nerve tissue severed. Sensory stimuli and motor impulses terminated. A final body spasm, and the guard was dead. The sudden odor of feces mixed with the night smells of jungle decay.

On hands and knees, Matt crawled away from the driver, feeling his way through the drenched undergrowth. Like Vietnam, he could smell the stench of feces rising from the corpse. "Not now, please," he whispered, pleading with the ghosts of years past to stay locked behind the farthest doors of his memory.

Finally, the present intruded. The flashlight! Quickly backtracking to the driver's body, he grabbed the light still clutched in the man's hand, pried it free and immediately snapped it off. But where was the weapon? Afraid to turn the light back on, he thrashed around with his free hand, searching through the undergrowth near the body, but nothing.

"'arry, s'at you? 'arry?" The voice came from somewhere back in the grove of trees.

"Damn it!" The oast house! No other choice. With the steel band groping tighter and tighter at his thigh and the pain now reaching up past his gut into his chest, Matt took as deep a breath as he dared and forced his way through the pounding rain.

It seemed to take forever, but finally he reached the side of the silo-like structure. Patience was no longer a virtue. Futility and desperation crowded out reason. "The door, damn it! Where's the goddamn door?"

The curvature of the brick wall suddenly gave way to a ramshackle slab of wood. Cramming the flashlight into his jacket pocket, he pushed with his shoulder until the door scraped inward, inch-by-inch. The odor of dried hop cones and decaying plant matter filled his nostrils, sour-sweet, sickening, but better than the smell of a dead man's bowels.

Almost through the doorway, Matt twisted sharply as he heard a shout from the edge of the clearing. "'arry, Pearly, I got 'im. 'e's trapped 'is self."

Two shots! The first smashed into the wall near Matt's shoulder, splintering fragments of brick against his jacket; the second thudded into the door just above his head.

Matt shoved the door closed against the white-smocked apparition now running toward the building. At the same time, the sound of the lorry's engine reached his ears, and he knew the odds against his survival had suddenly doubled.

"Fucking great!" Matt cursed as he felt his way along the circular wall, stumbling over piles of rotting hop vines, trying to get to the side of the room opposite the door, searching for a place to hide. Even a ladder to climb to the air vent at the top of the structure and onto what little roof there might be. Anything.

A sharp blow to his already injured ankle brought Matt crashing into a clump of hop vines. His teeth bit into his lower lip as he stifled the cry and grabbed for his ankle. Instead, he found the length of a metal pipe at least three-quarters of an inch in diameter. Feeling with his hands, he realized it was bolted at one end to the wall. It ran outward at least six inches above the floor for approximately two feet. At its farthest end, it was bent at a ninety-degree angle and driven into the concrete floor.

Halfway along the pipe, however, he felt the loosely knotted end of a rope that stretched upward toward the center of the structure's ceiling. Slipping the knot and taking the rope in hand, Matt stood and felt his way farther along the wall until he came to a wooden ladder also bolted to the wall.

He could hear the man outside shouting for the others and knew he had only minutes at most before the door would open and somebody would try to kill him. Though aware of the risk of the light being seen through cracks in the door, he pulled the flashlight out of his pocket and for a few seconds illuminated the ladder.

As he worked the beam upwards, he saw the ladder

extended up through what was left of three of drying floors, most of the floors and their supporting joists missing. Even from the limited glow of the light, he could tell that the kiln used for the drying process had been broken up and removed.

It was evident the oast house had long been abandoned. But it wasn't the ladder or what was left of the drying floors that sparked an idea. Centered in the peak of the conical-shaped ceiling, forty to fifty feet above the floor of the building, was a metal air vent. The rope was secured to the bottom of the vent, obviously used as a means of pulling the vent shut.

Without thinking, Matt stuffed the flashlight back into his pocket, wrapped the end of the rope around one wrist and started up the ladder. Each step along the way sent bolts of pain through his ankle. Slowly, awkwardly, hand over hand, grunt after grunt, rung by rung... It seemed there was always one more rung to reach for, to cling to. After what seemed a lifetime, he reached what he thought was between fifteen to twenty feet up and stopped just before the cone-shaped roof started its inward taper. Holding his position, he gasped for breath as if he'd just finished a hundred-yard dash.

Finally, he worked his way around so his back was to the ladder. Precariously balanced, he unwrapped the rope from his wrist. He first yanked the rope to make certain it was securely fastened to the closed air vent and would hopefully bear his weight. Judging distance solely by feel, Matt worked the rope to what he judged to be about eight to ten feet from the bitter end then waited, his eyes centered on the door, his mind rehearsing what had to be done.

The wooden door drug across the floor with a low growl as "white smock" pushed his way into the oast house.   Matt watched until the man stepped past the threshold, waited until he saw the silhouette against the gray darkness of the open doorway, and threw the flashlight to the far side of the oast house. As soon as the light clanged against the brick wall, "white smock" whirled about and fired at the direction of the sound.

With a howl dredged from deep in his gut, Matt pushed off the ladder and propelled himself into space. Praying the arc of his forward swing was sufficient to hit his intended target, he stretched his feet in front of him and aimed at the ghostly blob in the doorway. Out and down he swung.

More shots!   They ricocheted off the walls, creating deafening echoes as bullets splintered and splattered around the building. The last sound Matt heard before he made contact with the silhouette was three rapid clicks of an empty revolver.

Only the heel of Matt's right foot found its mark, and then only a glancing blow off the man's hip. The left foot slammed into wood rather than flesh and bone. To Matt's astonishment, "white smock" grabbed the sides of the doorframe for support and remained upright. His only reaction to the impact was a loud grunt.

Simultaneously, as Matt turned loose of the rope and fell to the floor, even as he felt a crunching sensation inside his chest, his feet continued to kick at the man. Groin, thighs, a knee. The targeted knee immediately snapped backwards, separation of bone and tearing of muscle sinews and cartilage the result.

A shriek, registering surprise as much as pain, echoed round and round the oast house. Losing his grip on the doorframe, "White smock" crumpled backward through the doorway into the rain and the deepening slush of mud and water.

Moving as fast as he could, his left foot and leg almost useless, Matt got to his feet and forced his way through the opening. Using his good foot, he first cracked down on one of "white smock's" ankles, shattering it and effectively preventing him from either standing or fighting back. As the man rolled onto his stomach and tried to rise, Matt straddled his back, forced him flat and pushed his head facedown into the water and mud.

"White smock's" arms flailed about. He bucked his body up and down, trying to dislodge the weight from his back, but Matt held on. Using that weight to pin down the man's upper back and shoulders, Matt kept both hands on the back of the head, refusing the man the ability to lift his head from the water and breathe. Matt shoved against the head, again and again until "white smock's" arms gave up their fight and the body grew still.

When there was no more movement and he could feel no rise of the chest to indicate the man's involuntary need for air, Matt released his hold, pushed to his feet and limped backwards until he felt the wall of the oast house against his back. Rain pelted his face, but there was no feeling, neither of the rain, the pain that had wracked his body, nor of the fear for his own life that had driven him to kill. All emotion was drained.

Even the sight of the crumpled fisherman's cap and the sailor's tattered pea coat standing before him in the gloom made little impression.

The fisherman's cap nodded toward the body in the growing puddle of water. "Poor Lemmie. Ya killed 'im, didn' ya, Mr. Berkeley?" The voice, deep and gravely, sounded as though it came from the grave. "En' 'arry? I suppose y'did the same ta 'im. No matter. Ya belongs t'me now, Mr. Berkeley."

For a moment, Matt watched as the barrel of the man's revolver moved up the length of his torso. He closed his eyes, took a deep breath and prayed to God that lightning would strike the sonofabitch before he could pull the trigger. Immediately sensing that divine intervention was not to be, Matt braced himself against the impact of a bullet.

He heard the shots, three of them, rapid, like the sharp ratta-tat-tat of a snare drum. Reflexively, he flattened against the oast house, trying to make himself as small a target as possible, then realized, something was wrong. No sledgehammer blows against his body. No searing pain in his lungs. No instant release of death.

Slowly, he opened his eyes. A flash of light from out of the darkness illuminated the last of the "hunters" lying across "white smock's" body. Three wisps of steam spiraled from holes in the back of the water-soaked pea coat, and the rain continued to pour. Matt blinked as the light stabbed at his eyes.

"You're safe, Mr. Berkeley." It was a woman's voice, soft and inviting. "Give me your hand, and I'll help you."

Matt squinted through the light's glare. Two shapes: one, a man, tall and thin with a pistol in one hand; the other, a woman. Her hand, outstretched, beckoned him forward.

Matt reached out and touched the offered hand. "Who are you?" he managed, but the answer never came. Consciousness deserted him. His knees folded; his body slumped; and darkness descended like the sudden arrival of a cold winter's night.

Chapter 13

At first glance, potted plants, patterned chaise lounges and a number of card tables strategically placed throughout the solarium might have given the impression of an English country hotel. In fact, the glow, created by a late October sun and filtered through broad windows looking past an outside terrace toward the Thames River, did little to discourage the illusion.

It was the people, however, who reminded Matt where he was and why – the uniformed attendants and their patients, some ambulatory like himself, others wheelchair bound and subject to the whims of their pushers. Most suffered in silence, while others complained about food, the staff or both. He hated hospitals.

As Detective Inspector Ian Stuart plopped down in a chair facing him, Matt said, "Three days, Ian. You forget where I was?" At the same time, he shifted his roller-mounted IV pole to allow the window cleaner room to work.

"Thanks, Gov," the workman said over his shoulder, simultaneously edging buckets of cleaning chemicals along the floor with his foot while squeegeeing a film of liquid from the window. His work, however, seemed to have no effect on hips that continued to sway to whatever music siphoned through earphones clamped over his head.

Matt nodded, easily recognizing the man as the one who cleaned his room the day before. And why not, since he was the only black male Matt had seen since his arrival.

"What've you found?" Matt asked.

Ian Stuart, seated across a small card table from Matt, looked quickly around to insure no one was listening before answering, "The man was a driver for the antiquities society. The woman? Leila Howard."

Matt repeated the name. "Howard." It was familiar, but from where? And then he remembered. "The note," he said almost under his breath before adding, "She was supposed to contact me."

"She and the driver had been to your hotel, learned from the desk clerk you'd gone to Chartwell in a leased automobile, and decided to follow."

"And?"

"They missed you at Chartwell, found your car in a roadside stream, heard shots, and the rest is history. I might add that the car leasing company didn't appreciate the way we returned your rental car. They did, however, say your insurance would pay for repairs."

"It ought to. I pay enough in premiums," Matt said as he straightened the transparent intravenous tube that looped down from a bottle of clear fluid on the metal IV pole and disappeared beneath a wide strip of adhesive covering the back of his left hand. Looking up, he said, "But the driver and the woman. The driver had a gun. I thought you Brits weren't supposed to –"

Ian cut him off. "We're not. He said he found the gun in the woods next to the man with the broken neck."

"Found it? C'mon Ian. You believe that, you believe in Christmas fairies or some kind of Robin Hood, taking from the dead and saving my ass. Fat chance. You know damn well –"

"What I believe and what I can prove are two different things, but as you say, he did save your life, didn't he?"

"Point taken. What about the three guys who tried to kill me? Who sent them? The Russians?"

Matt felt a nudge at the back of his chair and looked back to see the window cleaner shifting his buckets and squeegee.

"Sorry, Gov," the man said, still swaying to the music in his earphones.

Stuart watched the window cleaner for a moment before answering, "We don't know, but certainly not the Russians. Not their style. If they wanted you dead, they'd've done it themselves."

"Somebody sure as hell wants me outta the way," Matt countered, "and I'm thinking there's a helluva lot more to this thing than I'm being told."

"Why?"

"After all these years, two Americans, for different reasons, show up looking for the Churchill Icon. One disappears and the other gets ambushed. Uh-uh. Too much sudden interest in something the world has already forgotten."

Stuart sat for a moment, digesting Matt's rationale. "You may be right. As for the three men, two were nothing more than common street thugs from the East End, but the third? I've contacted INTERPOL to see –"

"Aw, man, would you look at that?" Matt cut in. "I must be dreaming."

"Look at what?" Ian asked, turning toward the double glass doors that provided entrance from the hospital proper.

"Talk about Christmas goodies, find her under your tree and Christmas could take on a whole new meaning."

Ian saw the woman and laughed. "Believe it or not, old son, Christmas may be a bit early this year."

"Huh?"

Ian stood and waved to get the woman's attention. "Miss Howard. Over here."

Matt's jaw dropped and his eyes grew wide. "That's Miss Howard?" he mouthed. A surprised smile spread across his face.

Bājī Leila removed the dark glasses that covered her eyes, dropped them in her purse and nodded her recognition as she started in their direction. The smile on her face, like a sudden ray of sunlight, made everything else dull and lackluster by comparison.

A hush fell across the solarium. Every eye followed her movements, not obtrusive, yet flowing and sensuous beneath the cream-colored jacket and matching skirt that highlighted the raven blackness of her hair and the rich smoothness of her skin. For Matt, luscious, maybe even delicious, were the only words that came to mind.

Leila accepted Ian's outstretched hand. "Inspector Stuart. Thank you for inviting me."

Quickly knotting the belt of his hospital robe about his waist and favoring what had been determined was a cracked rib in his right side, his thigh and swollen left ankle, Matt stood and extended his free hand as Ian said, "Matt, this is Miss Howard with the British-European Antiquities Society. Miss Howard, Mr. Berkeley."

Leila took Matt's hand. "Call me Leila, please, and I'll call you Matthew if you don't mind."

Matt felt the softness of her touch, her hand still cool from the outside air in comparison to the warmth of the solarium. He wanted to use the old punch line, "Call me anything you want; just call me," but decided on, "Matthew's fine, but plain old Matt would be better. And I'm sorry I didn't recognize you from the other night. Everything went kinda blank about that time."

"Sod off, old woman!" an angry voice carried from across the room. Everyone turned toward an elderly man in a wheelchair as he spun it around and placed his back to a nurse holding a bottle of pills. "I told you no," he shouted defiantly, "and I meant no, now go way and leave me alone, silly old cow."

"It's hot in here," Leila said, dabbing a tissue against her forehead, "and a bit noisy. Could we move outside?"

"No problem," Matt answered, immediately guiding the IV pole toward the door leading to the terrace above the hospital grounds. Unexpectedly, the window cleaner moved in front of him and pushed open the door, allowing Matt, his rolling IV, Leila and Ian to exit the solarium. He immediately followed with his cleaning equipment and started on the exterior side of the windows.

"Thanks," Matt said absentmindedly to the workman as Leila and Ian caught up and escorted him across the stone terrace.

"It's good to see you up and about," Leila said, "but you seemed surprised to see me, or perhaps perplexed is the better word. Have I said or done something wrong?"

"Not at all," Matt answered, lowering himself "sidesaddle" onto the low brick and concrete wall that surrounded the terrace, trees and a ribbon of river at his back. "I have to admit, you're not what I expected from the antiquities society."

Leila smiled. "I hope that's meant as a compliment."

Laughing, Matt answered, "Definitely, and I like the accent, too."

"My father was British, my mother from India.

116

Perhaps that is why the accent. More important, it seems Inspector Stuart has planned a trip for tomorrow. If you're well enough, that is."

* * *

The window cleaner pulled the squeegee down the length of the window and wiped the moisture from the rubber blade with a piece of rag, careful not to smudge the lens on the ultra-thin digital camera strapped to the underside of his wrist. Before repeating the process, he adjusted the tiny amplifier/receiver attached to his belt, smoothed out the wires running to the earphones, and listened to the voices from across the terrace. All the while his feet kept moving to an imaginary beat, only he could hear.

"A trip?" Matt's voice asked through the earphones. "Where? And why?"

"Do you remember a man named Henri Boulon?"

The window cleaner recognized Stuart's voice.

* * *

"Henri Boulon?" Matt stared at the stones beneath his feet as he tried to remember the name.

"Your Navy years," Stuart reminded. "The Mediterranean, ship visits to Marseille. Surely you haven't forgotten. Inspector Boulon thought –"

"Henry!" Matt said, snapping his fingers in recognition. "The Marseille Police *Judiciare*. Helped with shore patrol when the ships were in port. Worked with him when two of our Marines were murdered down in the Arab quarter. What's he got to do with us, or for that matter the lost icon?"

"He's now with INTERPOL. I called Interpol since they were involved when the icon went missing from Chartwell. They routed me to the Inspector. Spoke with him this morning. Boulon recognized your name and asked us to come over. He may have something concerning the icon and our third man."

"If he's with INTERPOL, that means Paris," Matt said.

Leila interrupted the two-way conversation. "Why not send the information through normal channels?"

"Something to do with INTERPOL'S constitution," Ian explained. "Forbids disclosure concerning certain areas of interest."

Matt was puzzled. "If that's the case, why –"

"Because of your past friendship, but it must be an unofficial meeting. That's the only way."

"Then we get me out of here and go to Paris. Simple as that."

"I'm not certain we should include Miss Howard," Ian said with some hesitancy. "In view of what's happened and the potential danger –"

"I disagree!" Leila interrupted.

"So do I," Matt said, nodding agreement with Leila. "If there's danger, it's in London, not Paris, and besides, it's her people and their money that are responsible for me being here. If not for them…"

Ian laughed and shook his head. "Very well. I know when I'm beat, Miss Howard, but first, neither my people nor I can accept responsibility for your safety and second, at the slightest hint of trouble –"

"I understand, Inspector," Leila said, moving closer to Matt and touching his arm. "Thank you for your support."

Matt placed his hand on hers. "I'm the one who oughta be thanking you. You saved my life."

Whether by accident or design, Matt felt Leila's fingers interlock with his own, holding for a moment as she smiled her acknowledgment.

"Anyway," Matt went on, nodding toward the IV pole as he pushed to his feet, "if we're going to Paris, I'd better get rid of my friend here. I wouldn't want people to think we're stuck on each other."

Matt started across the terrace, expecting and getting a soulful duet of moans and boos for his less than imaginative attempt at hospital humor.

* * *

After snapping a final picture of Matt and Leila with the miniature wrist camera, the window cleaner pulled a cell phone from his pocket, punched in a speed-dial number, waited to hear the first ring. When heard the word "Yes," he asked, "You get all that?"

He listened for a moment, then added, "Yeah, but if Berkeley's the best they've got, after a joke like 'stuck on each other,' maybe he's not as smart as we thought."

Chapter 14

The taxi waited at the curb as Matt, a pronounced limp in his walk, escorted Jenny Mason to the front door. "You really didn't have to, you know," Jenny said, holding up the new umbrella Matt had given her.

Matt chuckled. "From what I was told, I don't think the old one would have done you much good."

Reaching the front stoop, Jenny inserted a key into the lock and opened the door. The light from inside the entrance foyer provided a halo effect about her head and shoulders, offering just enough light to outline the invitation of a smile as she turned. "It was a lovely dinner, but the evening doesn't have to end at the door, you know."

Matt could smell the faint yet now-familiar scent of old lavender on her body, could feel the warmth of her touch as she took his hand, and the last thing he wanted was for the evening to end. "Nothing I'd like better, but tomorrow's an early start, and it's already past my ten o'clock curfew." He shook his head and exhaled his disappointment. "Doctor's orders."

"You will call when you get back from Paris, won't you? I really would like to help."

"Soon as I get back, and maybe a real night on the town. Deal?"

Jenny laughed softly, then leaned forward and kissed Matt lightly on the lips. "Deal."

Slightly less than eight hours later, with ankle, thigh and side each tightly wrapped, Matt stepped from the hotel entrance into a new day already laden with automotive exhaust and the sounds of an awakening city. Cautiously he looked around, surveying the street, sidewalk and upper windows of surrounding buildings.

They'd already tried to kill him, whoever they were, and he was damn sure they'd try again. Was it fear or simple self-preservation? Probably both. He learned in Nam that men who denied being afraid before venturing into unknown waterways and jungles were either out-and-out liars or downright stupid.

Seeing nothing suspicious, he shifted his overnight bag from his right hand to his left, stepped to the curb and waved, calling, "Taxi! Taxi!" At least half a dozen taxis passed, caught up in the growing rush hour traffic along St. Martin's Lane until finally, one pulled to the curb.

As Matt opened the car's door, two men in suits suddenly appeared from the hotel's doorway behind him. The men, one white, one black, moved rapidly, smoothly, like synchronized skaters, one to either side of him. Each grabbed an arm and pulled him away from the door and back to the sidewalk.

"What the hell!" Matt shouted, struggling to break free, at the same time recognizing the black man – the window cleaner at the hospital! "You're the –"

"Hospital flunky," the black man grunted. "Name's Mabry. Other guy's Honeycutt." Mabry sailed a ten-pound note through the taxi's open front window and yelled to the driver, "Get lost, Mac. He's with us!"

With a knot of onlookers already gathered only feet
away, Honeycutt twisted Matt's arm behind his back and snarled, "Free ride to the airport, Berkeley, so shut up and move."

A chauffeur-driven Chrysler 300 with a U.S. made left-hand drive, oversized for most London streets, edged into the space vacated by the taxi. Its rear door swung open as Mabry pushed Matt forward. The crown of his head scraped painfully against the top edge of the doorframe. "For chrissake, man! I can –"

"Move over," Mabry ordered. He shoved Matt forward, got in and slammed the door behind him, cutting off the outside world. Honeycutt settled into the passenger side front seat as the Chrysler pulled into traffic, drawing a chorus of angry horns in its wake.

"And who the hell are you?" Matt demanded, staring hard at a third man seated on his left. A man with a steel-gray crew cut; a man who, although older, instantly reminded him of Clint Eastwood in his "spaghetti western" and Dirty Harry days.

"Name's Hawkins," the man answered, his voice calm and deliberate, his expression that of someone in total control. "American Embassy. Sorry for the interruption to your transportation plans, but under the circumstances, figured it was the best way."

"Best way for what?" Matt asked. "Kidnapping? And what circumstances?"

"You think you woulda come with me if I'd knocked on your door and asked politely? No fucking way. Anyway, not my style."

Hawkins pulled a folded newspaper from the magazine pocket behind the front seat, and spread the paper open across Matt's lap. *The Times*, day before yesterday. What does the headline say, Mr. Berkeley?" Hawkins pointed to a line of bold capital letters running above a picture, which Matt instantly recognized as the one in his passport. It was next to a picture of his wrecked rental car. "Mr. Berkeley?" Hawkins demanded.

Matt read the headline aloud. "'Yank foils carjacking near Chartwell.'"

Hawkins grunted his amusement. "Carjackin', my ass. That's the spin your buddy Stuart put out, wasn't it? When a visitin' American kills three Brits, that makes me curious. A few phone calls to the right people about who you are and why you're here, and voila, whadda I find? The icon hunter."

"What business is that of yours?"

Hawkins leaned forward, tapped the driver on the shoulder and ordered, "Marble Arch." Sitting back, he said to Matt, "How 'bout a walk in the park? If I hear what I like, you're on your way to Paris. If not, you're on your way home. Simple as that."

Following instructions for the driver to locate a place to park as close as possible to Victoria Gate on Bayswater Road and a walk filled with rising antagonism on Matt's part, the two men reached a six-way intersection in the pattern of crisscrossing sidewalks some distance into the park.

In the background, Matt could still hear the drone of street noises and a man haranguing a lengthy cue of people waiting for a bus near Speakers' Corner. Except for an occasional jogger and a handful of maintenance people raking and blowing leaves from one pile to another, Hyde Park was relatively quiet for 7:30 in the morning. Matt's conversation with Royce Hawkins about his abduction, the icon and Hawkins' demands had been anything but quiet.

Shaking his head as they left the walkway and made their way across a broad stretch of green, Matt said, "You and that goon squad of yours remind me of some of the jerk-offs I worked with in Nam."

"Yeah?" Hawkins asked, a high level of irritation

already in his voice and on his face from their earlier conversation.

"Yeah. CIA. You sound alike, act alike, even smell alike. You and that phony insurance investigator who disappeared. He was yours, wasn't he? That's why I'm here, isn't it? Somebody took him out when he got too close, and now you need another gofer. Right?"

Waiting, but receiving only silence, Matt pushed on. "So, what's the icon to you?"

"Maybe we like pretty pictures."

"Bullshit!"

"You with us or not?" Hawkins asked pointedly.

"We both know there's more to it than just the icon," Matt went on, "and if the CIA's part of it, it's gotta be hot."

"Not your problem."

"The hell you say," Matt fired back. "If and when my ass is on the line, you better believe –"

Hawkins stopped and grabbed Matt's arm. "For the last time, goddamn it, you in or not?"

Matt shook off Hawkins' grip, took a deep breath and bit his lower lip in an attempt to control his anger before answering, "I'm already in too far to back out, aren't I?"

"Smart man. My rules," Hawkins insisted.

"And if I find it, what about the antiquities society and Scotland Yard?" Matt asked.

"You find the icon, I get first crack, then the Brits can have the damn thing. That's all you need to know."

"What if I like what I find and decide to cut you out?"

"Get tricky with me, and I'm on you like a pit bull after a bitch in heat. Nowhere you gonna run I can't find you. *¿Comprende?*"

Matt looked at his watch. "Stuart and Miss Howard are waiting at the airport."

"We'll gettcha there."

"Forget it, Hawkins," Matt said over his shoulder as he started in the direction of the park's Victoria Gate and his overnight bag waiting in the embassy sedan. "I'll find my own way. Last time your kind offered me help was in Nam. I lost two boats and half a dozen men. No thanks. Not this time."

Chapter 15

Paris

The London-to-Paris shuttle landed at Roissy/Charles de Gaulle shortly before eleven a.m. amidst a whirlwind of passengers. All were trying, it seemed, to get through the same customs and immigration gates, find the same exits, and use the same means of getting into Paris. But it was Leila, her smile and near perfect French, that swept away one bureaucratic obstacle after another.

It wasn't long until, miraculously, Matt found himself and his overnight bag squeezed between Leila and Ian Stuart on the B3 metro express. Their taxi driver, a man named Claude, drove like he was in training for the Gran Prix as they sped through the northern suburbs of Paris toward the Gare du Nord.

"Place de la République," Boulon had said, and the distance from the Gare du Nord along the boulevard de la Magenta had to be one of the fastest miles Matt had ever experienced. If there were historic sites or other places of interest along the way, he never saw them. In fact, he found himself staring straight ahead, braced for the inevitable impact.

Claude whipped the little Renault past delivery vans parked in the traffic lanes and wove through intersections jammed with cars, each jockeying for position to make its next turn. With loud beeps of the horn, he literally dared pedestrians to get in his way.

Getting there by taxi was bad, but getting across the street on foot from beneath the portico of the Holiday Inn where they were deposited was an even greater challenge. From the corner, Matt could see their destination. A small park enclosed by a wrought-iron fence just south of the square's central monument to the Republic of France and her various revolutions.

Clutching the overnight bag against his side and favoring his still swollen ankle and adhesive-wrapped thigh, he half-jogged, half-limped, following Ian, Leila and their carry-on's as they zigzagged their way through a steady procession of cars. Horns blared high-pitched warnings. Fists threatened through open windows. Middle fingers shot skyward in salute. Without fail, that most famous of Parisian greetings was hurled like rocks from a slingshot. "Out of the way, you stupid shit!" or so Matt interpreted.

Once to the other side and trying to catch their breaths after the wild race crossing the street, the three of them stopped and looked around. The park, a tiny shaded island in a never-ending flow of trucks, buses and automobiles, provided a noon refuge for workers from the surrounding business district. Each bench and patch of grass was filled with people, some eating from folded newspapers or bags while others talked, read or fed the squirrels and pigeons their leftover crumbs.

"See him?" Ian asked.

"Not yet," Matt answered above the traffic sounds as he moved farther into the park, "but where there's pigeons..." And there he was. Henri Boulon. A flurry of gray and white feathers surrounded a short, stocky man in a dark suit tossing breadcrumbs from a brown paper bag. His back was to Matt, but there was no mistaking the broad shoulders and full head of black hair, pomaded and combed to its owner's precise standard. It was the hands feeding the pigeons, however, that solidified the identification. Hands thick and heavy that could crush a man's face with a single blow. Matt had seen it happen more than once.

"Henry, Henry Boulon," Matt called as he moved closer.

Boulon emptied the remaining bread crumbs on the ground, tossed the bag into a wire trash container and turned, sending a bevy of pigeons rising into the air, only to immediately drop back to the ground as soon as he moved away.

Matt was surprised. Over twenty years had done little to change what he remembered of Boulon. A short, swarthy man, broadly built with a mustache that lay neatly across his lip and curled upwards ever so slightly at each end.

Boulon hurried forward, arms open wide, and clasped Matt in a warm, friendly hug. "Matthew, *mon ami*. It has been too long. Welcome to Paris, but how are your wounds? Inspector Stuart told me about them?"

Pulling back and taking Boulon's hands in an animated handshake, Matt said, "Healing, and you, that's still the greatest mustache in all of France."

To Ian and Leila, he added, "In Marseille, we called him *le pere de la mer pour les États-Unis*. Loosely translated, sea daddy for the U. S. as in Navy shore patrol."

"*Oui,* but now I am an inspector with INTERPOL," Boulon said, a grin breaking across his face. "No longer coddling young American naval officers and teaching them the back alleys of Marseille.

"But this," he said, nodding to Ian and extending his hand, "must be the famous Detective Inspector Stuart of Scotland Yard." Just as quickly, he disengaged from the handshake and turned his attention to Leila. "And you, Mademoiselle Howard. A distinct pleasure. Inspector Stuart has already spoken of your beauty."

Boulon took Leila's right hand in his, bowed slightly, and allowed the edge of his mustache to brush the back of her hand.

Matt laughed. "Same old Henry."

"How gallant, Inspector Boulon," Leila said, smiling in what Matt interpreted as her approval of Boulon's greeting.

Boulon released Leila's hand and nodded toward the boulevard du Temple, one of several streets leading away from the park. "But come. I have a table at *Chez bon Saveur*. We eat. Afterward, we talk about why I asked you to come to Paris and what might be of assistance in locating your missing icon."

Chapter 16

As the waiter cleared away the table, leaving a half-filled bottle of Saint-Louis Beaujolais and an accompanying quartet of glasses, Boulon snipped off the tapered end of a cigar and lit up, visibly enjoying the combined aroma of the match and tobacco as he inhaled. "Of the two younger men," he explained, "there is nothing in our files. Of the older one, a different story."

Boulon turned more to Matt. "The name you heard, *mon ami*, the name Pearly, was, as you would say, a nickname or as I would prefer, an alias. Our files show he had many, but his true name was John Wayne Humphry."

Matt laughed dryly. "John Wayne, huh? I bet the Duke would've loved that."

"From petty theft and assault with a deadly weapon," Boulon continued, "to gun running for the IRA in Northern Ireland and assassination of minor political figures on the Continent. His more recent activities, however, may be the possible connection with the Churchill Icon, and therein lies the problem."

"Which is?" Leila prompted.

Savoring the taste of his cigar and exhaling a rush of smoke toward the ceiling over an extended lower lip, Boulon explained, "There are several categories of social activity in which INTERPOL involvement is prohibited. One is religion, its forms, practices, and internal workings. That is why, if I am to speak freely, we meet at Chez bon Saveur."

Matt shook his head, offering, "Pearly didn't seem

very religious to me."

"Your Pearly or Humphry was part of a ship's crew taken into custody in Toulon less than a month ago. Selling heroin and various hallucinogens to a religious sect." To Matt, Boulon added, "You should be interested to know an American Drug Enforcement agent uncovered the arrangement."

"I'll wave the flag, but how come Pearly was out trying to kill me if he was caught peddling drugs?" Matt asked with one eyebrow lifted in question.

"Who knows," Boulon answered, shrugging his shoulders. "Many reasons are possible, but money is the most likely answer."

"How does this relate to the icon?" Ian asked.

"When questioned, a priest of the sect admitted congregational use of the drugs during certain rituals and gave as an example a forthcoming ceremony he's to attend in England."

"What kind of ceremony?" Matt asked while pouring more wine into his glass.

"Final rites of their leader and to pay homage to a venerated work of art entitled *Transfiguration*."

Matt plopped the wine bottle down on the table and snapped his fingers as though a light bulb had just popped on in his brain. "That's what Cavendish called it." Looking at Ian and Leila, he explained, "The icon's center panel, *Transfiguration of Christ the Savior*."

"Yes, the possible link," Boulon agreed, "but I was unaware of its potential relevance until Inspector Stuart's call. It was his mention of what you learned during your interview with the famous Dr. Cavendish of the Cortauld Institute and after I reviewed the Humphrey man's dossier and the case in question."

Leila raised a finger in Boulon's direction. "You

said England. Where in England?"

Boulon pulled at the cigar, exhaling smoke rings above the table. "Bear in mind, our interest was only in the sale of drugs, not the ceremonial liturgy of a religious group. There were, however, two place names given by the priest. Tavistock and St. Cyril de la Bot."

Sipping his wine, Matt looked at Ian Stuart over the rim of his glass. "Whaddaya think?"

Ian sat for a moment, considering the two names, then answered, "There's Tavistock Square in Bloomsbury, near the University of London. Also, a village called Tavistock in the southwest of England, north of Plymouth, but St. Cyril de la Bot? Never heard of it. Sounds more French than English."

"What kind of church are we talking about?" Matt asked.

"Originally from North Africa," Boulon answered. "An offshoot of the Coptic Church with congregations both in Europe and in England. As you would say, *mon ami*, it is a long shot, but hopefully I have provided information that will be of help."

"It's a helluva jump from where we were when we got here," Matt said, at the same time signaling the waiter for the check.

Stubbing out his cigar in a round, amber colored ashtray with the restaurant's name, *Chez bon Saveur,* displayed prominently from the bottom, Boulon pushed himself to his feet and shrugged his shoulders. "You will be returning to London, no?"

As Ian pulled back her chair for her to stand, Leila straightened her skirt and was the first to answer. "Not until tomorrow morning. Our wounded patient needs his rest, or so the doctor has insisted since he left the hospital under protest. They wanted him to remain for at least two more days."

Matt held his thigh and side as he eased his legs out from under the table and stood, complaining to Boulon, "Helluva way to spend a day and night in Paris, but maybe, when this is all over, before I head back to the States, I'll make it back, and we can chew over old times."

"I'd like that. You know, I never remarried after Nicole's death, and there's no one in Paris with whom to share the old memories. Yes, I'd like that very much." Boulon reached into his inside coat pocket and withdrew a small printed card. "My address and private telephone number if you need me."

Matt accepted the card. "Thanks, Henry. With my luck? One never knows."

On the way to their hotel, though the taxi driver's name wasn't Claude, Matt knew the man's driving habits must have been learned at the same school as their first driver.   Rounding the Arc de Triomphe, the taxi accelerated along the avenue des Champs Elysées, around Rond-Point before turning on what felt like two wheels onto avenue Montaigne. It finally screeched to a halt in front of a small hotel at Number Six.

After seeing the concierge to exchange British pounds for euros and going up to the room to be shared by Stuart and himself, Matt said, "Sorry, guys. After those two kamikaze taxi rides, the old war wounds are acting up. I'm gonna put it to bed for a while." He immediately removed his coat and tie, took off of his shoes and collapsed fully clothed on the bed.

Leila looked at her watch. "And I've time for some shopping and a short rest before dinner."

"What about you?" Matt asked Ian.

"Some calls to London, and then the Champs

Elysées to find a present for my wife. Not often I visit Paris at the Yard's expense."

Part way to the door, Leila reminded Matt, "Don't forget to change the dressing on your wound. The doctor said –"

"I know," Matt said, his eyes already closed, the pain in his side, thigh and ankle subsiding into a dull ache. "Now get outta here."

With a smile and a voice quickly fading into a much needed sleep, he waved them toward the door. "Scat! Go 'way. Spend your money and have fun. See if I care."

Already walking softly as she could, Leila put a finger to her lips. "Shhhh," and motioned Ian toward the door.

* * *

Unnoticed by Ian Stuart as he exited the hotel and turned right toward the Champs Elysées was a black Citroen sedan parked across the street. Inside the automobile were four men in dark suits and felt hats.

"There," the driver said, pointing toward Stuart.

Sitting in the rear seat, Damien, a large, powerfully built man in his mid-forties, nudged Brendan, the younger and smaller of the two. He ordered, "Get out. Stay and watch 'til we get back."

"But Damien," Brendan protested, "with the inspector gone, why not go to Berkeley's room and finish it?"

"No. Too confined and with the hotel's service people about. You saw them yourself. Everything in the open where there's room to maneuver, now go. The rest of us have work to do."

Chapter 17

"He is suspicious," Leila said, holding the telephone with her right hand, nervously sorting with her left the several, neatly wrapped packages that lay on the bed. "Not about me," she added hastily. "He's certain, however, there's something more than just the icon, but that doesn't mean I should –"

Strizhenko's words cut her short. "You have no choice. As the general has said, you must do whatever necessary to insure Berkeley's complete loyalty."

Leila paused, breathed deeply, then slowly exhaled to allow for a moment of thought. Finally, "Yes," she answered, the "yes" more a sigh than an affirmation. "I will think of something."

"See that you do!"

The harshness of Strizhenko's voice and the abrupt click at the other end of the line signaled both anger and an unspoken threat as Leila replaced the phone in its cradle. She stood, facing the room's double windows, thoughtful, seeing not the late afternoon sun that created a shallow curtain of dust motes in the air, but Matt's face and his smile from when they first met.

There was something – she couldn't explain what – that had drawn her to him in those early moments, and, she sensed, him to her. An immediate rapport, as if two separate rhythms had synchronized to form a single pulse. He trusted her, she knew, and she did not want to betray that trust any sooner than necessary. Never, if possible. If only...

It was Strizhenko's words, still echoing in her ears,

that reminded, *"You have no choice."* If the plans she and General Kazemi had made were to be successful, plans of which Strizhenko and Hajir must never learn, she knew he was right. She had no choice.

* * *

An automobile horn, its sound rising from the street and knifing its way through the open window, startled Matt from a sweat-soaked sleep. A sleep filled with icons, tattered old men in fishermen's caps, and a woman with raven black hair whispering from the dark, *"Give me your hand and you'll be safe."*

Thankful to escape the all-too-vivid dreams that dwelled on the fragile edge of existence, his especially, Matt forced himself out of the bed and into the bathroom. A quick shower, steamy hot to cleanse the oil from his pores; the water suddenly turned near scalding by the flush of a toilet next door; and a brisk toweling that brought new life to his skin.

It wasn't until he finished applying fresh layer of Polysporin and gauze to the wound in his thigh and started encircling his upper abdomen and still bruised and cracked ribs with an elasticized Ace bandage that his ears caught the sound. The scratch of a key against the lock; the turn of the handle; the hall door opening and closing; and the safety chain sliding home.

Quickly wrapping the towel around his waist to hold the bandage in place, he called, "Ian?" then stepped from the bathroom.

"Whoa!" he yelped, automatically tightening the towel about his midsection and almost dropping the roll of adhesive meant to secure the Ace bandage. "Ian never looked like that."

Leila, in a dress that hugged and massaged every curve of her body, smiled back. "I should hope not."

Gesturing toward the towel, Matt said, "Forgive my rather casual attire, but how did you get in?"

Leila laughed and held up a key before placing it on a table next to the door. "It's the one to my room. It seems one key fits all."

Matt laughed. "That oughta make for some interesting surprises. And that dress! Your shopping spree?"

"A Nina Ricci original. Also their latest perfume. I've come to model."

"By all means," Matt said, at the same time, trying to act as though his mind wasn't already boggled by the way she looked. "Why don't I get dressed, and then you can —"

"Why? Are you embarrassed?" Leila teased, suddenly stepping out of her shoes and executing a perfect pirouette, then another and another, stopping almost out of breath to admire herself in the full-length mirrors of a large mahogany wardrobe. "What do you think?" she asked, turning in his direction.

"It's beautiful," he said, then softly, "but it's you. You make it beautiful, not Nina what's-her-name."

"Although her name and creations live on, Nina died years ago, but thank you," Leila said as she stepped forward and took the adhesive roll Matt still held in his hand.

"Let me." Without waiting for his consent, Leila edged the towel lower on Matt's hips and placed one end of the adhesive over the end of the bandage.

Matt held his arms high as Leila worked her way around his side, the adhesive strip gradually encircling his back and stomach, finishing at the bandage where she had started. The stretching sensation of the adhesive across the wound was lost to the closeness of Leila's body and the caress of her hands as they moved over his chest and down to the towel. Her fingers slipped beneath the fold of cloth that held the towel close and pulled it free.

Suddenly Leila was against him, the material of her dress, gossamer to his touch. His arms circled her waist and pulled her close, her body warm against his, her lips open and inviting. Accepting the invitation, Matt's tongue probed lightly at first, its movements more insistent as she responded. He could feel her passion, like his, already on fire and expanding.

Without warning, Leila pushed away, her smile telling him it was for only a moment. With the sigh of a zipper and the soft rustle of cloth, the Nina Ricci original and a pair of flesh-colored stockings slipped to the floor, revealing a body clad only in the warm hues of a bedside lamp and the enticing fragrance of summer rose petals.

Matt eased himself onto the side of the bed, flinching at the pain in his thigh and side as he sat, the pain, however, as much aphrodisiac as discomfort.

Moving closer, her hands outstretched and reaching for his, Leila whispered, "Your wound. It hurts. I will make you forget."

Grasping Leila's hands, Matt pulled her forward until his lips touched her breasts and the lightly scented valley between. He could feel the surge of emotion spreading through her body as his tongue moved purposefully over each nipple; as his hand wandered to the velvet warmth between her thighs, the growing dampness an answer to his touch.

With words hurried by her breathlessness, Leila asked, "Before Ian returns... We do have time, don't we?"

"A lifetime," Matt whispered, taking Leila in his arms as he lay backwards on the bed. The weight of her body brought a sudden stab of pain from his ribs, but the pain quickly diminished as she raised herself, her knees bent forward along his sides. Her hair spilled like strands of silk across his face and over the pillow that supported his head.

With the touch of her hand, she guided him deep inside the satiny smoothness of her flesh, and the heat of her juices flowed over and around him. At first the movement of their bodies was slow and deliberate, each wanting to prolong the ecstasy of their union for as long as possible.

Matt's mouth sought and found Leila's. Their lips touched and parted; their tongues caressed and darted over and around, maintaining cadence with their growing passion. Her moans, rising from the well of her throat, grew sharper and more aggressive; her movements, matching his, became faster and more urgent.

Like floodwaters surging across a landscape, each found release, each cried aloud into the afternoon, and Matt knew it was a time in Paris he would never forget.

Chapter 18

Ian stood for a moment, the tree-lined avenue des Champs Elysées and its sprawl of mid-afternoon traffic reflected in the shop's window. Though several packages were already in hand, he debated which he should buy for his wife. The midnight-blue evening purse with the simulated pearl fleur-de-lis he knew she would prefer or, more to his liking, the flimsy, see-through nightgown in either wicked white, passion pink or seductive scarlet?

It wasn't until he heard the car door slam that he noticed, reflected in the window, a black Citroen sedan at the curb, two men inside and one walking in his direction.

"Inspector Stuart of Scotland Yard?" Damien asked with a plausible French accent as Ian turned toward the street.

"Yes, and you?" Ian asked, his eyes narrowed with suspicion.

Damien extended an open wallet in Ian's direction, quickly closing it as he replied, "My identification. Malraux, Paris police. Monsieur Berkeley said we might find you along the Champs Elysées."

"Is there a problem?" Ian asked, still unsure as to whether he should trust the man.

"An emergency, I'm afraid. Your office."

"My office? Why would they contact you?"

"I do not know, Inspector. I was instructed only to find you and offer my assistance."

"What's the emergency?"

"Your wife."

"Sophie?"

"Yes, Sophie."

Ian stared hard at the man. "My wife's name is Kathleen. Who are you?" Ian started backing toward the shop door when Damien grasped his arm and the muzzle of a pistol jammed against his side.

"It's fitted with a silencer," Damien warned without the French accent. "One word and you'll not see your Kathleen again. Understand? Put the packages down."

Ian nodded, dropped the wrapped boxes to the sidewalk and allowed Damien to guide him to the Citroen. The rear door opened from inside. Lowering his head to get in, Ian muttered, "Bastards! If you think –"

A sudden shove from behind forced him forward, head first into the knees of the man seated on the far side of the car. Before he could react, the crush of metal against the side of his head brought both an involuntary cry of pain from his throat and a kaleidoscopic burst of stars to his eyes.

Ian tried to push back, to get a foothold, leverage, anything. A second blow, this time to the back of his neck. It forced him down. His face slammed against the floorboard; his nose erupted in a rush of blood. He strained to get up, to see his captors, but the last thing he saw was the heel of a shoe. It rammed full force against his face, once, twice. And then the pain was gone, swept away in a wash of blood; consciousness folded into darkness.

* * *

Leila's head rested on Matt's shoulder, an index

finger tracing the slight depression in the center of his chest. "I hope this will not be our last."

He kissed her forehead lightly. "Doesn't have to be. And once I get out of these bandages, maybe I can play a more active part in our relationship." The softness of her laughter touched his ear as she nestled closer, the shape of her body a perfect fit against his, making him wish...

A knock at the door brought Leila upright as covers flew in every direction. "It's Ian," she hissed. Jumping from the bed, she gathered her dress, stockings and shoes from the floor and dashed into the bathroom. "Have him wait while I get dressed." The door slammed behind her.

Matt laughed at Leila's frantic movements as he eased off the bed, put on his shorts and pulled on his trousers. "Hold on a minute," he called.

"Monsieur Berkeley?" a voice answered from beyond the door. "It is me, the concierge." Matt recognized the man's formal school English. "I have an envelope for you, delivered only moments ago."

Minus shirt, Matt opened the hall door and took the envelope from the concierge, a stiff little man who Matt earlier decided would look more at home managing a mortuary than a hotel.

"Who delivered this?" Matt asked, noting "Berkeley" scribbled haphazardly across the front of the envelope.

"I do not know, Monsieur. I left the front desk for only a moment. When I returned, it was there."

"Thanks for bringing it up." Matt pulled a ten-euro note from his pocket and gave it to the concierge.

"*Merci*, Monsieur," the concierge answered as he

waved and hurried toward the still-open elevator down the hall.

Matt closed the door and called to Leila, "All clear. You can come out now," then walked to the window. Opening the blinds to catch what afternoon light still lingered, he fingered open the envelope and removed a single sheet of paper as Leila, fully dressed, stepped from the bathroom.

"What is it?" she asked.

"Sonofabitch," he muttered after reading the note. The sensation at the base of his skull was like the burr of a dentist's drill, faint at first, then grinding, faster and hotter.

"Damn it to hell!" he exploded, spinning away from the window and slamming his hands together. "I am not goddamn believing this!"

"What, Matthew?"

Matt held up the note. "This!"

"Read it to me."

Turning back to the window and holding the note to the rapidly fading light, Matt read aloud: "'Tonight, twenty hundred hours. Tour boat, Pont D'Iéna. Tell no one.' It's signed, 'Ian.'"

Leila took the note and read it silently to herself, then, "Ian didn't write this, did he?"

Grabbing his shirt from the foot of the bed and shoving his arms through the sleeves, Matt answered, "Hell no. A month's pay says it's the same people who wanted me killed at Chartwell, and I was the one who said there was no danger in Paris. What the hell's a Pont D'Iéna?"

"A bridge. Over the Seine to the Eiffel Tower," Leila responded, handing the note back to Matt and asking, "What will you do?"

Matt sat on one of the two straight-back chairs in the room, tugged on his socks and shoes then suddenly stopped. He shook his head and stared at the designs in the carpet as though he hadn't seen them before.

"I don't know. Do what they say, I guess." Looking up, he added, "But whatever I do, I'd feel a helluva lot better if I had a gun."

"What kind? Revolver or semiautomatic?"

"What difference does it make?"

"I'm serious. Which would you prefer?"

Matt laughed, still disbelieving. "If I had a magic fairy, I'd ask for a Beretta, nine-millimeter, with a fifteen-shot magazine, but we seem to be short on magic fairies at the moment."

Leila sat on the side of the bed and reached for the telephone on the small nightstand. She picked up the receiver, but held it without dialing. "I know someone who can supply such a weapon, but you must trust me. No questions. Now go. Find us a place to eat while I make the call."

"You're gonna get me a Beretta? Just like that?" Matt asked, simultaneously snapping his fingers. "Now I know you're kidding."

"Do what I ask, Matthew. The society has many contacts throughout Europe. I want only to help, so let me try. Please."

Slipping the belt through the loops of his trousers and tightening just enough to feel comfortable without putting undue pressure against his midsection and ribs, Matt opened the door, then stopped.

"You know, lady? I'm not sure what kind of antiquities society you folks are running, but one thing I do know."

"What?"

144

"I sure do like your style."

The smile on Leila's face and the clicking sounds of numbers being punched on the telephone's button pad faded as Matt closed the door and started down the hall.

Chapter 19

A chill mist rose from the river, attempting with only moderate success to smother the sights and sounds of the city. Two figures stood together in the shadow of the Palais de Chaillot, less a palace than a building housing four major museums. To their right lay a vast terrace lined with gilded statues, glittering in the dampness and serving as a lifeless barrier between Chaillot's massive twin wings.

Below, like a rare jewel in the mist, spread the gardens of the Jardin du Trocadéro. Lighted fountains formed delicate arches of spray and froth above the gardens' central reflecting pool, a silvery oasis in a world of perpetual light and motion.

Beyond the fountains and past the avenue de New York and its nighttime ebb and flow of head and taillights, lay their destination – the bridge, Pont D'Iéna, and the River Seine. The river's waters, like a strip of gleaming obsidian, reflected the brilliantly lighted lower half of Gustave Eiffel's "iron lady." The upper reaches of the nearly one-thousand-foot tower stood hidden above a wreath of fog and low-hanging clouds.

Stepping deeper into the shadows, Matt worked the slide on a blue-black Beretta to force a round from the fully loaded magazine into the chamber. He checked the "hammer drop" safety before stuffing the pistol under his jacket.

"It's time," he said, nodding toward the distant Pont D'Iéna.

"I know," Leila answered. She touched his hand

for only a moment, and then together, they descended from the terrace and made their way alongside the reflecting pool until they reached the intersection with avenue de New York. It was there that Matt made his decision.

"I'm sorry, Leila, but this is as far as you go."

"What do you mean, as far as I go?"

"I want you to go back. Wait at the hotel. No telling what's gonna happen over there. You've got Boulon's card if you need to contact him."

"I represent the Society, and I do not take orders," Leila said, her voice harsh and full of resolve. Her final words, however, took a softer tone. "I go where you go, Matthew."

He stood looking at her, wanting to take her in his arms and hold her close, but now was not the time. "Damn it, Leila, I just don't want –"

"I mean it," she said sharply. "Besides, after what we've shared, I have no choice, nor do you." She stepped off the curb and started across the intersection during a break in the traffic, calling over her shoulder, almost teasing, "Are you coming, or must I go alone?"

Matt laughed softly and shook his head in resignation. "Yes, damn it," he muttered. "I'm coming."

Halfway across the bridge, Leila stopped, leaned over the concrete balustrade and listened.

"What?" Matt asked, anxious to get to the Eiffel Tower side of the bridge.

Leila pointed to the river and a sleek, glass-topped tour boat nosing its way to a landing along the quay. The sounds of a string quartet drifted up from the boat. "Debussy," she responded as they continued across the bridge.

"Nice touch," Matt said with more than a little

sarcasm. "Musical accompaniment to a kidnapping and possible killing."

"Your optimism, so reassuring," Leila answered, her voice layered with cynicism, its tone much less confident than before.

At the end of the span on Paris's "left bank" nearest the Eiffel Tower, Matt rounded a large concrete abutment and led Leila down a flight of narrow steps to a small ticket kiosk. Sidestepping a line of passengers disembarking from the tour boat now tied to the quay wall, he read the sign above the kiosk: Bateux de Seine.

Matt searched for Ian's face among a group of people already boarding the boat for its next and final cruise of the night.

"I don't see him," Leila said.

"I don't either."

"Monsieur?" called a female voice from the kiosk.

"Yes? *Oui?*" Matt answered.

"Will you be going on the tour?" the young woman asked in perfect English.

Leila nodded, and Matt answered, "Three tickets. How much?"

"Ninety-five euros, Monsieur, but there are only two of you."

"Expecting a friend."

Matt handed the clerk two 50-euro notes, accepted the tickets and pocketed the change before leading Leila back up the steps next to the bridge and away from the quay. He stopped near the top of the stairs, partially concealed by the large abutment at the end of the bridge. From there he was satisfied they could observe every approach, be it from the bridge, the Eiffel Tower or along the Quai Branly, the wide avenue that ran parallel with the river.

"Eight o'clock, and I don't see a damn thing," Matt complained. At the same time, he flattened himself against the abutment to allow space for two people starting down the steps. An elderly couple edged by, the man in evening clothes, the woman wrapped in silks and furs. A small, jeweled tiara crowned the gray sweep of her hair. As they walked hand-in-hand, Matt followed with his eyes, envious of their whispered confidences, the laughter they shared, and the brief kiss at the foot of the steps. If only he and Leila...

From the boat rose the haunting strains of a Brahms sonata. Mixed with the tinkling sounds of champagne glasses, its melody floated on the slight breeze that coursed up from the river.

Before he could turn back to the street, one of the crew members, a small man wearing a waiter's jacket, walked to the kiosk, spoke briefly with the ticket clerk, then came to the foot of the steps. "Monsieur," he called, "we are leaving. Are you and Madame coming?"

Matt looked down at the man. "In a minute. We'll be there as soon as –"

"Matthew, look!" Leila grabbed his arm and pointed.

A black Citroen sedan pulled next to the curb along the Quai Branly, short of the entrance to the bridge but not more than fifty yards from where they stood. Matt eased the Beretta from beneath his jacket and released the safety. He counted five people in the car. Two from the back and one from the front got out.

From what he could tell using the lights of passing cars and nearby street lamps, each man wore black. Each head and face was concealed by a hat and scarf. One of the men turned back to the car and motioned to someone still inside. A fourth person, slumped in the middle of the rear seat, moved to the door and, with assistance from two of the men, stepped out and onto the sidewalk.

"My God, what have they done to him?" Matt whispered. Even though the face was swollen and misshapen, Matt knew immediately who it was. Ian Stuart!

To Leila he ordered, "Stay here."

He stepped past the safety of the abutment out onto the sidewalk and stopped as one of the men pointed in his direction. Ian looked up, his face, caught in passing headlights, even more distorted than it seemed at first. Ian nodded as the man said something in his ear, then started forward, his movements more stagger than walk.

Matt could see a sheen of tears along Ian's cheeks, the tremble of his lips, his effort to form sounds, and then the word, "*Matt*," silent, yet as loud to Matt as if spoken over a loudspeaker.

"Please, God, help him," Matt prayed, watching as Ian felt his way along the curb like a drunk in search of a used cigar butt in the gutter.

Suddenly, Ian broke into a run, his words shouted, loud and clear above the surrounding traffic moving onto and off the bridge. "Get away, Matt! It's a trap! Run!"

Matt watched helplessly as each of the men, still standing beside the Citroen, raised their arms, took aim and fired. He heard the shots and saw thin puffs of smoke escape the muzzle of each weapon, but made no attempt to count the number of rounds fired. More importantly, what he did see was Ian Stuart's back arching; his hands groping in vain for support that wasn't there. Then very distinctly, two more shots.

"No-o-o-o!" Matt cried. Ian's warning, the sounds of gunfire, the awful visual of certain death and suddenly, another time, another place etched deep in his memory.

< < > >

A moment, frozen in time and space; Matt's mind's eye in the past. Saigon, a dimly lit street and his Vietnamese contact. The boy, running toward him, shouting, "Go, Lieutenant. Is trap! Is trap!"

Two men, chasing. Automatic weapon's firing. His own voice. "No-o-o-o!" Bullets, tearing, ripping. The boy, flung forward. A passing truck. Metal against flesh!

< < > >

The impact of the bullets and the momentum of his forward motion drove Ian off the curb and into the path of an oncoming van. His body raggedy-anned through space, tumbling lifelessly beneath the tires of a truck
speeding in the opposite direction.

"Ia-a-a-an!" Matt cried, still lost halfway between a street in Saigon and a boulevard in Paris.

Hands closed about his arm and dragged him back to the present. "No, Matthew!" Leila pleaded. "There's nothing you can do. This way!" She pulled him toward the steps leading to the boat landing.

Bullets ricocheted off the sidewalk and the front of the abutment, splattering chunks of concrete like shrapnel from a grenade. As the men ran in his direction, the black Citroen jumped the curb onto a sidewalk then off, screeching to a halt at the south end of the bridge, effectively forming a roadblock against both ongoing and off-coming traffic, providing a metal barricade for the men.

Shrugging loose of Leila's grasp, Matt shouted,

"Get outta here, damn it!" He pushed Leila toward the stairs, then braced himself against the side of the bridge abutment and fired at the men and the car. The explosive sound of the Beretta, four times in rapid succession, echoed along the river.

The Citroen's windshield dissolved into a giant spider web of cracks and ripples; one of the advancing assassins crumpled against the car and slid to the asphalt. The remaining two, however, continued in Matt's direction, determined, he knew, to make the kill, whatever cost.

Clearing two and three steps at a time, Matt sprinted down the stairway toward Leila as the glass-topped boat pulled away, black water churning from beneath its stern. "The boat, Leila, get on the boat!" he shouted, pushing her toward the edge of the quay wall.

More bullets, like a swarm of hornets in search of human flesh, gouged out splinters of concrete from the top of the quay and punched holes in the tour boat's hull. "Jump, Leila, for God's sake, jump!" Matt shouted. At the same time, he dropped behind a large metal bollard and laid down a line of fire in the direction of the two men. Though part way down the steps, the bullets forced the men back onto the bridge.

Matt looked over his shoulder as Leila jumped, stretching over the water and landing half-on, half-off the boat's fiberglass stern cover. With feet hanging just above the river, Leila's fingers clung to a single cleat at the edge of the deck. He heard her cry, could almost feel the pain in her hands, the terrible ache in her arms and shoulders as she struggled to pull herself up.

"C'mon, Leila, do it," he begged, every muscle in his body straining as if he could somehow add his strength to hers.

Slowly, agonizingly, she pulled herself onto the deck. Still on hands and knees, she screamed, "Matthew, please..." but it was too late.

Matt watched as the boat made its way toward the middle of the river. The distance between himself and the relative safety it represented grew wider, too great for him to cover. Extracting the empty magazine from the Beretta, Matt slammed home the remaining clip and ran beneath the shadows of the bridge, a sanctuary from his pursuers that he knew would last only so long.

Chapter 20

"Other side, Damien," shouted the smaller man, waving his pistol in the air and running across the bridge. "He'll be following the boat, trying to get on."

A southbound driver, seeing the weapon in the man's hand and the Citroen blocking his way, immediately jammed on brakes, shifted into reverse and slammed into the car behind him. One after another, cars rear-ended the one behind it, creating a domino effect of broken fenders, crushed radiators and automobile horns crying in distress.

Damien forced a full magazine into the butt of his pistol, racked a bullet into the chamber and fired into the air. This created additional confusion and panic as he followed his companion to the opposite side of the bridge.

* * *

No longer able to see Matt, Leila worked her way along the narrow gunwale that ran just below the convex curve of the boat's glass top. When she reached the open entrance, she grabbed the handrail and swung down into the passenger compartment, startling both passengers and crew with her sudden appearance.

"What are you doing?" cried the little man in the waiter's jacket, reaching for Leila and trying to push her back through the opening. Larger and stronger than the waiter, Leila grabbed the man's wrist, spun him around and shoved him headlong into a phalanx of passengers coming to his assistance.

"Get off," shouted the helmsman from his position in the front of the compartment, at the same time maneuvering the wheel so as to keep the boat within the safety envelope of the bridge. "Those who were shooting. If you stay, they will kill us all."

"Go back to the wall," Leila cried.

"No, you must get off!"

Snatching the straps of a large leather handbag lying on top of one of the Formica-surfaced tables and, ignoring its owner's cry, Leila swung the strap above her head like a sling. The tightly packed, rock-hard bag, now meant as a weapon, sang through the air as it slammed against the side of the helmsman's head. Both helmsman and an explosion of lipsticks, compacts, combs, loose coins, Tampons and a wallet went flying across the compartment.

As the helmsman lay stunned and groaning on the deck, Leila took the boat's wheel in her hand, pushed the throttle forward and jammed the wheel to starboard, directing the boat downstream and out from the shadow of the bridge. Her objective – the quay wall and Matt, but the boat's movement immediately attracted gunfire from the bridge.

Bullets tore through the glass top and splintered the deck. Passengers and crew ducked for cover, some behind chairs, others under tables, while others, immobilized by fear, could only scream and cry for help.

* * *

Matt heard the gunfire and saw the boat toward the quay wall, the angle of its approach carrying it past the bridge and toward the wall in a sideswiping motion. It was now or never.

With a full magazine and a round in the chamber, Matt broke into a run. Firing over his shoulder, he directed the Beretta toward the top of the bridge where he thought the two assassins might be.

As the boat's hull crunched against the wall, it bounced away, then hit again, tearing out sections of gunwale as Matt jammed the Beretta beneath his belt, placed one arm over his face and jumped. The weight of his body carried him down and through the already damaged canopy, shattering glass and ripping away aluminum support rods as he fell.

The impact of his feet against the boat's deck was like two pile drivers rammed upwards into his hips and stomach. His ankles doubled under his weight and he rolled across the deck, feeling the crunch of glass beneath his body and hearing the screams of those trying to get out of his way.

Abruptly, he slammed to a halt against an overturned table, the breath expelled from his chest in a single whoosh. The pain in his ankles and knees screamed against further movement; his lungs begged for air. Even so, he forced himself to his feet and emptied the Beretta's remaining bullets through the opening he'd created before grabbing his thigh and dropping to the deck.

Abandoning the wheel to the helmsman, Leila crawled across broken chairs and shattered glass to Matt's side as another fusillade of bullets ripped through the boat. The bombardment was interrupted almost immediately by the shrill wail of police sirens converging on the Eiffel Tower and the Pont D'Iéna. Suddenly, no more shots; only the sounds of weeping from nearby passengers as the boat moved steadily down river.

"You okay?" Matt reached out and touched Leila's cheek.

"Yes, but you? Are you okay?" She held his hand against her face.

"Think that place in my thigh opened up again, my legs feel like busted match sticks, my ribs are screaming like hell, my lungs..." Matt drew a deep, painful breath.

"Other than that, wonderful. Help me up. We gotta get off this thing before the police get here."

"What about Ian?" Leila asked, her arm around Matt's shoulders as he pushed to his feet.

"You saw him. He's dead, and there's nothing we can do that'll bring him back. I don't like leaving him, but we've gotta move."

With Leila's help, Matt started toward the helmsman, pointing the Beretta toward the bridge up ahead. "Where are we?"

"Pont de L'Alma," the man answered.

"That's where we'll get off."

The helmsman shook his head and backed away from the wheel. "No, no, Monsieur. I will not help you."

"Then get out of the way." Matt waved the pistol in the helmsman's face, took the wheel, and steered the boat to the far side of the river beneath the Pont de L'Alma. He slowed as he made his approach, gently nudging the hull alongside the quay wall.

"Anybody hurt?" he asked loudly.

Several of the passengers pointed to an elderly man in dinner dress, slumped against an overturned chair. Blood seeped from what appeared to be an Ash Wednesday smudge of black in the middle of his forehead.

"Aw Christ!" Matt muttered under his breath, momentarily closing his eyes and remembering the steps to the boat landing. The couple in formal evening wear, their laughter, their kiss. But the woman? Where? And then he saw her, the man's companion, the woman in silks and furs, hunched beneath a table, the jeweled tiara in her hair hanging by a single clip along the side of her head. As though in a trance, she rocked back and forth, crying softly and cradling a fur stole to her bosom like she would a frightened child.

"I'm sorry," Matt apologized softly. "I really am."

He didn't know whether she understood or even heard what he said. But again, as with Ian and the young Vietnamese boy from his past, there was nothing he could do but add one more to the growing list of ghosts already hovering just beyond the veil of his memory. "Take the wheel," he ordered the helmsman.

Hesitantly, the man approached and assumed control of the tour boat as Leila helped Matt over the side and onto the stone walkway.

With the exception of the elderly woman still cradling her fur stole, all of the passengers crowded the side of the boat, straining their eyes for one final glimpse of the couple who disappeared into the darkness beneath the bridge. They were unaware the splash they heard was the Beretta striking the water and sinking to the bottom of the River Seine.

Chapter 21

London

U. S. Embassy

"I don't give a good goddamn what the hell you told Scotland Yard or anybody else," Royce Hawkins blasted from across the room. His index finger, pointed at Matt, shook in rhythm with the words that spilled from his mouth.

"The fact is, you and that lady friend of yours left Paris, left France, goddamn it, without so much as a 'go-to-hell-and-up-yours' to the Paris police. In the meantime, they're sittin' there with some old geezer on a tour boat with a hole in his head and Ian Stuart's body run over and shot to hell and back."

With one hand Matt stroked the stubble sprouting across his face after a night without sleep. With the other hand, he pressed against the gut-grabbing ache in his side reinforced by his plunge through the glass top of the tour boat, each breath a chore in itself.

As for the bullet wound in his thigh, it had been hastily re-sutured with only minimal local anesthetic by an embassy physician who Matt was certain had received his training from the team of Jekyll and Hyde. All after a bus ride from Paris to Coquelles near Calais, the Eurostar night train to Folkeston, Kent via the Channel Tunnel and a £150 taxi ride into London. Not only the lack of sleep but quite simply, he was a physical wreck.

His eyes followed Hawkins' erratic movements about the office, a room, which seemed to mirror Hawkins' personality, or at least the personality he wanted to project. Desk littered with papers and documents, some wreathed with what appeared to be weeks of accumulated dust; file drawers open in stair-step fashion with no apparent thought to organization; and credenza and desk edges scarred by the lengthy embers of forgotten cigarettes.

An analyst might conclude it displayed an attitude of rebellion, a lack of attention to detail, a slackness unbecoming the CIA's Chief of London Station, but Matt knew better. Even having met the man only once, Matt was convinced that, despite outward appearances, the "Hawk" did and said nothing without purpose and without planned and anticipated results. That's what concerned Matt most of all.

"Don't know who they were unless the ones behind what happened on the way back from Chartwell and I don't know how the hell they found out we'd be in Paris, but what about the kidnapper?" Matt asked. The pain in his side jabbed like a heated tong with each intake of breath.

Hawkins stopped in front of a framed poster of Clint Eastwood mounted on the wall between the room's two windows overlooking Grosvenor Square. Along the top of the poster in bold print, "**CLINT EASTWOOD IS DIRTY HARRY IN MAGNUM FORCE**." In "Dirty Harry's" right hand, a .44 Magnum revolver followed by the words, "Go ahead, make my day." Handwritten at the bottom, "To Hawk, my almost double. Best wishes, Clint."

"What about which kidnapper?" Hawkins asked out of the side of his mouth as he studied the picture.

"After they shot Ian, I hit one of the kidnappers."

"No shit!" Hawkins blurted, spinning in Matt's direction. "And how'd you get somethin' to shoot with? Better yet, don't answer. I don't wanna know." Shaking his head, he continued, "You're a regular killin' machine, aren'tcha? They got two bodies. Stuart's and the old guy in a tux, period. And so far's I'm concerned, it's all your fault."

Matt eased himself from the chair and limped around the desk to the credenza and a coffee maker that bore the stains of days, if not weeks, of neglect. Inside the glass carafe, a brownish-black liquid that smelled like a combination of used motor oil and burned rubber lay heavy over a residue of coffee grounds. As he poured, he said, "If I'd known Ian was gonna get kidnapped, I would've put a leash on him, but unfortunately –"

"Fun-ny, fun-ny," Hawkins said, his voice thick with sarcasm.

Bypassing the cup of sugar speckled with what appeared to be either coffee grounds or roach droppings, Matt returned to his chair, sipping as he went, his face suddenly drawn into a sheet of wrinkles, his eyes shut tight against the revolting bitterness. "Jesus Christ, Hawkins, what've you got in this stuff? Toad piss?"

"Brush your teeth once in a while, and maybe things'd taste better."

"Forget it," Matt said, shaking his head and wiping his lips with the back of his free hand as he lowered his tortured body into the chair. "You still haven't answered my question."

"Which one? All you got is questions."

"The icon. It's tied to something people are willing to kill for. Kill me for, damn it, and I want to know what. Secret formulas? Diamonds? Russian war plans? Just what the hell are you looking for?"

With a final glance at his "almost double" in the photograph, Hawkins stalked across the room and settled on the edge of the desk, bending forward to the point that his face was only inches from Matt's. "They call it, 'need-to-know,' and that you don't have."

Leaning back and folding his arms across his chest, he continued, "What you do have, however, is the U. S. Ambassador, the British Home Secretary, and even the Prime Minister yellin' their heads off wantin' to know who the hell you are and what the fuck you're doin', and I don't like that worth a damn!"

Matt stood and pulled his jacket from the back of his chair. "Then it's time you go your way, I go mine."

"The hell you say," Hawkins shot back. Jumping to his feet, he moved to the door. His lanky frame blocked Matt's way. "You do it my way, or not at all."

Matt slammed his coffee cup hard against the top of the desk and started for the door, ignoring the crack in the side of the cup and the stream of black liquid that sloshed across the desk. "I didn't wanna get involved in this thing in the first place, but now that I am, I may not find what you're looking for, but I'm sure as hell gonna find the people who killed Ian Stuart."

"And what good'll that do, Mr. Special Warfare tough guy?" Hawkins challenged. "Get even for all the ghosts that've been chasn' you for the last thirty years? I know all about you, Berkeley. Two tours in Nam and a fuckin' basket case when you came back. And yeah, since then two dead wives."

Matt stopped, muscles tensed, fists clenched in white-hot anger. "You bastard! You rotten, self-centered old bastard! I oughta..." Matt caught himself. "Get the hell out of the way." As Hawkins shifted to one side, Matt yanked open the door and stomped into the hallway, turning immediately toward a nearby stairwell.

From the doorway, Hawkins aimed a finger at Matt's back and shouted in his best theatrical voice,

"Walk outta here, Berkeley, and you're through. You hear? Through!"

One by one, heads popped from doorways along the corridor as Matt turned and smiled his contempt. "Almost forgot, Hawkins. Since I didn't tell the Paris police, I'll tell you." The smile disappeared. "Go to hell and up yours."

Ignoring the impromptu audience and instant buzz of "ooo's" and "ah's," Hawkins exploded, "Go to hell yourself, you pigheaded, sorry-ass sonofabitch! Nobody fucks with Royce Hawkins. Nobody. Y'hear?"

Chapter 22

The door slammed behind him as Hawkins returned to his desk, a broad grin on his face. "Like takin' candy from a baby," he said to himself, at the same time flipping a switch on the office intercom. "Helen, you there?"

Almost immediately, he heard, "Yes, sir."

"Get me Langley. Herb Samuelson."

"It'll be a few minutes," Helen replied, her words as mushy as the lunch she was trying to swallow.

"No sweat, and Helen?"

"Sir?"

"What the hell you got in your mouth? A banana or somethin'?" He laughed suggestively, remembering the one and only night he'd spent with the woman. "I can think of somethin' a lot better."

Her response, "Royce, please!" was followed by the sound of embarrassed laughter and a whispered, "If somebody hears you, and my husband found out..."

Laughing to himself, Hawkins switched off the intercom and poured himself a cup of coffee. Looking up at Eastwood's Dirty Harry poster, he raised his cup in toast and said, "You gotta admit, Harry baby. With Berkeley, even you couldn't've played it any better."

Hawkins' grin went sour, however, as he tasted the coffee. Catching it halfway down his throat, he spit as much as he could into the metal waste can next to his desk before admitting, "That sonofabitch was right! It does taste like toad piss."

Laughing to himself, this time at the thought of Berkeley's determination, Hawkins pulled open the large drawer at the bottom right side of his desk, lifted the boxy-shaped, leaden-colored phone from the drawer and set it on his desk. After insuring that the phone's signal strength through its wireless connection to the embassy's master router was in the Excellent range, he snapped the phone's 5.6-inch video screen into its upright position.

He then rotated it such that the screen and its quarter-inch camera lens, centered above the screen, faced in his direction. With that done, Hawkins dropped his six-foot-three-inch frame into the swivel chair and swung his legs onto the top of the desk. Papers he had no intention of reading scattered, but he was careful to avoid the puddle of Matt's coffee already eating its way through the desktop's several layers of varnish.

Helen's voice from the intercom punctuated the silence. "Mr. Samuelson's on the line. He's at home, but he wants to go secure mode. He's patched into a video-audio scrambler unit at his residence."

"Thought he would be," Hawkins responded, watching the blinking red light on his cryptographically covered videophone suddenly turn to a steady green. Hitting the ON buttons for both the speakerphone option and the monitor screen, he said, "Hi, Herb, how the hell are ya?"

The screen turned from a deep blue to a paisley printed pajama shirt, then tilted upward to Herb Samuelson's sagging jowls. The man's face was still flush from sleep and hair, sparse as it was, spiked haphazardly. Samuelson whined, "For chrissake, Hawk, do you know what time it is? Seven in the morning, Saturday morning, to be exact. One of only two days out of the week I get to sleep past four-thirty."

Hawkins had to bite his lower lip to keep from laughing at the face on the screen. "To be honest, Herb, you look like hell. Stead of doin' a comb-over with what little hair you've got, maybe you oughta think about gettin' outfitted with a wig or somethin'."

Hawkins watched Samuelson's eyes narrow and lips grow tight with anger at what Hawkins called one of his *Herb jabs*. Before Samuelson could find the words to shoot back, he went on, "But for now, time to get it in gear. Berkeley's on the hook, tighter'n a well digger's ass in January. Couldn't pry him loose if you wanted to."

"What've you got?" Samuelson asked, at the same time smoothing his hair back and across his head with one hand.

"Quick and dirty. First, on a tip from Interpol, Berkeley's got tabs on some kinda off-the-wall church group that might have the icon, but we'll have to wait and see how that plays out. Second, the antiquities society he's workin' for, it's a fake."

Samuelson suddenly came alert. "A fake? What do you mean?"

"Checked it out. *¡Nada!* Not a damn thing. Then I thought, maybe it's the Russkies. It's their style. Remember a KGB agent named Strizhenko from Berlin? Late seventies and into the eighties?"

"The one they called, 'The Leopard?'"

"That's him."

"So?"

Hawkins knew what he was about to say would get a rise out of Samuelson when he answered, "I got hold of your old buddy, Klebinov, at the Russian Embassy."

Samuelson jumped to his feet, the paisley print pajama shirt suddenly back on the screen before the man's face reappeared, its size as though the video camera had zoomed in for a close-up. With eyes wide and a voice at least two octaves higher, Samuelson screamed, "You fucking did what?"

Hawkins couldn't help but laugh as Samuelson, clutching his forehead, nearly fell as he tried to sit back on the side of his bed or chair or whatever he'd been sitting on.

"Careful, Herb, or you'll bust a hemorrhoid. Seems Strizhenko was on the wrong side and went AWOL from the KGB right after the attempted coup in ninety-one. Right now, he's in London, workin' for the Iranians."

"You're sure?"

"Yeah, somethin' about usin' a Russian embassy license plate, and what Klebinov's gonna do if he ever gets hold of him. Anyway, the Iranians make sense. We and the U.N. pretty much tear up their economy with our embargoes which, except for the Russians, cuts off most everything they need for their nuke program, puttin' 'em back I don't know how many years.

Hell man, they need somethin' that goes boom, somthin' they think we can't stop 'em from gettin'. Like a friggin' laser gun or two or three. Who gives a shit if it came out of World War Two. If they can get hold of the plans and if they can make it work, it's better than nothin'."

"How would they have known?" Samuelson's voice had yet to resume its normal vocal range.

"What if, like we did, they found out from a former KGB comrade? Strizhenko, for example. And what if your boy Roberts gave the show away and somehow Strizhenko got on his tail?"

"A lot of 'what ifs,'" Samuelson said, his hesitancy to accept Hawkins' theory abundantly evident as shown by a raised eyebrow and a sideways glance at the camera.

"Awright, Herb, one more 'what if,'" Hawkins said, swinging his legs to the floor and pulling open the desk's top right drawer. Shuffling through a stack of folders and papers, he lifted out a large envelope stamped "SECRET" and scattered several recently processed color photographs and a collection of grainy black and white, 8x10 enlargements on the desk. He made sure none fell on the corner of the desk where Matt's coffee had turned the surface into a puddle of varnish-bubbling sludge. After sorting through the pictures, he picked out two, one color and one black and white and held the color photo in front of the videophone's camera lens.

"In addition to this shot of Berkeley at the hospital and the broad who calls herself Leila Howard, … Yeah, that's her hangin' onto his arm and looking like she's ready to hop in the sack with him already. What if I said we got photographs of the Iranian president, the one and only Mahmoud Ahmadinejad, and his family at some kind of social event right after he was elected. Like this one."

Hawkins dropped the color photo and held the black-and-white picture up to the camera. As you can see, Ahmadinejad's got his arm around the same Leila babe who's playin' up to Berkeley. Known as Bājī Leila. The Lady Leila. Only thing, she's the president's younger sister, a graduate of some Russky university back in the eighties, early nineties with an advanced degree in physics and related subjects."

Samuelson went silent for a moment, his face taking on a somber expression as though he was deep in thought. Finally, he asked, "Berkeley know this?"

"By now, he prob'ly knows her bra size and the

inside of her knickers, but this? I doubt it."

A slow "Hummmm" came from Samuelson, this time gnawing his upper lip in thought before saying, "No mistakes, Hawk. Make sure you've got all the angles covered."

Hawkins laughed. "Don't worry, Herb. I'm like the whore you always wanted. On top of everything right up to the climax."

"Why do you always have to. . ." Samuelson stopped in mid-sentence, finishing with, "As for Berkeley, if he tries to double-cross us for this Leila woman, do whatever's necessary, but do it discreetly."

"Yeah, Herb. Discreet's my middle name, and unless you got somethin' else you wanna talk about, you can go back to bed, but don't forget what they say down in Texas."

"What's that?" Samuelson asked, his voice leery with suspicion.

"If you don't want splinters up the ol' sphincter, don't take any wooden dildos."

"Goddamn it, Hawkins," Samuelson erupted, "someday you'll go too far with that mouth of yours, and when you do, –"

Hawkins reached forward and punched the OFF buttons for the speakerphone and the video screen, breaking the connection. With a smile on his face, he leaned back and swung his legs to the top of the desk. "Too far, my ass," he said to the autographed Clint Eastwood poster on the wall. "As the Joker once said to Batman, brother Eastwood, they ain't seen nothin' yet!"

* * *

Even the traffic noise seemed far in the distance,

cloaked as it was by the six-foot-high stone wall and line of willows surrounding the garden. A mixture of poorly maintained hedges and walkways ran between tight little patches of roses. A few of the rosebushes still held a diminishing number of late season petals, a smattering of tarnished pink and yellowed white among leaves caught unawares by London's first cold snap of the season.

As he thought of the man called Berkeley, the pruning shears in General Ahmad Kazemi's gloved hands moved swiftly from stem to stem, snip-snip-snipping each bush into little more than a stiff, thorn-laden stub.

"By his own hands and resourcefulness, two men dead south of London," Kazemi said over his shoulder, the rhythm of the shears never missing a beat, "and one of Inspector Stuart's abductors in Paris. It would seem your Mr. Berkeley is more formidable than you earlier implied."

"And perhaps he has only been very fortunate," Strizhenko responded, the sudden defensive tone in his voice not lost on Kazemi, "but of more importance, I am convinced he grows closer to the icon with each passing day. If his progress continues, I anticipate the use of your people within the next twenty-four to forty-eight hours."

"They will be ready, but what of Bājī Leila?" Kazemi asked, tucking the shears underneath one arm and removing the leather-work gloves from his hands as he turned to face Strizhenko. "She appears... distant, shall we say, after her trip to Paris."

"It is my impression Berkeley may have had more influence on her than she on him."

Kazemi thought for a moment before deciding, "In that event, she will see him no more. There must be no hint of disloyalty to her brother or the Supreme Leader."

Strizhenko laughed quietly, a shallow sound edged with cunning and the threat of exposure. "It would complicate your plans, would it not?"

Kazemi was suddenly alert. "What plans?" he asked, his own defense mechanism whispering in his ear, *He knows, he knows.*

"Forgive me, General," Strizhenko said, the laughter lines on his face fading into a sneer. "Perhaps I am wrong about you, Bājī Leila and what I sense to be your plans for her brother. And then again... but no matter. Once our goal is achieved, what is to become of the American?"

"He must die," Kazemi answered without hesitation.

"So be it."

As Strizhenko turned and walked toward a line of French doors at the rear of the Iranian Embassy, Ahmad Kazemi took the shears and very carefully, very methodically snipped off the top of the nearest rosebush, at the same time promising under

his breath, "And so must you, my Russian friend. So must you."

Chapter 23

After sleeping virtually around the clock, it was the next day when one of the hardest things Matt had ever done was a visit to London's Fulham Road area and Ian Stuart's wife, Kathleen, to express his sorrow for what happened in Paris. He assured her he would remain in England and do whatever it took to find those responsible for Ian's death.

But now, it was time to restart the hunt for the icon and, with that, those whose hands were wet with Ian's blood. Not for the antiquity society, not for Royce Hawkins and the CIA, but for what he hoped would be his own peace of mind.

* * *

The high vaulted ceiling above Westminster Abbey's great nave was lit by aisle and clerestory windows as well as numerous glittering chandeliers. Their light, however, seemed to fade with age before reaching into the countless niches and crevices created in the building's thirteenth- and fourteenth-century stonework. In the nave below, Jenny Mason sat in the pew behind Matt and a young minister clad in clerical garb.

Her attention was divided between the men's conversation and the continuous mutterings of hundreds of tourists, milling from one chapel to the next among an overwhelming array of ornately carved stone sarcophagi and engraved memorials. Even so, Jenny's eyes and ears quickly focused on Matt as he explained to the Most Reverend Joshua Rutherford...

"I've been told one of their churches might be located in a village called Tavistock, near Plymouth, but the chief constable there said the only churches in the area were Catholic and the Church of England. I've also been told you're an expert on comparative religions. Especially the various sects established in England over the last fifty years. That's why I'm here. Can you help?"

"*Umma Coptya,*" Rutherford said.

"Say again?"

Jenny leaned forward on the wooden bench, intent on hearing the minister's answer.

Rutherford seemed aware of her movement and shifted so he could address both Matt and Jenny. At the same time, he smiled at Matt's questioning expression. "Umma Coptya, Society of the Coptic Nation. In response to Moslem persecution, large numbers of Christian Copts fled Egypt in the nineteen thirties and early forties. Though still active in Egypt and Ethiopia, they continue to be targets of Islamic fundamentalism.

"In addition to the earlier migration, during more recent years vastly different, 'theologically modernized' Coptic congregations, as they refer to themselves, have been established in southern Europe and the British Isles. A rather large number of converts appear to be in London and the south of England."

"Is that what they're called?" Matt asked. "Society of the Coptic Nation?"

"Actually, as in Europe, they're known as the Church of the Coptic Reformation. You're certain these are the people you want? Their teachings really are quite peace loving."

"I'm not certain of anything, Reverend, but right

now, they're the only game in town. There's a place called Tavistock Square in London. Would that be –"

"Yes. They've a church, an old converted townhouse located just south of Euston Station. I found the address after you called. Number sixteen Tavistock Square. Do you know it? The Square, I mean?"

"Not really," Matt admitted.

Rutherford glanced back at Jenny. "Perhaps the young lady?"

Jenny answered immediately, "Yes, Reverend. I've volunteered to be Mr. Berkeley's transportation while he's in London. I am familiar with Tavistock Square."

A short time later, with the engine idling, Jenny's small white Ferrari sat beneath the shade of a large plane tree. Its spread of autumn-touched branches created a spider web of shadows across the car and over the street.

Hardly noticed by those driving or walking along the thoroughfare was a horse-drawn funeral carriage rounding the corner. Its driver wore mourning clothes complete with top hat, its huge black stallion in funerary trappings more common to an earlier time. What appeared unusual to Matt in this largely residential neighborhood on a Saturday afternoon was apparently commonplace to others.

The sharp cloppity-clop of the stallion's hooves faded into a drift of fallen leaves as the carriage came to a halt in front of a stone and brick townhouse across from the Ferrari where Matt and Jenny watched and waited. The building, one of many clustered about the square, stood at the end of a row of nineteenth-century, five-story façades aged in a collaboration of browns and yellows, their doors in gloss-black conformity.

"I hadn't planned on this," Matt said, silently

counting the six men who suddenly appeared and eased a steel gray casket from the rear of the carriage. With precision movements, the pallbearers, each hooded and hidden beneath a black, ankle-length robe, carried the casket up a short flight of steps and through the double front doors of Number 16 Tavistock Square.

"Then don't go," Jenny offered. "You could come back another time, you know."

"Uh-uh, and besides, a funeral's probably as good a cover as any." Matt opened the door, adding, "I appreciate your help, but you don't have to wait."

Jenny shook her head. "No. I'll be nearby when you come out."

Matt got out and closed the door, his "thanks" muffled by the low growl of the Ferarri's engine and gears as the car pulled away and disappeared around the corner.

Turning up the collar of his coat, he crossed the street and stopped in front of Number 16. With the empty funeral carriage at his back, its driver perched in his seat seemingly oblivious to the passing world, Matt stood for a moment and studied the building's entrance.

Embedded in stone above the arched doorway was a cross, Latin in shape except for a modified fleur-de-lis at each of the four extremities. Immediately below the cross, inscribed in the same stone, the words, *"Umma Coptya,"* which he mouthed, each word mentally repeated and mulled over for its significance. Maybe he was wrong. Maybe the whole thing was a misinterpretation of what Boulon had said. Maybe... but the sniffing and impatient pawing of the stallion in the leaves along the curb interrupted his thoughts and spurred him on.

Climbing the steps, he pushed open one side of the

double doors and entered. As the door closed with a pneumatic hiss, he found himself in a small windowless foyer. The closeness was relieved only by the glow of a three-branched candelabrum on a side table. The walls were host to several lines of wooden coat racks and a small number of neatly hung robes, some black, others white.

He stood for a moment, allowing his eyes time to adjust to the dimness. Simultaneously, his ears strained to search out and identify the sound from beyond a massive curtain of heavy black velvet that blocked his way. He could hear it, almost feel it in the floor beneath his feet, a mournful hum, female voices, joined by male. The sound gradually dissolved into a low chant and repeated over and over: "Kyrie eleison... Kyrie eleison..."

He pictured the church of his youth, the choir, the call to God, "Kyrie eleison... Lord, have mercy upon us."

It was the odor that seeped from beneath the curtain that suddenly demanded his attention, not unpleasant, but it was there. Familiar yet, at the same time, strange, like a hand beckoning him to enter. And he did.

Slipping into a black robe and pulling the hood partially over his head, Matt eased the curtain aside just enough to step past. He edged his way along the wall at the rear of what he recognized to be a religious sanctuary converted from what had to have been several apartments of sitting and dining rooms, bedrooms and hallways. Once past the curtain the chant became stronger, the odor more intense. The atmosphere, bathed in a mist that seemed to settle in his nostrils and along his eyelids, was like a fine layer of dust.

"Good God," Matt whispered to himself, wrinkling his nose and holding back a cough. "Hashish oil."

From a ceiling at least two stories high hung an array of chandeliers, each supporting dozens of finely tapered candles. They provided a soft, almost eerie glow across the chamber.

Meanwhile, along the two outer walls, wisps of smoke, saturated with the evaporate of hashish oil, rose in tiny swirls from torch-heated censers, glass beakers placed at intervals among floor-to-ceiling murals portraying the life of Christ.

Matt remembered. The icon! The burnished copper backing and its scenes of Christ the Savior. From birth to death, from death to resurrection, from resurrection to ascension, yet somehow these murals were different. Not only the colors, but the figures, the background and the heavens above – each scene painted with a brush coated in mysticism and North African folklore.

Through eyes already watering from the scented haze gradually enveloping the sanctuary, Matt probed the faces of the congregation, at least those few he could see from where he stood. Men in black, full-length robes like the one he wore, hoods lying loose about their shoulders. Women in white, their hoods pulled protectively about their heads and faces. How many? Fifty? Sixty? A hundred?

What mattered more, however, was the fact that no one in the congregation had noticed his entrance, or if they had, they made no outward sign. Not even the men positioned at each end of a cloth-draped bier at the front of the sanctuary on which rested the casket he had seen taken from the carriage.

Settling into a chair near the foyer curtain, Matt watched as, slowly, almost painfully, a priest, his robe different from all the rest – ash-gray with scarlet trim – rose from behind the casket and swept the congregation with his eyes. When they fell upon him, Matt sensed the gaze as it traveled the contours of his face, touched, memorized, but gave no sign of recognition before moving on until each member of the congregation had been so blessed.

Matt likewise studied the priest. He was tall, yet thin and stooped beneath the weight of too many years. Eyes and cheeks were sunk deep within a face more common to the grave than to the living. His hands seemed mere bones covered by glassine skin, their knobby fingers wrapped tight around the shaft of a large wooden cross. The man was old, very old, but there was something more, a sickness that already seemed to have claimed its victim, yet held at bay by some inner strength only the man could know.

With the wave of the cross in his hand, the chant abruptly ceased. There was silence until the priest spoke, his voice, like his body, old, yet filled with a power that comes only with the staunchest of faith in one's beliefs.

"It is with sorrow that we bid farewell to our brother, Brendan, who only two night's past gave his life on the streets of Paris to protect what is rightfully ours. He precedes us to that other life. A life of goodness, peace and love. A life we've striven so diligently to achieve in this world and which we will achieve despite those who offer opposition to our faith."

The streets of Paris? The words hit Matt like a stone hurled into the middle of his chest. The man he'd shot on the Pont d'Iéna? No, it couldn't be, but there was something wrong. Whether it was the voice of the priest or the vapors rising from the censers, he didn't know, but something was happening. Numbness had settled over his legs and arms; a slow dizziness was drawing halos behind his eyes. Suddenly, he knew he shouldn't be there. He wanted to leave, but his body refused to respond.

"Yes, my people," the old priest continued, "I, the Redeemer, will lead you and all of humankind from darkness into light. The breaking of our silence will reveal to all the Universal Oneness of God and bring about the everlasting brotherhood of man."

Again, underlying the Redeemer's words, a steady monotone of voices from the congregation lent its support as the old man raised his arms above the casket and cried, "The Night of the Angels is upon us. When the angels spread their wings above this earthly orb as they will soon do, the darkness of greed and hatred will be transformed into the light of tolerance and forgiveness.

"And I say unto you, nothing will stop the Night of the Angels. When their light issues forth over the islands of the sea, the world will experience an awakening never before seen."

Matt could hear the mournful sound rising from the congregation, rhythmic and soulful, spreading through the sanctuary like a creature generating its own life force. Flames beneath the smoking censers increased in intensity. As the atmosphere grew heavier, the sweet moldiness of hashish began to erode Matt's awareness. A sudden chill gripped his body while, at the same time, he could feel a definite quickening of his heartbeat, a beating so severe and so loud, he was afraid the congregation might hear.

Dryness constricted his mouth and throat. He squeezed his eyes shut against the penetrating haze, drew the side of the hood across his nose, but the odor persisted.

From the past, something he'd wanted to forget, something he'd shut away in the back closets of his mind forced its way into his consciousness. He wanted to shout, "For God's sake, stop," but he couldn't, and then...

He was there again. M-60 machine gun, its ammunition belt heavy in his arms; river scum to his waist; leaches sucked tight against his skin. Squalid little villages mired deep within the Mekong Delta; stifling heat along the rivers My Tho, Ham Luong and Co Chien. Again, the odor, always mixed with death.

Down river from Vinh Long, a smoldering village, its temple gutted. A Buddhist monk in burned and tattered robes; hashish smoke, rising from a glass water pipe. A Vietnamese farmer, clothing caked with dirt and blood. A filth-stained canvas, hiding the "unhideable."

And again, for the thousandth time, he asked, "What happened?" As always, his words, fraught with fatigue, battle weary like himself.

Each time, the farmer's cry never changed. "You bombs kill my family!" The canvas, jerked away. A woman, two children, charred, shriveled lumps of once living flesh and blood. The same cry; the same hate; the same accusing finger. "You bombs! You kill. You! You!"

Just as quickly, the dank haze of the temple merged with the present, the Coptic sanctuary, the old priest, and the smell of hashish. As in a dream, through eyes blurred by the mist, Matt watched the lid of the casket swing open. A chimeric hand reached out and grasped for support as the chant, "Kyrie eleison," like a snake charmer's voice, drew it forth. An arm, and then the head and chest of the corpse, its eyes blackened, blood tears trailing down its cheeks. They fell and burned their way into the casket's white satin lining.

Matt shook his head and closed his eyes against what he knew had to be an apparition, a phantom of his own creation, but when he looked again, the corpse remained. Only now, one hand gestured toward bullet wounds in its chest, the other, like the hand of the Vietnamese farmer, pointed an accusing finger and cried, "You-u-u-u!"

"Oh, God," Matt breathed. The finger pointed at him. This time, it was the man from Paris, the man he'd shot to death, the man they never found.

Using all the strength he possessed, Matt pushed up from the chair and braced himself against the rear wall as the Redeemer raised his hands above the corpse and sprinkled earth through open fingers. The particles blossomed outward and floated down like a waterfall in slow motion.

"From dust thou came, and unto dust shalt thou return," the Redeemer cried, his voice tremulous, his words bouncing off the walls of the sanctuary and echoing through the corridors of Matt's brain.

All at once, the corpse began to disintegrate before Matt's eyes, a metamorphosis from lifeless flesh to a boiling, billowing cloud of dust, rising from the casket like a miasmic fog, filling the air with its foulness.

As Matt watched, the congregation turned in his direction. Arms and hands, suddenly elastic like gum rubber, stretched outward from beneath the sleeves of their robes, reaching and grasping for his soul, seeking vengeance, he knew, for their fallen brother. Faces, each a death's-head come to life, stared at him through eye sockets glowing with the fires of hate and damnation.

Sweeping the hood from his head, Matt tried to shout, "No! He killed Ian. I had no choice." But his words were silent cries, lost in the swirling cloud of dust as the death's-heads drew closer, and the chant became louder and stronger.

"Kyrie eleison, Kyrie eleison..." The chant crushed him against the wall with its power as the underlying hum became a low, angry wail, quickly scaling upwards into a piercing, high-pitched shriek of lamentation, the shrill warble of the zagreet, a cry of death echoing from across the ancient sands and hills of North Africa.

Matt's breath became shorter, more ragged, until he found himself fighting for air. He knew he was on the verge of panic, the same reaction he'd felt from the stench of blood and death and the horror of men, his men, torn apart on the rivers and in the jungles of Vietnam.

Blindly feeling his way along the wall, he made his way back to the curtain, through the foyer, and out into the afternoon overcast of Tavistock Square. Staggering down the steps and across the sidewalk, he slammed into the funeral carriage, the sweet odor of hashish locked in his nostrils. It saturated his clothing, followed him like a stalking animal.

He pushed away from the hearse, fought to keep his balance, stumbled, almost fell as he threw the robe from his shoulders. Free of the robe, he rushed forward, trying to escape the torment of his past and the hellish nightmares of the present.

"Matt, what's wrong?" Jenny called as she ran

from across the street.

Her hand reached to give him support, but he sidestepped and swiped it away. "Leave me alone!"

"It's me, Jenny. Jenny Mason. Don't you remember?"

Matt wrapped his arms around a light pole and stared hard at Jenny's face, sucking in great slugs of air while trying to remember. "Jenny?" He closed his eyes and shook his head, fighting the dizziness and mental sludge that eroded his memory. "Can't you smell it?"

"What?" Jenny asked, shaking her head.

Tears poured from Matt's reddened eyes as he pointed toward the funeral carriage and the casket now being carried down the steps of number 16 Tavistock Square. "Vietnam, Jenny. Vietnam and the smell of death."

"Come with me." Jenny pried his arms from the lamppost and led him down the street to the small white Ferrari, its top up, windows down. "I'll take you to a doctor."

"No doctor," Matt said, allowing Jenny to open the door and help him down onto the leather-covered seat.

Jenny hurried to the driver side of the car, snuggled in beneath the steering wheel and started the engine. "You're certain you don't need a doctor?"

"I'll be okay," Matt answered. He leaned back against the head rest and closed his eyes, inhaling through his mouth and forcing out long rivers of air in an effort to clear his lungs of the pungent narcotic. "Lots of air. That's all I need. Air."

Soothed by the motion of the car as Jenny steered away from the curb and out into the traffic, Matt heard her say, "Your hotel then."

Once the car turned onto Woburn Place and

Southampton Row, he allowed his mind to lapse into neutral until the smell of perfume, the soft scent of old lavender, further ignited his memory. Abruptly, he raised his head and looked at Jenny. "What the hell are you doing here?"

"Don't you remember?" she asked, keeping her eyes on the traffic ahead. "I was with you. I told you I'd be waiting. If you'd only let me..."

Jenny's words floated on the sounds of traffic as Matt drifted between car horns and distant sirens until, "Here we are, London's most efficient taxi service." Jenny eased the car alongside the curb across from the Jubilee Hotel.

Matt shook himself awake. "Sorry. I must've dropped off. You were saying?"

Jenny laughed. "Whatever it was, it wasn't important."

Matt sat for a moment, mentally preparing his body for movement before very slowly opening the car door. "Thanks for finding me."

"You do remember who I am, don't you?" Jenny asked, a smile forming a question mark across her face.

Matt laughed softly as he pulled himself out and closed the car door, bending to look through the open window. "Yes, ma'am. Jenny Mason, the umbrella girl, but... but how did you know I was staying here?" he asked looking up at the hotel's marquee and name.

"You told me. Don't you remember? And changing the subject, when you feel better, will you tell me what happened in the church?"

"Not sure myself, but when the fog clears, I'll call. Tomorrow at the latest."

"And you also remember my address and telephone number?" Jenny asked with a slight tease in her voice.

Matt tapped his forehead and winced at the thumping sound, a miniature jackhammer against his skull. "Engraved in stone, and that's pretty much how my head feels."

"Until then." With a smile and a wave, Jenny maneuvered the Ferrari into a flow of cars and buses in the direction of Oxford Street, leaving Matt on the curb, watching as the car disappeared in the traffic.

He stood for a moment, his mind traveling back to Tavistock Square. The man in the casket, and the man he'd shot in Paris. Were they really the same, or hashish vapors playing tricks with his brain? The old priest who called himself Redeemer and the Coptic Church. What did they know about the icon? And what was the Night of the Angels? And yes, when did he tell Jenny he was staying at the Jubilee? He didn't think he had, but suddenly, it was all too much. His brain registered overload; his body demanded rest.

First sleep, he told himself. Then, if he could find it, a photograph and the face of a dead man who, God willing, might speak to him from the grave. A dead man who might provide the missing link to the Churchill Icon.

Chapter 24

The travel clock on the bedside table read 6:45 in the evening. Hours lost, but he'd needed the sleep. Bed unmade, clothes strewn across the floor, still shrieking the odor of hashish, but finally a mind able to focus on what had to be done.

If there were those who knew who he was and what he wanted, they'd know where he was staying. They could be watching, listening, waiting for their next chance. Paranoia or common sense? Whatever it was, Matt knew he had to learn more about the Church of the Coptic Reformation. He also knew that time had become his enemy.

Remembering his conversation with Lord Alanbrooke at Chartwell, he knew what that next move would be. But he had to find a place where those who might be listening couldn't hear, where he could lose himself in a crowd and not be seen. He remembered seeing such a place only a few doors down from the hotel that would serve each of those purposes.

* * *

It was the third phone call he'd made over the past hour. The first to Royce Hawkins; the second to Jenny Mason to tell her he'd recovered from that afternoon's ordeal and express his thanks for her help. For this call, however, the swelling laughter and conversations from an oversized bar on the other side of the latticework partition forced Matt to turn against the wall and hold the telephone tighter against his left ear. He pressed the heel of his free hand against his other ear to reduce the noise.

"If you don't mind, sir," he said. "Tonight, if you can arrange it." Trying to hear what was being said on the other end of the line, he tightened the muscles of his face and ears against a sudden round of cheers and applause from both the television mounted over the bar and an enthusiastic roomful of patrons.

Matt laughed softly, squinting through the latticework at the television and a replay of the British National Soccer Team scoring a goal against the Italians. "No, sir, I didn't see the goal, but I heard it, loud and clear and saw the replay. Anyway, I appreciate your efforts. Nine o'clock will be fine. And Lord Alanbrooke, I'll let you know what I find."

Matt replaced the telephone receiver and returned to his booth and an empty, froth-coated glass with the brewer's logo on its side. He was still hungry, but the partially eaten steak-and-kidney pie and pile of fried potatoes on the side tasted too much like the odor of hashish which had thus far refused to vacate the linings of his mouth and nose.

"Anything else, Gov?" It was the young waiter who had originally served him.

"Another pint and some –"

"Hey!" the waiter yelped, suddenly pushed aside as Royce Hawkins slid onto the bench on the other side of the table.

"Pint of stout, waiter. Now!"

The waiter complained, "Y'didn't have to –"

Matt held up his hand, silencing the young man. "You're wasting your breath on this guy. Just get what he wants, and if we're lucky, he'll drink up and leave."

Shrugging his shoulders and rolling his eyes to

demonstrate his dislike for Hawkins, the waiter turned and walked in the direction of the bar.

"How was Tavistock Square?" Hawkins asked. "You looked like you'd seen a ghost when you came outta there."

"Dull life you lead if all you've gotta do is follow me around."

Hawkins leaned back in the booth, a satisfied grin splitting both corners of his mouth. "We got you covered like a blanket, buddy boy, but one thing we missed. The little lady from the Antiquities Society? What happened? Did she lose interest, or'd she just get tired of playin' beddy-bye after Stewart cashed it in?"

"You really are an A-number-one asshole, aren't you," Matt snapped, the curl of his lip showing his disgust. "If it's any of your business, the society sent her up to Edinburgh this afternoon. She'll be back Monday or Tuesday. As for Tavistock Square, let's just say I didn't find the icon."

"You're sure about that?"

"You don't hear very well, do you? And what if I had and didn't tell you?" A sly grin crept across Matt's face. He liked goading he hawk.

Hawkins leaned forward across the table. "You find that sonofabitch, you damn well better tell me. Scotland Yard's about had it with you, and I'm the only one standin' in the way of them sendin' you back to Paris for questionin' and maybe a stretch in the *Fleury-Mérogis* where prisoners commit suicide just to get out. You double-cross me and there won't be a goddamn rat hole in London or anywhere else you can hide."

Matt grunted his amusement and said, "After what I've already been through, those kinda threats don't mean a damn thing to me, Hawkins."

Just then, the waiter returned with the drinks, hurriedly placed them on the table and left under the sullen glower of the man who ordered stout. "Buncha goddamn poofs," Hawkins growled in an obvious attempt to vent his anger in a different direction. Matt knew the Hawk needed whatever information he had to give and could only push so hard.

"So?"

"You heard me. Poofs. Queers. This pub's lousy with fag actors and homo queens. That waiter's about as queer as a three-dollar bill." He waved his arm toward the bar. "They're all queer. Didn't you know that?"

Matt cupped one ear toward the cheers at the bar. "They don't sound too girlie to me. Anyway, different strokes for different folks. They leave me alone; I leave them alone."

"Especially as long as you're gettin' it from Leila babe, huh? And what about that cute little chickie with the white Ferrari? Word of advice. Keep your pants zipped and your mind on the icon. Now, why'd you wanna see me?"

Matt sipped his ale, considering his options: tell Hawkins to go to hell, or knuckle under and play by the rules? Hawkins' rules, damn it! He already knew the answer. "I need information," he said.

"Whadda I look like? A fuckin' library?"

"More like a burned-out spook with a limited vocabulary," Matt fired back as he pulled an envelope from inside his jacket and slid it across the table to Hawkins. "A summary of what I learned from a minister named Rutherford at Westminster Abbey and what happened at the funeral in Tavistock Square.

"There's also a list of questions I need answered, like, Church of the Coptic Reformation... locations outside of London? A man called The Redeemer... who is he? What's the Night of the Angels? And in relation to all the above, what's the significance of 'islands of the sea?'"

"What the fuck, Berkeley?" Hawkins chugalugged his remaining stout, slammed the heavy mug against the top of the table and scooped up the envelope before getting to his feet. "Why should I do this?" he asked, waving the envelope in Matt's face. "You walked out on me, remember? If you think –"

Matt cut Hawkins short. "You want to see the icon as bad as I think you do you'll get whatever I want. And one other thing," Matt went on, "tell your bloodhounds, if they're going to follow me, keep their distance. If it looks like I've got a bunch of rent-a-cops on my tail, it could blow this thing wide open, and me with it."

"Just remember what I said, Berkeley," Hawkins warned. "Screw me on this, and we're gonna hang your balls from the highest point on the goddamn London Eye Ferris wheel, and I don't give a shit whether you're with 'em or not."

* * *

Hawkins paused as he passed through the door of the pub onto St. Martin's Lane, looked quickly over his shoulder to insure Matt wasn't following, then crossed the street to a car parked in front of the English National Opera. As he walked past the front of the car, he slapped the hood for Agent Mabry to lower the window.

"Sir?" Mabry asked as Honeycutt leaned from the passenger side to hear Hawkins' instructions.

Keeping an eye on the pub's front door, Hawkins ordered, "You and Honeycutt stay close. That sonofabitch's just about there, and I don't want anything goin' wrong.

"And don't forget, the Iranians, and maybe even the Russkies, are watchin', so be careful. I wanna keep the competition as friendly as we can for as long as we can."

*　*　*

Matt stepped onto the street ten minutes later, leaving a chorus of groans and curses aimed at the Italian soccer team which had just scored their second goal in as many minutes against the British. The early evening chill nipped at his cheeks and caught him by surprise. The beguiling warmth of the pub and its patrons quickly turned to a wariness that irritated and angered him.

He knew they were there, somewhere, watching and waiting: a parked car, a store entrance, a window in one of the buildings across the street. Everywhere he looked, faces, expressionless, eyes immediately turned away, but he knew. Somewhere among those faces were men who, for whatever reason, wanted the missing icon. Then again, there always seemed to be the others, the ones who wanted him dead.

Chapter 25

A stiff breeze swirled up from the River Thames and through the streets, and the temperature felt sharper since darkness had descended. Enough to make him zip up the front of his jacket as he stopped on the steps of St. Martin-in-the-Fields, overlooking Trafalgar Square.

The usual Saturday night crowd of tourists and buskers, punks and hustlers had already gathered. Passing car horns, boom boxes and live entertainers competed for the attention of those who had come to talk, to be seen, to panhandle and to pick pockets, or, for a fee, to find a willing partner for the night.

It had been his intention to avoid the square altogether until he saw the two men, loitering on the steps of the National Portrait Gallery across the way. Though not looking in his direction, he remembered the faces and the names. Honeycutt and Mabry. Salt and pepper. CIA. And for tonight, his assigned keepers.

"All right, guys," he said, issuing a whispered challenge, "let's see how good you really are."

Without looking back, Matt made his way across the street and down into the square, quickly losing himself in a world of perpetual motion. A world peopled with scam artists on the make, prostitutes, drug pushers and of course, the innocents, the ones preyed upon by all the rest. It was the punks, however, who stood out in all their individualistic glory: hair-spiked, "Mohawked," corn-rowed, frizzed, curled, and dyed various shades of pink, orange, green and purple. He thought they'd gone away after the sixties, seventies and eighties, but there they were, in his mind, a gaggle of multicolored clowns.

Their clothes were a mixture of Hell's Angel leather, tight enough to raise the voice by at least three octaves, and oversized coveralls worn with army-issue, Iraq War jackets. Each jacket sported anti-war and anti-American slogans on the back. Beaded headbands, some above facial tattoos, seemed to be a mandatory part of their uniforms.

Blending as best he could with such an amalgam of humanity, Matt was careful to avoid the more lighted areas, in particular the reflecting pools and the quartet of sculptured lions at the base of Lord Nelson's lofty effigy. He zigzagged his way toward the south side of the square.

Head low, he moved with the crowd before sidling into a group of people clustered about one of the many buskers performing for handouts. At the group's center, an elderly woman played an Irish jig on a button-studded violin. Her accompaniment was the clanking of coins tossed into an aluminum pan at her feet.

He glanced quickly over his shoulder. Seeing neither Honeycutt nor Mabry, he hurried on, again stopping near the edge of the square. Another group, larger than the last, applauded two whiskered old men in moth-eaten army uniforms. One was blind, singing war songs, the other squeezing an ancient accordion with hands and fingers as gnarled and ragged as the accordion itself.

Matt searched the crowd once more. Satisfied he had lost his "shadows," he knew there was nothing to gain by waiting any longer.

* * *

"Which way?" Honeycutt asked, turning first one way, then another, sometimes standing on the toes of his shoes to see over the crowd.

"That way," Mabry pointed, shouting over the ear-rending sound of a nearby saxophone that climbed the scale, then wheezed a cracked reed into a duet with an off-key trumpet.

"C'mon, freaks, move it," Honeycutt shouted at a group of punks who pushed their way across his path and blocked his view of Matt.

"Who you callin' a freak?" dared an overweight giant of a man with purple and lemon colored hair spiraled upwards like springs in a discarded mattress and a definite New Jersey accent. With a doubled fist, he shoved Honeycutt in the chest. "Want me to break your fuckin' neck? Huh? Huh?"

Mabry shouldered his way between Honeycutt and "spring head." At the same time, he grabbed Honeycutt by the arm and pulled him free. "When the hell you gonna learn to keep your mouth shut, damn it? We got more important things to do than screw around with a buncha juiced-up air heads."

Mabry moved toward the center of the square, climbed up beside one of the bronze lions at the foot of Nelson's column and looked out over the crowd.

"See him?" Honeycutt called up.

"Hell, no!" Mabry shouted back. "Sonofabitch's gone!"

* * *

Hoping Lord Alanbrooke had made the necessary arrangements, Matt hurried along the sidewalk, past the Horse Guards Building with its clock tower showing seven forty-five, past the entrance to Downing Street and on toward Parliament Square.

Midway to his destination, he stopped beneath one of the trees lining Whitehall and looked back. With exception of automobile lights moving in both directions around the Cenotaph memorial in the middle of the boulevard, the only other life form along the street was a homeless bundle of rags, a remnant of lost hopes, shuffling aimlessly behind him. The thing stopped, searched its lower regions, then directed a stream of urine at the side of the building that bordered the sidewalk.

As though prompted by the flow of urine against stone, the rain began to fall. Light mist at first, then heavier, forcing Matt to turn away and double-time his movement along the sidewalk, pushing against the wind as it moaned through the trees and around the corners of nearby buildings.

* * *

The forlorn-looking creature finished emptying his bladder against the wall, zipped up the fly of his pants, then reached inside the ragged overcoat covering his body. He pulled out a cellular phone, punched a series of buttons and asked, "Damien?"

He listened for a moment before answering, "Right you are. The bunker. That's where he's headed."

Chapter 26

Matt turned before reaching Parliament Square and walked up King Charles toward St. James Park and the Great George Street Government Offices housing the Cabinet War Rooms, Churchill's wartime bunker. Rounding the corner, he followed Horse Guards Road to the building's west entrance and knocked on the glass double doors. The uniformed guard seated inside looked up from his magazine.

"Name's Berkeley," Matt called, he through loud enough for the man to hear through the glass. "I'm meeting a Mr. Desmond. Is he here?"

The guard stood and moved to the door. "Wha' d'you say?"

"Desmond. Is he here?" Matt shouted.

"Wait." The guard picked up a phone and dialed four numbers, spoke into the mouthpiece and listened. After dropping the instrument back into its cradle, the guard unlocked the door and let Matt enter.

"'e's on his way," the guard said out of the corner of his mouth as he walked back to the magazine centerfold and its overwhelming spread of feminine attributes laid out across the top of the desk.

Within minutes, a casually dressed, very serious young man entered the foyer. The curve of his nose reminded Matt of a large bird; the frown on his face telegraphed his irritation at being called out on a Saturday night. "Mr. Berkeley?" he asked in an imperious tone.

"Yes. You Desmond?"

196

"Quite.   Lord Alanbrooke said you needed admittance to the old War Rooms this evening. Most unusual, but here we are. I represent the Imperial War Museum, which manages the facility.   What's so important you couldn't wait until normal hours?"

Matt answered, "Lord Alanbrooke asked the same question, but seriously, it's about photographs. Lord Alanbrooke spoke of photographs in the War Rooms."

"Photographs? That's why I'm here?" Desmond groaned his displeasure, then, "Very well, let's get on with it. I do have a life, you know."

Matt followed the man into a long hall almost the length of the building. After descending a flight of steps to a locked metal door, Desmond opened a small, wall-mounted cabinet from which he removed both a ring of keys and a flashlight.

"No lights?" Matt asked.

While unlocking the door, Desmond answered, "The main light switch for the corridor beyond is near the public entrance some distance away. We'll need the lantern until we get to the Cabinet Room and a switch. We'll be slightly more than ten feet below ground level and there are no windows to admit light, even during daylight hours."   Pushing open the door, Desmond directed, "This way."

Following the light's beam, they made their way down a second flight of steps to a subterranean passageway, through several open doorways and past slabs of concrete jutting out into the corridor. "Blast walls," Desmond explained. "Built to diffuse the effects of shock waves from bombs during the Great War. Thought you'd be interested."

"Thanks," Matt answered, shrugging his disinterest. "Never know when you might need a blast wall or two."

At the same time, he glanced over his shoulder into the darkness that followed close at their heels. Only the sound of their footsteps and the irregularity of their breathing interrupted an almost suffocating silence, a silence made even more ominous by the occasional groan of aging pipes and ceiling supports. He never liked caves, and he sure as hell didn't like being ten feet underground with no windows. The sooner he was through...

"This is it," Desmond said, stopping abruptly before a door with a small glass window and inserting a key into the lock. At the sound of a click, he pushed the door open and, as if conducting a guided tour, announced, "The Cabinet War Room." Desmond flicked a switch at the side of the door, and the room instantly filled with light.

"I'll be upstairs, so you'll be on your own," Desmond explained, at the same time, pointing to an alcove in the wall on the far side of the room. "Though it might not look so, the phone there's a working phone. When you're finished, ring four-double-oh-two and I'll be down. I'd recommend against trying to find your way in the dark."

Desmond started to leave, but stopped and asked, "By the way old man, you wouldn't touch anything, would you?"

Matt read the suspicion in Desmond's voice. With an eyebrow arched in mock disbelief, he responded, "Who me? No way." He laughed softly as Desmond, more irritated than ever, retreated from the room, the echo of his footsteps disappearing down the hall and into the darkness.

Matt quickly scanned the space: its bright red pillars and cross beams supporting the ceiling; almost claustrophobic, box-like configuration of baize-covered conference tables; its dozen or more green leather-upholstered chairs crammed together around the tables, making it almost impossible to move about.

There was one chair, however, that was different from all the rest, and he knew immediately why. Churchill's chair sat at the head of the table arrangement, a plain wooden chair with rounded arms and a plump cushion on its seat. Several feet to its rear hung a wall map of the world, while on the table immediately in front rested four glass inkwells, a red dispatch case and an ornamental dagger.

Giving in to a sudden urge and after a quick glance toward the door, Matt circled the arrangement of tables and eased into the Prime Minister's chair. A smile of remembrance crept across his face. As best he could recall, the words repeated so often in radio transcripts, newsreels and war movies spilled automatically from his mouth. "We shall fight on the beaches and on the landing grounds, in the fields and in the streets. We shall fight in the hills. We shall never surrender...."

Touched by the memory, he sat for a moment, looking at framed photographs mounted on the walls of the room. An aerial view of destroyer escorts and a convoy of merchant vessels in the North Atlantic; a squadron of spitfires flying over the chalk-white Cliffs of Dover; a diesel submarine, its decks awash as it angled up from beneath the waves of the English Channel; a column of tanks raising dust devils across the Libyan desert; but where were the ones Lord Alanbrooke had mentioned? The ones from Yalta. The ones of Churchill and his staff.

"Damn it," Matt cursed.   Another mistake? Another dead-end?

Exhaling his frustration, Matt shoved the chair away from the table and stood. As he did, the back of the chair accidentally nudged the wall map behind it, pushing and creasing the map inward as though there was only empty space for a backing. Not wanting to damage the map any more than already done, he moved the chair back into place and very gently pressed against the material with the flat of his hand to hopefully smooth the crease.

Instead of the expected stone wall for support, the map pushed farther inward. Pulling back the edge, he was surprised to see a recess in the concrete wall, an area resembling an oversized fireplace except there was no chimney. Only a large cardboard box sealed with masking tape. "WW II PHOTOS" was scrawled across its top in broad, black letters.

"Well, well," he murmured, "a regular little treasure-trove."

Pulling the box from behind the map, Matt placed it on the table and slit the tape with Churchill's ornamental dagger. He opened the lid and lifted out a stack of unframed photographs. "Bingo!"

He rummaged through the pictures as quickly as possible, trying to find a particular face and name that might have some relationship to the icon. Each photograph – some of individuals, some with two or more people, usually gathered about Churchill – contained the names of the person or persons typed neatly across the bottom margin.

As he lifted each to the light, he read, "Brigadier Stewart Menzies, Head of Secret Intelligence; Anthony Eden and Cordell Hull, British Minister of Foreign Affairs and U. S. Secretary of State, respectively; General Dwight D. Eisenhower, Allied Commander-in-

Chief; Field Marshall Sir Bernard L. Montgomery..." and on and on, one after another. But where was Yalta? Surely...

Suddenly he stopped. There they were, a packet of pictures tied with a string and labeled "Yalta, February 1945." The top photograph showed Stalin, Roosevelt and Churchill, each seated and smiling at something or someone off camera. Matt cut the string and started through the pictures, one after another until finally, he found it. A print containing Churchill and four men whose faces he did not recognize. But the names? Ah yes, each one familiar.

Placing the photograph on the table, he read from the lower margin of the picture the names of the men standing behind the seated Prime Minister, his right index finger touching each figure as he read aloud. "General 'Pug' Ismay, Primary Aide; Lord Moran, Sir Charles Wilson, Private Physician..." He laughed softly, shifting his finger to an unrecognizably young and slender, "Jeffrey Chatterton, Earl of Alanbrooke, Private Secretary..." The laugh turned into a quizzical *ummm* as his finger tapped against the fourth image. "And Colonel Edward Mason, His Majesty's Royal Marines."

Alanbrooke had been right, but now that he'd found a picture of those with Churchill at the conference, he realized it did him little good. As with Alanbrooke, the likeness of each would have changed over the last sixty plus years, and besides, all but Alanbrooke were dead.

Still, there was something about Mason, the tall, perilously thin Marine colonel, that bothered Matt, something strangely familiar yet so distant his mind was unable to make an immediate connection. Was Churchill's choice of the ascetic looking Mason to guard

the icon on their final day in Yalta one of convenience
and not purposeful in design? Or was there in fact
something that linked the colonel, later General Sir
Edward Mason, inextricably to the missing icon?
Mason's extreme thinness, large protruding cheekbones
and sunken eyes haunted Matt, but it was the eyes more
than anything else.

"Couldn't be," Matt said aloud, shaking his head.
"He's dead." But the vision persisted: the funeral, the
casket, and the old priest who promised, *"Yes, my people,
I the Redeemer, will lead you."*

"Mason?" Matt asked himself, studying the
picture as mentally, Mason's photographic image
merged with the remembered impression of the priest.
Again, "No way. He'd be damn near a hundred years
old."

He was now more certain than ever that there had
to be something other than the icon itself that caused
Churchill to hide the thing from public view. Sealed
away behind a layer of wallboard in a closet. Something
of tremendous importance to interest Hawkins and the
CIA over six decades later. Something undoubtedly
shared by the Prime Minister and General Sir Edward.
But what? Where was the connection? How did it
involve a retired general who supposedly committed
suicide, how long ago? Nine, ten years?

Leaving the photograph on the desk, Matt started
for the telephone only to freeze in place. His ears stood
at attention, his breath on hold. He listened, consciously
attempting to wrap around and decipher the shuffling
sounds he heard.

"Desmond?" he asked. There was no answer.

Stepping quickly to the light switch next to the
door, Matt snapped off the lights and stood in the ink-

black darkness, scarcely breathing for fear of alerting someone to his presence.

Again, the faint shuffle. His diver-honed senses could almost feel the sound. Was it from above, penetrating through more than ten feet of concrete? Impossible. Or was it coming from farther back in the winding labyrinth of tunnels, corridors and rooms? An inner voice warned him it was not the incidental noise of someone making security rounds or coming to escort him back to the surface.

Matt moved silently across the small open space between the door and the conference tables, and then he remembered. The box of photographs! But there was no time. Sounds from the passageway grew louder, forcing him forward. With one hand to guide his way along the edges of the tables, he was doubly careful not to stumble against something, which might create a noise. Maneuvering around Churchill's chair, he quietly lifted one side of the wall map, slipped into the false fireplace and eased down into a crouched position, his backside jammed against cold stone at the rear.

From beneath the bottom edge of the map which hung at least a foot and a half above the floor, Matt watched the glow of light from the passage grow brighter as two men, carrying large, battery-powered lanterns, stepped into the room. From his position, Matt could see neither man, but could hear their conversation until it stopped as more pronounced footsteps sounded from the hallway.

"That you, Damien?"

"Aye." A third person entered the room. "Any sign of Berkeley?"

"Not a hair," one of the men answered. "He's here, lookin' for something. He couldn't have got past us. Hidin' somewhere back in the bunker, I'll wager."

Matt held his breath as a cone of light swept the room. Its beam finally centered on the table, the glow creating a reverse latticework of rivers, boundary lines and place names across the map. Could they see his outline through the heavy grained paper? His body tensed as he heard the scraping of a chair and the sound of photographs and a box being swept to the floor.

"Damn!" It was Damien's voice. Through the map, Matt could distinguish the upper silhouette of a man holding a single photograph, and he knew immediately which one.

"Now I know why he's here," Damien said. The harshness in his voice sent chills along Matt's spine.

"Why?" asked one of the men.

"Never you mind," Damien growled. "You, check the public entrance way, and you," he ordered, the silhouette of an arm, hand and finger pointing at the second man, "retrace your steps and be quick about it. We've got to stop him before he spreads the word."

The sound of grunts acknowledging the order and footsteps moving out into the hall were overshadowed by the scuffling of Damien's shoes against the floor. As he walked about the room, he muttered, "Bloody bastard! If ever I get my hands on him, I'll..." The click of a switch returned a flood of overhead light to the space. More photographs fluttered against the map and scattered to the floor from an apparent swipe of Damien's hand. "I told 'em not to leave the damn things lyin' about, but no..."

Damien's voice trailed off as the sound of paper being torn apart and ripped into quarters, reached Matt's ears. He knew without thinking it was the picture that included Colonel Edward Mason. Suddenly, beneath the bottom edge of the map, Matt saw Damien's shoes, not more than six inches away. They turned in his direction. Fingers slid beneath the side of the map and began to pull it away from the wall.

Operating on survival instinct, Matt shifted forward to give himself better purchase on the balls of his feet. With a grunt born from the pit of his stomach, Matt lunged from the fireplace, tearing the map from its overhead rollers and sweeping it down on top of the man called Damien.

With head and shoulders like a battering ram, Matt smashed into Damien's groin and shoved the man up and over the conference table. The clatter of chairs and the breaking of glass inkwells as they fell to the floor echoed through the subterranean chambers.

Leaving Damien cursing and wrapped in the map, fighting to get free of the tangle of chairs and table legs, Matt grabbed the man's lantern and sprinted out into the corridor, running as fast as he could for the door that led to the building above. Two bullets shattered against a concrete blast wall immediately behind him.

The sounds of running feet, shouting voices, and more gunshots followed him up the narrow staircase. When he reached the top of the stairs, he threw aside the lantern and bolted down the hallway, running toward the distant point of light that he knew was the foyer and escape. As he swung around the corner to the exit, he pulled up short.

"Aw, shit!"

The guard lay partially spread-eagled across the top of the desk. Blood had oozed from a gash in his head and worked its way over the centerfold's erotic charms. It was the sight of Desmond, however, that stopped him cold. Slumped between the desk and the wall, Desmond lay motionless, eyes open in a glassy stare, neck severely twisted and head lying disjointedly on one shoulder.

"Stop him, damn you, stop him!" echoed from the hallway.

Matt pushed against the glass doors, but they refused to budge. "Goddamn it!" Matt cursed as the voices drew nearer. Looking quickly around, he saw it. His only chance. Shoving the guard's body out of the way, he grabbed the desk chair, lifted it over his head, and hurled it against the doors. The glass exploded outward, the chair forming part of its destructive spread. Without looking back, Matt dove through the opening and over the chair as gunshots tore out the remaining glass and a security alarm screamed in the night.

Over and over he rolled. The glass crunched beneath his body; concrete steps scraped skin from his hands and face; bullets splattered off the sidewalk. Operating on near panic, Matt pushed himself to his feet and sprinted across the street. It was Paris all over again until finally, he submerged himself among the growth of shrubs and beneath the trees of St. James Park, running and running until the shrill cry of the alarm and bleating of police sirens fell silent.

Only the pumping of his heart and the fire deep within his lungs forced him to stop. Bent nearly double, hands resting on his knees, he tried to catch his breath as he listened and scanned the surrounding darkness. No human sounds; no shadows; no movement. Except for the wind and the still falling rain, he was alone, and best of all, alive. But for how long?

Chapter 27

Matt hesitated a moment, watching the taxi pull away from the curb, its taillights rapidly blending into the city's nighttime patchwork of color. It was the taxi driver who had insisted on stopping at a chemist's shop for the rubbing alcohol that still burned like hell as he made a final effort to clean away any remaining blood from the scrapes on his face and hands. His handkerchief, stained with diluted reds and pinks, offered patterns even the good Dr. Rorschach would have appreciated.

At his back lay the glistening, rain-washed surface of Kensington Road, and farther on, the barely visible entrance to Flower Walk and the Kensington Gardens/Hyde park complex.

Shrugging off the light drizzle that inched down his neck, Matt pushed open the wrought-iron gate, involuntarily cringing at the high-pitched cry of rusty hinges, and started up the walk toward Jenny's house. Three days since he'd left Jenny standing on the front step, but it felt like forever with all that had happened. The house made little impression at the time, but now, its architecture seemed to stand out from all the other homes along the street.

A stark white, nineteenth-century, three-story creation, its walls were cast of thick masonry and stone. To Matt it resembled a fortress more than a home. Its mullioned windows were tall and narrow, all dark except for two on the second floor.

It was the entrance, however, that made it unique. The door was cut into an unusual, hexagonally shaped turret jutting out from the face of the structure. The turret itself extended upwards past a line of third floor windows, the apex forming a castle-like battlement overlooking the park and gardens across Kensington Road. He imagined the gaunt form of General Sir Edward Mason standing high on the battlement, preparing for an attack from enemies that no longer existed.

A light next to the door was on, and the brass, lion's-head knocker in the center of the door seemed to leer in its anticipation of his touch. He could almost feel the hot breath of its nostrils on the back of his hand as he knocked, three times in rapid succession. Within seconds the door swung open.

A young woman in a maid's uniform stood in the doorway. "Good evening. May I –" Suddenly speechless, her eyes darted from the freshly made scratches and scrapes on Matt's face to those on his hands.

"I'm Matt Berkeley, and believe it or not, I'm a friend of Miss Mason's. I know she's not expecting me, but I need to see her."

"I... I'm not certain. Miss Jenny's... she's uh, already retired for the evening."

Jenny's voice and footsteps sounded from a flight of stairs that wound around the inner walls of the turret. "Anna? Who's there?"

Imagination or not, Matt inhaled the aroma of old lavender as Jenny entered the foyer. Turning from the stairway, the flared skirt of her knit dress swirled about her knees, reminding him of Chartwell and a cotton print dress pressed tight against her body by the autumn wind.

"Matt!" Jenny gasped, her mouth open in surprise. "You're the last..." To Anna, she said, "It's all right, Anna. I'll –"

Jenny stopped in mid-sentence, her attention shifting to Matt. "What in heaven's name happened to your face and hands? You smell like a surgery, and you're soaked clear through."

"Right place, wrong time, I guess," Matt answered, automatically wiping the backs of his hands with the soggy handkerchief even though the cuts had stopped bleeding.

Quickly recovering her composure, Jenny ordered, "Take his jacket, Anna, and dry it in the kitchen."

Matt worked the jacket off his shoulders and handed it to Anna who apologized. "I'm sorry if I made you feel unwelcome, but the way you looked, I –"

"Don't worry about it," Matt said. "If somebody came to my door looking like this, I'd probably shoot first and ask questions later. No offense taken."

Anna smiled and nodded with what Matt interpreted as her appreciation for his understanding before disappearing toward the back of the house with his jacket.

Jenny took Matt by the arm. "Let's go into the drawing room. Much more comfortable than standing out here."

"I can't stay long, but we do need to talk."

A momentary frown crossed Jenny's face as she led Matt down the hall and into the drawing room. "You sound so serious. Talk about what?"

"Your father," he answered, looking for a place he could stand without dripping on the carpet.

"My father? I thought Lord Alanbrooke would have told you. You spoke of Yalta, didn't you? He took his own life shortly after the Churchill Icon disappeared."

"That's what I want to talk about. I just saw a photograph of Sir Edward who looked like a man, an old priest, I saw at the funeral, only –"

Matt's words were interrupted by the shrill ring of a telephone in the hall. "Wait a moment," Jenny said before calling, "I'll get it, Anna," and hurrying from the room.

* * *

Looking back toward the drawing room door, Jenny picked up the telephone and answered softly, "Yes?"

The male voice at the other end responded with a simple, "Sorry. It's up to you, now."

Still watching the drawing room door, Jenny answered, "What should I do?"

* * *

Matt walked slowly about the room, fascinated how so many things could be stuffed into one small space. The ultimate in Victorian. Each table, and there were several, each standing chest, the sills of windows and the mantlepiece over the fireplace, every available surface packed with flower arrangements, small statuary, ornately framed photographs, books, vases, lamps and virtually every type of memorabilia he could imagine. Even the walls, very nearly every inch, were covered with framed lithographs, sketches and oils. A perfect opening scene for Masterpiece Theatre.

Missing, however, were photographs, war medals and anything else connected to Sir Edward. He thought it odd in light of all the pictures of Jenny and those whom he assumed to be her mother and several generations of relatives crowded onto the top of a linen and lace-draped baby grand piano.

He didn't hear Jenny return until she spoke, referring to the phone call. "For my mother, but she's in the Cotswolds for the weekend."

Matt gestured toward the cluster of pictures on the piano. "Family?"

"Yes. A rather stuffy lot, really."

"But none of your father."

Matt caught the strained look on Jenny's face as she answered, "My mother had almost everything either destroyed or donated to the war museum. She feels such reminders do little but bring back the sadness of his death."

"I'm sorry. I shouldn't've asked, but about Sir Edward. I've got a problem, and you're the only one who can solve it. After that, I'll get out of your hair."

"I won't hear of it, leaving before your jacket's dry, or getting out of my hair, as you call it. Besides, if the rain has stopped, there's still time for a walk in the park. I usually do each night. Mother and I, when she's here."

"Sounds great," Matt admitted, "but it's been a long, tiring day and an equally, shall we say, punishing evening. I really need to be getting back to the hotel."

"Please? Otherwise, I won't feel safe without someone with me, and didn't you say you'd tell me what happened at the funeral this afternoon? Afterwards, I could answer whatever questions you have."

Matt laughed softly and shook his head. "The things I'll do for a beautiful woman. It's against my better judgment, but okay. A short walk, a couple of questions, some answers, and then I'm gone."

"If you'll take off those soggy things you're wearing, I'll get some of father's old army things. Afraid that's all mother allowed me to save, the rest going to the

Salvation Army and such, but at least they're dry. I'll be back in a moment, and then off we go."

Chapter 28

The rain had stopped and the wind faded to little more than a whisper as they walked, hand-in-hand. A single umbrella was raised to ward off drops of water still falling from tree limbs stretched above the footpath.

"...and that's when you came along and rescued me. You're sure you never heard of the Church of the Coptic Reformation?" Matt asked, guiding Jenny from one side of the path to the other to avoid puddles accumulated in the dips and crevices of broken asphalt; puddles dimly lighted by distantly spaced street lamps.

"I do recall hearing something, but there are so many religious groups in London. It's difficult keeping up with them all." Turning loose of Matt's hand, she pointed and said, "Over there, the bridge over the Serpentine, or is it Long Water? Quite silly, actually, same lake, but different names on opposite sides of the bridge. Like Kensington Gardens on this side of the water and Hyde Park on the other. The same park, really, but come, close the umbrella and I'll race you to the bridge."

Two other couples strolled beneath the canopy of century-old chestnut trees, nodding as Jenny and Matt jogged along the path toward the bridge and the deserted restaurant sitting off to the right. Slowed by a pronounced limp, he finally caught her at the center of the bridge, both laughing, both breathing heavily from the chase.

Trying to catch her breath, Jenny pointed toward the far end of the Serpentine. "Look."

Matt's eyes followed the direction of her arm, down the length of the lake, its normal flotilla of boats and sails conspicuously absent. Over the distant trees he could see the majestically lighted towers of Westminster. "Quite a sight, but its time you answered some of my questions."

"About my father?"

Matt nodded. "When he died. What happened?"

"Mother found him. A single shot and he was dead. It must have been awful."

"Where were you?"

"Working. At Chartwell. An unpaid volunteer with the National Trust at the time, but let's walk. I'll show you where he used to take me when I was a girl."

Jenny took Matt's hand and led him across the bridge to the Hyde Park side of the Serpentine, continuing along the lakeshore, past the boat hire station and a second restaurant at the southern end of the lake. Turning off the main path and away from the water, Jenny explained, "Concerts in the park each Sunday afternoon, and as usual, Mother would be away."

Matt detected a hint of anger in her voice over what he perceived as her mother's frequent absences from the family fold.

"We'd come, my father and I, mostly to get away from the house, but also to hear the music. Everyone recognized him from his years with Churchill. I was always so proud."

"You loved him?"

"Very much. He was both father and mother much of the time, perhaps trying to make up for all the years he was away, but here we are."

They entered a clearing softly lit by several park lamps of old English design, the bird- and weather-stained heaviness of their globes creating as much shadow as illumination. It was the conical-roofed bandstand in the center of the clearing, however, that for Matt brought back visions of his own childhood in Charleston. Sundays in the park, the foot-powered merry-go-round, and the band in their bright red jackets and white trousers. A Sousa march, a medley from Broadway musical, *Oklahoma*, the concert always ending with "God Bless America."

But this bandstand, built in the shape of a large octagonal gazebo, was empty, the sounds of summer music stolen by the winds of autumn. The edges of its protective banisters and railing, once a glossy white, were flaked and peeling; its plank floor littered with fallen leaves, discarded popcorn bags and the loose pages of an old newspaper. The drooping remains of what might have been bright yellow and white chrysanthemums encircled the bandstand, insulating it from a broad expanse of grass and trees and memories.

"Up here with me," Jenny invited as she ran up the steps to the wooden platform. Matt followed.

"So many wonderful times," Jenny sighed. At the same time, she moved close to Matt and placed both arms around his waist. "We could have wonderful times, also."

The soft glow of the nearby park lamps made Jenny even more beautiful and more desirable than he had imagined, but it was an afternoon in Paris that flooded his mind and the thought of Leila and what they had shared that made him resist. "As beautiful as you are, Jenny, there's –"

"The Howard woman? Forget her, Matt. She's wrong for you. I know."

Matt leaned back, eyes narrowed, a frown on his

face. "What do you mean you know? And how'd you know her name?" Shaking his head, he added, "I never told you about Leila."

"Hush," Jenny insisted. Suddenly, her lips were against his. Her arms pulled him close, and then it happened.

Without warning, an indescribable weight slammed against the back of Matt's head. Jenny's face evaporated in an instant flash of light, an eruption of hot, searing, blinding light that spewed out instant pain. Then numbness as his brain automatically closed off the brilliance and rejected the sensation. He felt himself slipping away. His knees buckled. The front of Jenny's skirt brushed against his face. Another blow and another, and then the pain returned.

Matt clawed at the wooden floor, trying to pull himself toward the steps, trying to escape the brutal assault. A new torment erupted in his side and stomach, someone kicking and punching. From somewhere far off, an angry voice snarled, "Take that 'n that," as the blows rained down. "You're the devil's own trouble, but you'll not get away from us again, ya bloody bastard!"

Too much! A dull glow formed behind Matt's eyes and swirled in a wild vortex of irresistible energy that sucked the strength from his body. He reached out, but found only emptiness. No sound, no feeling, no sight, and no Jenny as he slipped into the black hole of unconsciousness.

Two men stood over Matt as Jenny stepped silently from the bandstand and faded into the nearby trees. It was a man dressed in ragged clothes, the homeless man Matt had seen on Whitehall, who spoke first. "This may be our last best chance. If we kill him now, that'll be the end of it."

Drawing a hypodermic syringe from his pocket and removing the protective cover from the point of the needle, Damien shook his head and knelt next to Matt's body. Once the sleeve of Matt's borrowed jacket was pushed up past the elbow, he responded, "There's been a change."

That said, the needle penetrated Matt's arm and sent its vial of clear liquid speeding into the vein. After he pulled the needle clear, Damien took a deep breath and sighed. "There. That'll keep him from runnin' away again. This time we leave it to the angels. That's what Redeemer wants, and that's how it'll be."

Chapter 29

Matt lay very still, enveloped in a cocoon of dampness. The invasive odor of mildew and sweat seemed to rise in waves from the padding beneath his body. "Awwww man, that's bad." His brain resisted all efforts at rational thought, but there was sound. A steady *hummmm*. From within his head, or somewhere outside his sensory awareness?

Without opening his eyes, he first moved his fingers, his hands, and finally his arms, each movement generating lightning bolts of pain which stimulated the awakening of his senses, yet the movement was there. Everything whole; nothing broken... so far.

He tried his toes and then his ankles and knees. The joints popped like the teeth of a ratchet wheel, but they worked. A deep breath told him his ribs, though still sore to the touch if not more so now, were intact. The sutures in his thigh, however, were no longer tight, slipping through needle punctures in the surrounding skin if he stretched the leg or moved too quickly. Only the gauze and adhesive around his thigh held the wound together.

A dull throb inside his head coincided with the beating of his pulse as he reached back and felt the swelling at the base of his skull. Finally, he opened his eyes. Darkness. The only light was a sliver of moon glow slanting through a circular window. It danced through snake-like ribbons of paint, peeled from the overhead after years of moisture and neglect. Like eels, upside-down in an ocean surge, they waved, hundreds, back and forth in a stagnant sea of air.

Matt closed his eyes tight, hoping it was an illusion, but when he opened them, the "snakes" still danced, their unnerving presence the catalyst that swept away the final vestiges of drowsiness that had blanketed his consciousness. Objects, odors and motion began to register. The window – a porthole; the metallic smell of rust and black oil superimposed above that of mildew; the dizzying sharpness of what he recognized from his Navy years as stack gas; and finally, the gentle roll of the room from side to side. A ship? But why? And where?

Pressing one hand against the wound in his thigh, the other against his side, he forced himself on one elbow into a sitting position and worked his legs, inch by inch, over the side of what had to be a bunk and mattress until his shoes touched the deck. It was slick with moisture, but the vibration against his feet told him the hum he was hearing was not inside his battered skull, but from the ship's engineering plant somewhere below decks.

Unsteady at first, Matt pushed off and took very deliberate, very measured steps across the room. At the same time, he used his arms to clear a path through the paint strips, sweeping them away from his face and hair until he reached the porthole. Its rounded slab of glass was streaked with salt crystals and dirt, yet clear enough for him to make out the moon and stars and a weather deck running fore and aft.

Groping his way along the bulkhead, he discovered the frame of a watertight door, each of several "dogs" or handles tightened to the extent it took every ounce of strength to force them free. When he finally broke the seal, the door creaked outward on weathered hinges and allowed a breath of cleansing sea air to sweep through the soured compartment.

Matt hesitated, asking himself why his captors had failed to tie him to the bunk or lock him in the compartment? Stranger yet, why hadn't they killed him? Unable to find an answer, he stepped over the coaming that formed the lower frame of the doorway and out on deck. He stood quietly in the chill darkness and listened for the sounds of human habitation. Stars hovered above, the moon dipped toward the horizon, and lights shimmered on a distant shore. On the ship, however, there was no sign of life.

Moving cautiously to the rail, he looked down at the wake and its occasional smear of phosphorescence. The ship's speed? Four, maybe five knots he calculated. Based on the position of the north star, the ship's course was east by northeast. A gentle roll caused by long, low swells pushed up from out of the south.

With eyes acclimated to the night, Matt crept silently along the deck, past the superstructure and its darkened pilothouse, around the foremast toward the foc'sle in the forward part of the ship. He stopped and listened, hearing neither voices nor other sounds that would indicate life. There was only the whisper of wind moving through the ship's rigging, bringing with it a faint sea mist that forced him to pull the old army coat closer.

Army coat! It hit him like a slap in the face. General Sir Edward's coat! Jenny! "Sonofabitch!" Matt cursed. "You let her play you like a goddamn –"

He stopped, his body tense as he forced the anger back into its cage. No time for recriminations. That and Jenny would come later, if there was a later. And if there was...

He found the anchor windlass, felt along the edge of the capstan top and down to the wildcat where anchor chain links would normally be engaged. "That's what I thought," he muttered, seeking the company of his own voice. "No chain, no anchor."

Moving back to the rail for a less obstructed view, Matt scanned the dark, his eyes straining to pick out the shape and outline of equipment and superstructure in the forward part of the ship, then down the main deck toward the stern. A coastal steamer, he decided, an old two-stacker, 200 to 220 feet in length and approximately forty feet at the beam, but there were no lights, not even the normal running lights required of a ship at sea.

The lack of life sounds and movement and the absence of an anchor and running lights provided the explanation. Except for himself, the ship was deserted, a derelict, yet still under power. But under whose direction? And why was he on board?

Cautiously, he picked his way along the cluttered deck, careful not to fall over scattered coils of rotting hemp, gutted motors and various other pieces of junked equipment. Reaching the superstructure, he climbed a narrow ladder to the catwalk that wrapped around the forward part of the pilothouse. Like a rime of crystallized frost, salt spray coated everything: ladder, catwalk, metal railings, bulkheads, and now his hands as he wiped clear a small place on one of the windows and peered into the pilothouse.

Except for a bank of tiny, pinpoint-size lights – red, green and yellow – spread along the after bulkhead and casting an almost supernatural aura over the space, the pilothouse was deserted. It was as though the crew had suddenly abandoned ship, leaving it to steam through the night with neither purpose nor destination, but Matt knew that couldn't be. There was purpose and an ultimate destination, or he wouldn't be on board. Of that he was certain.

Pulling the door open, he stepped out of the wind and into a room warmed by a wall of electronic equipment stacked in metal frames at the rear of the space. The lights he had seen through the window played hypnotically across the front of each piece, while cables ran across the deck, one to the base of the ship's wheel, another to the engine order telegraph which indicated, "AHEAD SLOW." Other cables stretched from the tops of the electronic equipment through a hole in the overhead to the flying bridge immediately above.

Using what light was available, Matt's eyes traveled the space: an ancient captain's chair, bolted to the deck and raised to window level; a jury-rigged chart table, the design in its linoleum surface faded and split beyond recognition; an empty binnacle and hood, the compass bowl and gimbals long since removed, its once black "mariner's balls" or quadrantal spheres scratched and rusted with age. Finally, on a brass nameplate, darkened from exposure and mounted on the centerline of the forward bulkhead above the windows, were the barely
visible words:

STEEPHOLM
Newcastle-on-Tyne 1907

"Okay, *Steepholm*," Matt whispered, "let's see just how much alive you really are."

Taking hold of the ship's wheel, he spun it to the right as far as it would go, then to the left. Nothing. Still not satisfied, he moved to the engine order telegraph and shifted the two levers to AHEAD HALF, then AHEAD FULL, waiting for a change in the ship's vibration to indicate an increase in speed. As with the ship's wheel, there was no response. Only the steady hum of engines deep inside the ship.

Remembering the lights glittering along the horizon, one, maybe two miles distance, Matt checked his watch and thought for a moment. If he could stop the ship and wait until daylight, no more than an hour away, he could swim ashore, but which of the equipment would he have to disable?

His eyes settled on the coil of tightly bunched cables extending through the overhead to the flying bridge, and his mouth formed a single word. "Antenna!"

There had to be an antenna receiving signals that directed course and speed and whatever else was planned for the ship. If he could break the cable connection, end of game.

Decision made, Matt backed out of the pilothouse and onto the catwalk, this time climbing a set of rungs bolted into the bulkhead. He inched his way upwards until, finally, he pulled himself over the edge of the deck and onto the flying bridge.

With the moon now past its zenith and the stars his only light, Matt made his way across the deck on hands and knees, searching the darkness. It wasn't his eyes, but his hands that found the cables, three of them feeding up from the pilot house, heavy with insulation and damp with sea mist, but which one led to the antenna?

Allowing his hands to be his eyes, he followed the cables until they split in opposite directions. Tied together, two of them ran aft along the deck toward the base of the first of two exhaust stacks and a tiny glimmer of light he hadn't seen. An opening was cut into the stack's metal casing for entry of the cables. For what purpose, he didn't know, but it would not be for the antenna. The antenna would be as far forward as possible to prevent signal blockage by the stack. It was the third cable he wanted.

Matt grasped the only remaining cable and started forward, feeling his way until, suddenly, a steady clicking sound from the pilot house below interrupted his movement. It grew louder, more strident, then ended, immediately giving way to a noise similar to that of fuel siphoning under great pressure.

Spinning around, his jaw dropped as he watched the front of the stack began to open, two sections opening in opposing directions. The glimmer of light he had seen became larger and brighter as each section of the stack swung outward on runners installed in the deck.

"That the hell!" Matt breathed, forcing himself to believe the unbelievable. Inside the stack stood a cylindrical object, its cone-shaped head more than twice as tall as him. Its silvery skin glistened in the light. Metal straps and harnesses held it in place. Wisps of smoke curled from its base.

The increasing roar of igniting fuel – gas, diesel, oil or whatever – and the acrid stench of smoke drove Matt toward the side of the flying bridge and the ladder leading below. He moved, slowly at first, then with greater urgency, as the realization rammed home. "That sonofabitch's gonna blow!"

Chapter 30

Dropping over the edge of the deck and using only the top rung, Matt gritted his teeth at the sharp stitch of pain in his ribs as he swung down to the catwalk, grabbed the rails of a ladder leading aft and literally catapulted himself through the air. His feet were already moving as he hit the main deck.

With equipment edges snapping at his legs and arms, creating obstacles that seemed to rise up and block his progress, Matt slipped and stumbled along the moisture-laden deck toward the stern of the ship. He was convinced *Steepholm* was determined to deny him flight from whatever fate she awaited.

Matt looked back only once as he fought his way around and past rusted winch motors, disassembled boom posts, empty oil drums and great lengths of heavily greased wire snaked along the deck. Already, huge torrents of steam billowed from the forward stack. As he reached the relative safety of the fantail, a sudden shudder passed through the ship, knocking him off his feet. The sound of thunder rolled across the decks as an expanding red and yellow flame illuminated the ship's superstructure. It forced him to look away, to hide his face against the sound and heat borne on the night wind.

He waited for the final burst of power, which would lift what he thought was some kind of missile from its launch position, yet there was no upward movement. Only the steady roar of fuel igniting in the tail of the cylinder as flames, like a giant acetylene torch, cut deep into the heart of the ship.

Pushing to his feet, Matt hung as far over the rail as he could, trying to escape the smoke and steam that boiled around him, driven down on the fantail by *Steepholm's* forward motion.

He saw them – lights on the far shore, at first steady and bright, then on and off as though affected by an alternating loss and surge of electrical power. He blinked at what appeared to be a single ray of light. It rose into the night sky at a speed almost too fast for him to follow. Jerking his head up and around for what could only have been the smallest fraction of time, he watched the beam of whitish, blue-green light disappear into the heavens. Almost as quickly, it reappeared, this time, streaking down toward the ship and its captive missile like a lightning bolt thrown down by the hand of God.

Before he could react, a deafening explosion rocked the *Steepholm*, followed immediately by a second explosion from somewhere amidships. It threw him to the deck, his body flung savagely against one piece of equipment after another as the ship's midsection buckled and began to split apart. Both forward and after sections at the point of separation seemed to rise up to meet the sky. In Matt's case, this caused a severe downward angle in the direction of the stern. Immediately he was out of control, sliding and rolling with the angle of the ship.

Frantically, he grasped for a handhold to stop his movement. A pad-eye, a cleat in the deck, a bollard, but everything too wet. His hands scraped across sharp edges, unable to maintain a hold. He felt the impact of his ribs against metal, the thrust of his legs over the side of the ship, the flaking rust of a rail stanchion in his hands, tearing and biting into his fingers and palms, but he refused to let go. And directly below his feet, *Steepholm's* massive twin propellers churned and pushed what was left of the ship toward its now inevitable doom.

Matt clung to the stanchion as the stern righted itself, then inched his way back on deck, his hands wet with blood, salt and flecks of rust. It was the ship itself, however, that sent an additional surge of adrenaline racing through his body. The forward quarter of the ship, containing jagged reminders of the superstructure, was torn away on the starboard side. Its port side now aligned at a forty-five-degree angle to the remaining and larger stern section where he lay. *Steepholm* was dying, and there was nothing he could do.

He could feel and hear the tearing of metal as the bow, sinking deeper in the water, leaned farther to port, its weight and downward movement ripping great sheets of steel away from what was now the ship's main body. With propellers still turning, the stern section pushed onward, refusing to give up. At the same time, it dragged the rapidly flooding bow in its wake. With a final wrenching tear and the sound of ancient rivets popping like rifle fire, the hull separated into two distinct parts. The bow sank almost immediately.

Matt knew only minutes remained as the stern rose steadily in the air. The forward section began to dip beneath the waves, the sea relentlessly filling compartments that had been gouged open by the initial explosions. Much of the fire was gone, but great columns of steam filled the night sky, creating a halo effect about the dying hulk.

Without thinking, he shrugged off the old army coat that already felt like it weighed a ton and kicked off his shoes, at the same time searching for something that would float. He saw it, partially covered by a coil of wire rope, a life ring of wood and canvas, grease stained and scarred, probably rotten, but better than nothing.

Fighting the ever-increasing incline, Matt tugged the life ring free and struggled to the side of the ship. With the stern counter now completely clear of the water, its propellers rotating in midair, he threw the life ring as far out from the ship as he could, climbed over the railing and pushed away. He dropped feet first, one hand over his crotch, the other hand shielding his face.

Like a mouth opening and closing, the water's chill enveloped him and swallowed him whole. It pulled him down as pressure waves from another explosion inside the ship hammered at his ear and sinus cavities and twisted him over and around. He tumbled and rolled through the darkness. His lungs screamed for air.

Disoriented and praying he was swimming up and not down to his death, Matt fought for his life. Hands and arms swept out and down like opposing sails of a windmill; feet and legs in a hard scissors kick against the water's resistance. With a final shove, Matt broke surface within arm's reach of the stricken hull. The ship's creaks and groans were loud in his ears. The silhouette of the stern pointed high into the sky, almost at right angle with the sea.

Gulping air into his lungs, Matt pushed away from the hull, but suddenly, his forward movement was stopped, his body dragged back and down. He was pinned against an open suction valve drawing in huge torrents of water as the hull slipped deeper through the swirling maelstrom. *Steepholm* was determined to share her grave, but he resisted, his hands and feet braced against the hull to keep from being suctioned into the opening. He knew only seconds remained as the increasing water pressure stabbed like ice picks at his eardrums and oxygen starvation began to drain his strength and ability to think.

He felt it at first, like an avalanche, its power building as it coursed down a mountainside. And then he heard it – a low gurgle, quickly transposed into a thunderous eruption of air. A gigantic air bubble, trapped inside the hull under enormous pressure, exploded from the valve. Its tremendous thrust forced him away from the ship and propelled his body like a torpedo.

Matt cleared the surface as the stern took its final, agonizing gasps, the sounds cutting across the water like the cries of a dying animal. He clenched his teeth against the clearly audible wrenching and tearing of boilers and engines being stripped from their foundations, the crushing boom of steel bulkheads being forced apart by increasing pressure, and the steam-whistle hiss of compressed air shooting spray into the sky. All at once, silence, followed by a single, resounding gulp. *Steepholm's* after section disappeared into the ocean depths.

Matt lay on his back, cold and shivering, filling his lungs, coughing, sinking, and moving arms and legs to remain afloat. Most of all, he had to recoup his strength and concentrate on what had to be done.

A mist hung over the water as pieces of debris drifted past. Too small to bear his weight, they nudged him in their aimless journey, teased him with their buoyant lightness, then moved on into the night. The life ring, but where?

Ignoring the sting of salt water on the cuts that seemed to cover his body, Matt turned on his stomach and began to move with a slow breaststroke, allowing the swells to carry him from crest to crest. He hoped, somehow, he would find the life ring, but the longer he swam, the more exhausted he became and the fewer pieces of flotsam he encountered.

One swell, shorter in length than the rest, lifted him and shoved him forward, then abruptly dropped him into its following trough. His body slammed hard against something large and metallic. Momentarily stunned, he treaded water. While one hand grasped a seam protruding from the end of the object, the other hand touched and explored. The thing was round, its body rough with rust but no apparent marine growth. As it rode the swells, only a few inches of its bulk remained above the surface, and from inside came the sound of sloshing liquid. "Thank God," Matt breathed. A partially filled oil drum. It had to be one of those he'd seen on the ship!

Slowly, so as not to start a rolling motion, Matt pulled his upper torso over one end and along the body of the drum. Straddling it with both arms and legs, he inched forward until he could feel his knees against the side, all the while watching for lights on the shore each time the drum rose on the crest of a swell. Three times the drum rolled, submerging him, and three times he pulled himself back on. Each time, the fatigue in his arms and legs ate a little deeper into his mental and physical reserves.

The lights – were they closer, or farther away? If he kept his head up, he could see them at the top of each swell, accompanied by the first gray fingers of dawn that played along the eastern horizon. And then they were gone as the oil drum made its slide into the valley between crests, rising again on the next swell, then falling, rising and falling. The rhythm played on his imagination.

Twice he thought he heard voices only to decide it was exhaustion taking its toll. Twice he rested his head against the drum only to be revived by the slap of water against his face. And again, voices, chanting, in and out like the tide, or was it surf against the shore? So near, so far away. If only he could sleep.

"Don't sleep," he told himself, but the sea played its lullaby, and he did.

Chapter 31

Strizhenko stood on the steps of the Hyde Park bandstand as two nanny's pushed oversized prams across the clearing toward the lake and the boat hire station. Several horses trotted on a nearby equestrian trail, their riders dressed in identical riding habits. Each bounced and swayed with the movements of their respective mount; each resembled a puppet on invisible strings, raised and lowered by an unseen hand from above.

General Ahmad al Kazemi waited outside the ring of withered chrysanthemums that surrounded the bandstand. As the riders and the two nannies with their infant wards moved farther away, he asked, "And this is the place?"

"Hajir watched from the trees," Strizhenko answered, "then followed as they took what appeared to be an unconscious Berkeley to an airport in the north of London. The same ones who tried to kill him in Paris. They filed a flight plan to the island of Guernsey."

"And Hajir?"

"He is on the island. Arrived this morning and has learned many things."

"What about Berkeley? Alive or dead?"

"I don't know, but should we find him alive, do you still want –"

"Dead," Kazemi said without hesitation. "When do we go?"

"After Hajir makes his next report. Certainly, tomorrow night at the latest."

"Very well," Kazemi answered, "but remember,

Major. Our success will be your success, our failure yours, and you know the price of failure."

Ahmad al Kazemi turned on his heel and walked away, leaving Major Viktor Mikhailovich Strizhenko to contemplate his future.

* * *

"What the hell're you trying to tell me, Hawk?" Herb Samuelson's facial expression and voice over the secure videophone line was a study in misunderstanding and impatience.

Hawkins looked at Samuelson's image glowering from the monitor screen on the desk in front of him. He shook his head. His response was more that of a parent to an inattentive child. "Okay, Herb, one more time, slow and easy. Berkeley's gone. Slipped surveillance, but we tailed his Iranian shadow. I know who's got him and where."

"The Iranians?"

"For chrissake, Herb, the religious cult I told you about."

"I can't believe some bunch of religious loony-tunes would –"

"You're still not listenin', Herb," Hawkins cut in. His own level of patience nearing the saturation point, Hawkins pushed up from his chair and, trying to get away from the videophone and the inquisitive eye of its camera,
started pacing.

Directing his words back at the device, he said, "Berkeley saw one of the priests or ministers or whatever the hell they call themselves at Westminster Abbey. The guy's an authority on weirdo religious sects. I talked with him this morning. Everything he says and everything that's happened so far jibes with what Berkeley told me."

"Where the hell did you go," Hawkins heard Samuelson shout. "Get back where I can see you."

"Stretching my legs, damn it," Hawkins called over his shoulder as he stopped at a window overlooking the traffic along North Audley Street and across at the Roosevelt Memorial in Grosvenor Square. Or was it South Audley Street? Hawkins never knew where one began and the other ended, nor did he really give a shit.

Continuing his explanation about the religious cult, Hawkins added, "Besides a place here in London, these people've got a retreat on Guernsey, one of the Channel Islands. Some character callin' himself the Redeemer runs the church from there."

"I knew it," Samuelson blurted. "Religious cults and Redeemers and God only knows what else. You're on the bottle again, aren't you? Why don't you just admit you've blown the whole damn thing. Now get back over in front of the camera so I can see you."

"And you're talkin' outta your ass, goddamn it!" Hawkins spun on his heels and stomped back to the desk. Dropping back into his chair, he pointed an index finger at the camera and said, "I'm tellin' you, they got Berkeley, and I'd bet the crown jewels they also got the icon, or why the hell kidnap him?

"Unless I miss my bet, we'll also find Strizhenko and the Iranians when we get there. In force, if the movement we're seein' at the Iranian Embassy's any indication."

"When you get where?"

Hawkins threw up his hands in frustration. "Jesus Christ, Herb! Guernsey! Haven't you heard anything I've said?"

Samuelson was silent for a moment, then, with an audible sigh of surrender, he said, "You'll need support. Men, logistics, weapons –"

"Already got it," Hawkins cut in. "The Ambassador and I are scheduled for a final session with the Admiralty and the British Foreign Office in less than an hour."

Samuelson's face went red with anger. "You must be out of your mind," he shouted. The two speakers on the sides of the videophone crackled with the sudden volume. "This is a company operation. I'll have you –"

"You won't have me anything," Hawkins interrupted, his voice and emotions under tight control. "If I find the icon and the plans, you, Herbert Indigo Samuelson, will be the first to get a medal. If I don't, fire me! Now, fuck off and let me do my job." With the touch of a button, the monitor screen went blank and Samuelson's screamed rebuttal never reached its mark.

Looking up at the autographed poster of his look-alike, actor Clint Eastwood, Hawkins grunted and said, "Sure could use your help on this one, Clint my man. If I'm wrong, it'll be my ass hangin' from the highest yardarm they can find."

Chapter 32

Voices faded in and out as Matt worked his way free from the bonds of sleep, the throb in his side pushing and prodding its reluctant host back into the world of reality. Light slipped through the granular glue that had sealed his eyelids, and forms began to take shape. The first thing he noticed was that his lower body, covered by a sheet, was naked.

A table, an oil lamp casting a subdued glow of yellowish-orange, an empty straight-back chair and the bed he was in – a narrow cot, actually – seemed to be the only furniture in the room. A heavy woolen curtain covered the room's only window. The walls were bare except for a wooden crucifix mounted on the far wall. Two figures stood beside the bed, a man and a woman, both in monks' robes.

"He wakes," the woman said, then turned and left the room.

"Where am I?" Matt asked, surprised at the sandpaper scratch in his voice.

"St. Cyril de la Bot," the man answered. "On the island of Guernsey."

"My side?" Matt felt the tightness around his midsection when he tried to move.

"Your ribs, badly bruised, have been wrapped with fresh adhesive. The wound in your thigh has been cleansed and re-bandaged."

"Who are you?"

"Damien, a follower of the Redeemer."

Matt stared at the man. "The Cabinet War

Rooms?"

"Yes."

"And the woman?"

"She brings food. You've not eaten for two days."

"Two days?" Matt shook his head. "No way." He pushed back the sheet and tried to get up.

"First, eat," Damien ordered, forcing Matt back onto the cot, "and then, the sacred ground."

"The what?"

"You will see."

* * *

Though the shirt and trousers given to him were comfortable enough, the shoes Matt had been given were at least two sizes too large. His heels rode up with each step as he shuffled along the village's main street, a mixture of hard-packed dirt and cobblestone worn smooth by years of wear. If the blisters forming on his heels weren't enough, his wrists, extended in front of him, chafed from the fibrous cord that bound them together. But he'd be damned if he would show the pain.

Damien followed close behind him, a chrome-finished 45-caliber semiautomatic pistol concealed by the sleeve of his robe. From the set of Damien's jaw and narrowness of his eyes, Matt knew the man was more than willing to shoot if he varied so much as a foot from the prescribed route.

Along both sides of the street were cottages, large and small, as well as a church farther on, all of stone, all tarnished a yellowish gray by the late afternoon sun. Even the people who stopped to watch seemed cast in similar pallor, but it was their silence and the instant condemnation in their eyes that was unnerving. A small girl, held tight in her mother's arms, extended a tiny cross in Matt's direction as though warding off something vile and evil.

As he moved farther along the street, a group of children in robes with hems that dragged the dirt suddenly broke the communal silence, chanting, "Sinner, sinner, go away. For your soul, this night we pray."

The chant continued as he approached the church, the children falling behind, but the meaning of their words? A children's rhyme, or an omen? He shunted the thought to one of the more obscure crevices of his mind and concentrated instead on the church immediately in front of him.

It was larger, much larger than it had seemed from a distance, its stones much grander and more precisely cut than those of the cottages he had passed. Its roof of dark slate was steeply angled, a cape of blue-green moss thrown across its northern slope. Its stained-glass windows were alive with the passion of Christ the Savior as He trudged the path to Golgotha.

Matt's thoughts were interrupted by Damien's words, "The walkway." At the same time, Matt felt a hand nudge his back and direct him toward a path that disappeared into a row of hedges running alongside the church. "The sacred ground lies at the end of the path," Damien explained.

As Matt reached the rear of the church, he could see the "sacred ground," a cemetery spread across a narrow valley and an adjoining hill with footpaths wandering along its slope and fading into the trees. It was the sameness of the graves, however, that immediately caught his eye. Each grave marker a stone cross; each cross of Latin design, a modified fleur-de-lis at every point, replicating the one above the doorway in

Tavistock Square. Each cross, the symbol of Christ's crucifixion, stood watch over the sculptured shape of a sleeping lamb.

On the hill beyond, partially hidden by the trees, rested the rounded dome of a massive concrete building, distinctly different from anything Matt had thus far seen. But why here? Why the cemetery? The children's chant, *"For your soul, this night we pray,"* slipped from its hidden crevice in his sub consciousness and taunted him. Was his grave to be among those that lay along the valley floor?

"There," Damien said at his shoulder. "The statue of our Redeemer." Again, a hand nudged him forward.

Near a large stone that looked more like a monolith taken from the circles of Stonehenge than the statue of the Redeemer, or what he remembered of the one who called himself Redeemer, Matt saw the back of a man, or was it a woman? Very small, robed and hooded against the chill now moving in from the sea. The figure stood before an easel and canvas, a pallet in one hand, a brush in the other. As Matt approached, the figure turned.

"Ah, Mr. Berkeley. I'd hoped we'd not meet again, but here you are."

"Cavendish!"

"Yes, but perhaps, since you're here, a walk and certain explanations are in order." He nodded toward Damien and pointed to the easel and other equipment. "If you would be so kind, Damien."

Matt walked along the path with Cavendish explaining the purpose of the *Steepholm*. Damien brought up the rear, carrying the boxed pallet, brushes and canvas in one hand, the easel in the other.

Afterwards, Matt said, "And the laser that destroyed the ship, the test of your so-called angel's light.

That's really what the CIA's after, isn't it? Not the icon."

"Without a doubt," Cavendish answered, "as are many others. For example, the Iranian Embassy with their Russian friend, a former KGB operative, acting as your Antiquities Society. I'm afraid you've been duped all along."

"You don't know the half of it," Matt muttered, preferring not to think how many times he had been misled and lied to by how many people. "But if the laser was such a big deal, why didn't Churchill do something with it?"

Cavendish laughed knowingly. "Timing, my dear fellow, timing. The war was drawing to a close. Only months remained. And then he was voted from office almost immediately following Germany's surrender."

"That still doesn't –"

"Perhaps bitterness was the reason. Getting even for the loss of the election after all he'd done for England, or, in the confusion of it all, he simply forgot. Only Churchill could say for certain."

"Forgot?" Matt laughed sourly. "Hidden behind a closet wall? C'mon. Get real. At any rate, Colonel Mason didn't forget, did he? He's probably the one who hid the icon in the first place."

"General Sir Edward, you mean?"

"You know damn well who I mean," Matt said as he abruptly stopped, knelt and removed his shoes. With fingers growing numb from the bindings around his wrist, he touched the blisters that had formed on his heels, then stood and moved on, barefoot, shoes in hand.

"When the icon made its reappearance, Mason took it and dropped out of sight. He didn't commit suicide. He's here. He's the old priest I saw in the church. The Redeemer, risen from the grave like some

Messianic savior. But if he's such a holy man, why does he need a weapon?"

"Much like our religion, the icon has languished over the years. Sir Edward, young Jenny's father, being a convert to the true religion since his years in Egypt, saw his opportunity to give to the icon the prominence it deserved.

"With Jenny's help, he removed it from Chartwell. In addition to the joy and happiness it has brought our people, it provided an even greater treasure, which was known only to Sir Edward. The design for a weapon that, if used wisely, could be for the good of all mankind."

"Like killing Ian Stuart and trying to kill me was for the good of mankind," Matt shot back, the bitterness of Ian's death like the taste of bile in his mouth. "That's a crock, and you know it."

"Think what you will," Cavendish went on. "To further our cause, we've done no more than the world church has done for centuries."

"What cause?"

"Peace. After tonight's display, should the world refuse to heed our call for total disarmament, we'll have no choice but to turn the beam against them."

"Somebody's jerking your chain, Cavendish. If the laser's really that good, the rest of the world's gonna come in here, stomp your ass, and take it. End of story."

"We have faith that will not happen. Much has been sacrificed for this moment. Not only by our own people, but members of an international organization known as Scientists United for World Peace. Even researchers associated with your own government's beam and particle weapons program have secretly given of their time and knowledge, providing, if you will, our major innovation."

"What I saw the other night," Matt said.

"Correct. The use of lasers in space. An orbiting satellite equipped with laser reflectors, or mirrors, if you like. Infrared telescopes for sensing and targeting heat sources, either in space or on earth; computing equipment; beam regenerators; and of course, our equipment here on Guernsey." Cavendish pointed toward the dome-topped building behind the trees on the far hill. "Our operations center where the laser cannon is housed."

Matt looked toward the sky. "How'd you get the satellites up there?"

"A private European consortium known as *Spatium Arcturus*. We used the Arcturus rocket fired from the consortium's launch site in South America, but come. Up ahead, there's someone waiting."

Looking almost directly into the sun as it slipped toward the horizon, Matt could distinguish the outline of a statue, a shepherd boy with a lamb in his arms, and a group of robed followers gathered at its base, their collective heads suddenly turned in his direction. As he approached, all but one began to move away. The remaining follower pushed back the cowl from her head.

"Hello, Jenny," Matt said. As he drew near, the faint scent of old lavender brought the memories of Chartwell and the bandstand in the park flooding back. "I thought I'd find you here. Now all we need is your father, Sir Edward."

Jenny's smile disappeared. Her face assumed a solemnness Matt had not seen before. "Sir Edward is no longer my father," she said. "He is the Patriarch of our religion. The Great Redeemer. Man in flesh, only; god in mind and spirit."

"Pretty heavy stuff for a retired army officer,"

Matt said, searching Jenny's eyes to make sure she was serious.

"You must accept the fact, Mr. Berkeley," Cavendish explained, ignoring Matt's flippancy, "Sir Edward is no more. His body is but a god-vessel used to spread our gospel. Through him, mankind will live, if not in peace, at least in coexistence."

Taking up the explanation, Jenny continued, "Tonight we celebrate the Night of the Angels. Once each thousand years, the angels spread their light across the heavens to rid the world of evil. Before tomorrow, the nations of the world will know the Redeemer's power and rid themselves of the useless trappings of war."

"In other words, the laser," Matt said, nodding his understanding. With a short laugh, he added, "I think you people have been sniffing too much hashish."

Cavendish shook his head, his disappointment with Matt readily apparent. "Sadly, however, the Redeemer's earthly body has grown old and malignant. Tonight, he will leave this world, but his son will take up the burden, and our followers will accept and honor his presence."

Matt looked at Jenny, his brow furrowed in question. "I thought you were Mason's only –"

"His only child?" Jenny said, finishing Matt's question. "Yes," she answered, "but as I said, to us General Sir Edward Mason no longer exists. Only the Redeemer, father to a son. Our son. I am the child's mother. To insure purity of bloodlines for our coming Lord, the Redeemer impregnated me."

Stunned, Matt looked at Jenny for a moment before saying, "I thought what happened in Waco was sick, but this one's right up there with it."

"Waco?" Jenny asked.

"Forget it."

"Come," Cavendish ordered, taking Matt by the arm. "Put on your shoes. The Redeemer has asked to see you."

"And after that?" Matt asked.

"That, young man, is a decision only the Redeemer can make."

Chapter 33

Two miles off the southern coast of Guernsey a small coastal steamer, running lights conspicuously absent in the rapidly fading twilight, began to slow. It gradually lost steerageway before drifting with the currents. Almost immediately, the ship's forward boom swung out over the side, its cargo a large, rigid hull-inflatable boat powered by two massive outboard engines. Four times the boom made the journey, each time lowering an inflatable and its operator to the water. Once each boat touched the surface, the operator quickly released the boom hook and maneuvered the boat to a debarkation point midway along the ship's side.

General Kazemi and Leila observed the offloading from a wing of the pilothouse bridge. Two levels below on the main deck, Strizhenko watched from the rail as men dressed in camouflage fatigues of the Iranian Revolutionary Guard's Quds Force filed past.

Using what little light remained, he checked each man's equipment as they passed his position: a Kalashnikov 7.62-millimeter AK-47 assault rifle with three hundred rounds of ammunition, a Makarov PM 9-mm automatic pistol, six hand grenades and a spring-loaded knife. All were of Russian make and similar to the complement of weapons once carried by Spetsnaz forces of the old Soviet Union. Moving down a metal debarkation
ladder, they quickly filled each of the first three boats.

As the fourth inflatable pulled alongside the bottom of the debarkation ladder, Strizhenko looked toward the bridge wing and called, "General, we are ready."

On the bridge, Leila argued, "But why, General? I can verify the plans once you return to the ship. You do not need me on the island."

Kazemi admonished, "No, Bājī Leila. It is your duty, as it is mine. Strizhenko and Hajir know what your brother has ordered. Should you remain on the ship, they would grow suspicious, and that could be dangerous for us both."

"But you don't understand."

"More than you think," Kazemi said, his voice less harsh than before. "If it is love for the man Berkeley that causes your reluctance, and he is still alive, I will do what I can to spare his life if..." Kazemi raised his finger to emphasize the point. "... if it will not endanger you, myself, or our plans for the future of Iran. I pledge. Now come. The boats are waiting."

*　*　*

One after the other, four Wessex assault helicopters, each carrying ten fully armed Royal Marines, and a fifth helicopter with Royce Hawkins, Marine Colonel Angus McDevlin, and two Marine sergeants, lifted off the flight deck of the amphibious assault ship, *HMS Fearless*. Hawkins watched the lights of Guernsey's capital city, St. Peter Port, pass below as his helicopter climbed up from the harbor and over the hills before turning southwest
toward the central part of the island.

Within minutes, Hawkins saw what he hoped was a line of runway lights as each of the helicopters banked, one after the other, and began their descent. "What the hell kinda airport is this?" he grumbled. "Where's the terminal?"

"Closed.   Runway's used... at night for... for emergencies, only," McDevlin answered, spacing his words with the thump and bounce of the wheels against the tarmac.

Hawkins spotted two, open-bed, scum-encrusted farm trucks in front of the darkened terminal building, their lights blinking like beacons to guide the offloading troops. "If that's our transportation, they're gonna smell us comin' a mile away. They look like fuckin' manure carriers."

McDevlin shouted over the sound of the rotor blades as the door slid open. "No military vehicles on Guernsey, but if it's cow manure they haul, I'd think a hard-boiled Texan like you would feel perfectly at home. Right?"

Hawkins caught the joke on himself and laughed. "Damn right, Colonel!   Like good ol' home, sweet home!"

* * *

Matt's wrists burned beneath the bindings as he followed Jenny and Cavendish down the central aisle of the church, its interior, from floor to vaulted ceiling, lighted by hundreds of candles. Its walls were graced with the stained-glass windows he had seen from the path leading to the cemetery. The candlelight, however, seemed to soften the lines of Christ's face as He bore the cross on his shoulder along the road of suffering, yet sharpened those of the soldiers who mocked him.

Damien prodded Matt's back with the pistol partially covered by the sleeve of his robe and shoved him forward along the aisle that led to the front of the church. As they neared the chancel, he grabbed Matt by the shoulder and ordered, "That's far enough."

Cavendish moved beside Matt. "What do you see?"

Matt surveyed the area before him. To his right, a choir stall, enormous in size, designed to seat at least fifty, maybe more. To his left, a Baptistry, its backdrop a life-size painting of St. John performing the act of baptism. Straight ahead, the chancel railing, a communion table and chair, more throne than chair, large enough for two, and farther on, darkness.

"I don't know what you mean," Matt said. "What do you want me to see? The Redeemer? The icon?"

"Exactly, my friend. Below the cross."

"What cross?"

As though by divine order, Matt felt a breeze sweep through the church, followed quickly by a robed figure. One moment the figure was there, the next, gone, leaving behind the sudden glow of candles at the head of the church. The shimmer of their flames reflected along the length of a magnificent golden cross, fastened to the wall and reaching to the ceiling.

Below the cross, an altar, and on its marble surface, an icon made of three hinged partitions, its wings open. The paintings on the wings were too small to distinguish from where Matt stood, but the center panel was like a beacon. The white robes of Christ on the mountain resembled a star in the wilderness of night. As Cavendish had said, the icon's colors were vibrant with energy; its detail, even in the candle glow, intricate and lifelike.

"*Transfiguration of Christ the Savior*," Matt whispered, immediately captured by its beauty. "No wonder –"

248

"The fruit of all your labors, Mr. Berkeley," Cavendish said with false sympathy in his voice, "but alas, too late to claim your reward."

"Matthew," Jenny whispered in his ear, "the Redeemer."

Matt followed her gaze as the aging priest from Tavistock Square, accompanied by several younger men in robes and a small boy of five or six, entered the sanctuary. Jenny and Cavendish knelt briefly while the old priest and the boy climbed the steps to the throne. Matt felt Damien's hands close over his shoulders and press downward, but he refused to kneel.

With the young boy standing on the right side of the throne, the priest sat and stared at Matt as though attempting to peel away his soul. Matt stared back.

The resemblance was there. Though the years had drawn the old man's neck and shoulders forward into a permanent slump, it was the cheekbones and hollow eyes that identified this man, the Redeemer, as Colonel, later General Sir Edward Mason. *Yes,* Matt said with a silent voice, *it's him, the man in the photograph.*

The Redeemer's hands rested on the rounded arms of the throne. Barely visible in the candlelight was the shape of a cross tattooed in blue on the back of each hand. Beads of moisture coated dark circles beneath his eyes, while a pronounced tic pulled spasmodically at the muscles in his cheeks and upper throat. As the Redeemer pushed back the robe from his left arm to rub an apparent irritation, Matt saw long scars and sores running along the inner arm.

Surprised, Matt whispered to Cavendish, "Track marks. What's he shooting? Heroin?" Cavendish made no reply.

After several moments of silence, the Redeemer

spoke. "You've become a nuisance of extraordinary tenacity, Mr. Berkeley. Would that your perseverance be more righteously directed. Your actions have caused much death and sorrow."

Matt countered, "You seem to be pretty good at that yourself, Sir Edward, not to mention drugs and a little incest for dessert."

The old man ignored Matt's reply while others in the room glared their hatred at him.

"I am a forgiving god, and you will be the lamb of my forgiveness. As a symbol of my great love and mercy, you will be allowed the privilege of accompanying our beloved icon and me on an eternal journey. You will represent both the sins of the world and God's capacity, my capacity, to forgive."

Matt shook his head. "Somehow, I don't think Sir Edward Mason's forgiveness is gonna do me a helluva lot of good."

Jenny's hand was little more than a blur as it slapped his face. Her fingernails scraped lines of skin from his lower jaw and chin. "He is not Sir Edward Mason!" she shouted. "He is the Redeemer, our god incarnate."

Stepping forward, she placed an arm around the small boy that stood next to the throne and added, "Ibrahim, my son, will follow in the Redeemer's footsteps. You are blind to the truth, Mr. Berkeley, but as you walk the path to eternity, I will pray for your salvation just the same."

Whether from outside the church, or from inside his mind, the chant of children filled Matt's ears. *"Sinner, sinner, go away. For your soul, this night we pray."*

Chapter 34

For Matt, it seemed like a tale lifted from the pages of biblical lore; even more, a nightmare from which there was no escape. Torches lit the way, held high by men and women in robes and hoods. A chant, soft and mournful, echoed across the night hills. Up ahead, the Redeemer trudged wearily along a path cut through stands of waist-high bracken beneath a canopy of trees, their branches and trunks shaped and bent by the prevailing winds. Behind, the Redeemer trailed Jenny with young Ibrahim in her arms and a priest carrying the icon.

With wrists still bound, the cords damp with sweat and blood from the chafing strands, Matt made his way along the path. The center point of his spine ached from the barrel of Damien's pistol that prodded him along.

Was this the way to his own personal Golgotha, or just another way to die? More important in Matt's mind: how would it happen and how quickly would it be over?

* * *

Beneath the cliffs and overlooking the Gulf of St. Malo, the all-seeing eye pierced the darkness from high in the tower. Its field of vision changed with deliberate slowness as its lens searched along the rocky shore for signs of life. Only intermittent splotches of heat registered in its receptors. Not enough to activate its defense mechanism, but enough to maintain vigilance against unwanted activity within its mandated sphere of responsibility.

The open room at the top of the tower was dimly lit by the greenish glow of a target-data display screen. The eye, a heat-sensing scope, was directed at the narrow beach and adjacent waters through one of several sentry ports in the room.

Mounted on the side of the scope, a laser, lethal in its purpose. It ultimately took its commands from the "brain," a bank of computerized equipment that calculated and interpreted input from the scope. Of its two methods of operation, automatic and manual, the "brain's" command module was set on MANUAL FIRE MODE, thus requiring human participation to activate the deadly laser gun.

*   *   *

It was the second night Hajir had waited, hidden among rocks on the eastern up-slope of the valley, the second night he had watched the ancient tower that protected the seaward approach to St. Cyril de la Bot. Shortly before dark, he saw a robed man come down the opposite hill, approach the tower and enter. He expected electric-powered lights to go on, but the tower remained dark. That being the case, Hajir focused on the sentry ports and the glare of a flashlight as the robed man climbed the circular staircase that clung to the tower's inner walls. Satisfied the man had come alone, he followed.

As Hajir hoped, the man left the tower unlocked. In fact, much to his amazement, there was neither a lock nor even a keyhole for securing the heavy wooden door. Entering, he moved silently up the steps.

Once he neared the top, he drew a knife from the

scabbard inside his jacket.   The five-inch blade momentarily reflected the greenish light of the target-data display screen.

As he edged upwards to the final step, he saw the man in the robe, standing at an open sentry port, a set of binoculars pressed to his eyes.

With the speed of a striking cobra, Hajir sprang forward, grabbed the man and spun him around, then pushed him against a wall and shoved the knife, hilt deep, into the upper abdomen.   A high-pitched squeal of surprise turned into a struggled grunt of pain, escaping the man's lips as Hajir twisted the blade, causing it to scrape against rib bone as it angled upward in search of heart and lung.

Hajir held the body in position until he felt it grow limp and the warmth of urine against his leg from the man's loosened bladder.   He released his hold and allowed the weight of the body to slump against the wall and slide to the floor.

Satisfied with his own thoroughness and certain the robed man no longer presented a threat, Hajir pulled the knife from the man and wiped the blade clean on the sleeve of the man's robe. He then removed a flashlight from his pocket, stepped to the sentry port and blinked a prearranged signal.

* * *

With motors silenced, the four rigid-hull inflatable boats drifted with the current less than a mile off shore, their occupants waiting for the signal that would tell them it was safe to proceed. Strizhenko was the first to see the light. Two short flashes and two long, repeated at three-second intervals.

"There," Strizhenko said, pointing toward the shore. "Hajir, from the tower. Everything is ready."

Ahmad Kazemi watched the final flashes and said, "Then let us go, and may Allah be with us."

* * *

The two open-bed farm trucks crunched to a halt along the only street that ran through the village, their tires grinding against ancient cobblestones and filling the air with dust. Except for the church at the far end of the village, the street was dark, each cottage shuttered and empty.

"Deserted," Hawkins said, joining Colonel McDevlin in front of the lead truck. "Gotta be the church."

"Dismount, and spread out," McDevlin shouted to the Marines, a small map and flashlight in his hands. "If they're not in the church, then it has to be the high ground above the sea. Where we saw the lights from the air. Now move!"

Chapter 35

Ahead and slightly off the path, Matt could make out the outline of a large circular building of stone and concrete. "Your control center?" Matt asked as Doctor Cavendish edged past Damien and moved to his side.

"Yes," Cavendish answered, his breath short from the increasing steepness of the climb, "and this is where I will leave you."

"Damn good of you to see me off," Matt cynically replied, "but there's still one little detail."

"Oh?"

"How am I supposed to die?"

"Oh, dear, I thought you knew. The angels. Their light, of course."

"Of course, the laser, but what's the heat source for targeting the beam? Not the same thing you used on the ship I hope."

Cavendish laughed softly. "You'll see."

"Sounds like a real blast, but I still don't understand how zapping me is going to make an impression on the rest of the world."

"In addition to 'zapping you' as you so crudely put it," Cavendish answered, "I feel certain we've the capability to provide an adequate demonstration of our resolve to mandate peace throughout the world. It will show our power, a power none others have, and our willingness to use it. For the moment, however, I'll leave that to your imagination."

"And if tonight's demonstration doesn't work?"

Matt asked as they reached an intersection in the path, one way leading up the hill, the other to the circular concrete building.

"A firestorm will be brought upon their heads. I assure you mankind will have no alternative but to live as the Redeemer would have them live, but now I must say good-by, hopefully for the last time. May the Redeemer bless you and keep you, may the Redeemer lift his countenance upon you and –"

"Knock it off, Cavendish. Go play with your toy, and let's get it over with."

Cavendish looked at Matt, shook his head as though to say, "You foolish, foolish man," then turned and walked toward the control center.

Torchbearers moved quickly ahead as the procession continued to a large open area high above the sea. The sound of wind through the trees mingled with the chant of several hundreds of followers who spread out across the clearing.

"My God," Matt muttered as he emerged from the tree line. Before him, near the edge of the promontory, stood a surprisingly large structure in the shape of a pyramid. It was constructed of at least twenty-five narrowing tiers of stone. A flight of steps led up to a small wooden platform, which Matt judged to be a good twenty-five to thirty feet above the pyramid's base.

Encircling and protruding only inches from the lowest level of the structure were dozens of small tubes, each sending forth a sharp hiss as torchbearers stepped forward and lowered their torches. With a loud swoosh, each tube ignited, spewing forth an orange and yellow flame that shot up past the first and second layers of stone. A single break in the line of flame granted access to the flight of steps and the platform above.

Taking the closed icon from the priest and holding it against his chest, the Redeemer moved to the pyramid's steps. Accompanied by two priests, he began to climb with excruciating slowness, his body bent, his face drawn. His determination to reach the summit, however, transmitted itself to his followers and drew upon their combined strength. Even Matt could feel the power of a man who would not surrender until his mission was completed.

Finally, the Redeemer pulled himself onto the platform. As the two priests started their descent from the pyramid, he stood for a moment, facing the open sea, heavy with fatigue, chest heaving as he sucked in much needed air.

Matt sensed a rising concern among the followers until suddenly, the bend in the old man's back seemed to disappear, his shoulders straightened, and his head rose from his chest. When he turned, Matt was shocked. The man suddenly appeared tall and straight as if the years had been stripped away. Though the face still reflected the gauntness of incurable illness, Matt was more certain than ever that it was the man from Yalta, once Churchill's aide, the army colonel. It was the Redeemer's own transfiguration.

The chant, almost disappearing during the man's torturous climb to the top of the pyramid, began again. A soft moan served as an undercurrent for his words as he unfolded the icon and held it above his head. The colors of the *Transfiguration* danced in the fire's light, the figures alive with adoration for their Savior.

His head held high, the Redeemer proclaimed, "I say unto you this night, this night of a thousand years, this Night of the Angels, the veil shall be rent and the world will witness God's power. The machines of war will grind to a halt, peace will reign, and you will be the standard bearers for all mankind. Bring forth Ibrahim."

The chanting and moaning grew stronger as Jenny stepped forward, carrying the small child in her arms.

Lowering the open icon to his chest, the Redeemer beseeched his followers, "This is my beloved son in whom I am well pleased; hear ye him and follow him." And to his son, "O Ibrahim, thou art of my blood, my flesh, my spirit. Thou art god. Lead thy people through the valley of the shadow, and they shall surely find rest amongst thy vineyards. And now, deliver unto me the forgiven one that he may share the eternal life."

With Ibrahim held close to her body, Jenny stepped back as Damien took hold of Matt's arms and forced him onto the lower steps of the pyramid. A second man removed the blood-soaked cords from his wrists and pushed him forward, uncaring of the layers of skin and flesh the cord pulled away. "Son of a bitch!" Matt cursed, his teeth gritting against the pain.

Part way up the steps, Matt looked back at Jenny and the hundreds of eyes staring at him from the crowd and knew there was nothing he could do but climb the pyramid and share the Redeemer's "eternal life."

"What now?" Matt asked as he reached the platform. "A little hocus-pocus to please the followers?"

Ignoring Matt's remark, the old man whispered, "Beyond the trees."

At the same time, he nodded toward the control center's roof as two sections of concrete and steel slid back, the whirring sound of motors barely audible above the continuing chant. It was, however, the turret and barrel-shaped rod rising from the opening that sent chills along Matt's spine and into the base of his skull.

"Take the icon," the Redeemer ordered, "and clasp

it to your bosom as a sign of my forgiveness."

Matt accepted the icon, folded its wings and held it tight against his chest, aware that at last he was in possession of the treasure that had brought him nothing but pain and an opportunity to die at least twenty years too soon.

The Redeemer spread his arms toward the heavens and cried, "Behold the sky, my children. The Night of the Angels is upon us."

As though on cue, a beam of light, blue-green like the one Matt had seen from the ship, streaked heavenward from the opening in the control center's roof. The light was powerful enough for him to see despite the glare of flames at the base of the pyramid. It pulsated on and off, again and again.

Matt waited, expecting to see the beam on its return path, feel the initial burst of heat as it slammed into the pyramid, but there was nothing. He thought at first the orbiting reflectors had failed to properly function, but then, short blasts of light spotted the heavens, one after another, like star bursts a thousand light-years away. Their numbers grew. Suddenly he understood. Satellites! Weather, navigation, communications, photographic reconnaissance – all bombarded by beams now invisible to his eyes; all exploding around his visual horizon. A lightshow to impress, not only the Redeemer's followers, but the rest of the world as well.

At Matt's side, the Redeemer whispered, "Now do you believe?" before calling to his people, "Rejoice, gentle flock. You have witnessed the Night of the Angels. And now I leave you."

It was only a slight movement, but Matt saw it: a control lever in the floor, the Redeemer's foot, a push, and then the roar of flames. They rose like a volcanic eruption from the center of the earth. Their white-hot tips stabbed at the platform beneath his feet. A windstorm of air rushed to satisfy the fire's insatiable appetite as the entire structure of the pyramid began to tremble from the pressure building in its base. It had to be. It was the heat source for the laser's return to earth.

"No damn way," Matt growled through clenched teeth. Suddenly mobilized for survival, Matt threw the icon across the flames, toward the edge of the cliff and away from the crowd of followers.

"What are you doing?" the Redeemer cried. He grabbed for Matt, but Matt swatted his hand away.

"Declining the invitation," Matt shouted as he closed his eyes, said a prayer to his own God, and jumped through tongues of fire already licking over the edge of the wooden platform. The last words he heard from the Redeemer's mouth were, "The icon! You can't..."

With knees bent to cushion the impact on his feet and legs, Matt hit the ground only inches from the pyramid's bottom tier of stones. He immediately fell forward, right shoulder rounded to absorb the upper body's initial contact with the ground, rolling, over and over. A distant explosion sent tremors through the earth as he grabbed at rocks, weeds, anything to reduce the momentum of his body. His fingers dug into the dirt, finally stopping his forward movement at the very edge of the cliff.

From somewhere past the pyramid and the roar of flames, he heard the sounds of gunfire and screams, but they registered only peripherally to his more immediate need. Primary was getting away from the pyramid before the "angels" sent down their deadly beam.

It suddenly registered: automatic weapons fire, exploding grenades, cries of wounded and dying. Past the flames and smoke enveloping the pyramid, he saw the Redeemer's followers, many running for the trees and false security of the village. Others fell before a barrage of bullets fired by combat troops charging up from farther along the cliff.

"Holy Christ," he hissed to himself, his head shaking in disbelief.

And then he saw her, Jenny, with Ibrahim in her arms, trying to break free of the crowd, trying to reach the pyramid. Just as quickly, she was gone. Jenny, Ibrahim, caught in a hail of gunfire, falling and crushed beneath the stampede.

Shaken yet knowing there was nothing he could do for Jenny or the boy, Matt pushed to his knees and began searching for the icon. He had come too far to leave without it, and then he saw it. Its copper backing gleamed in the firelight; its Christ figures summoned him to its side.

On hands and knees to avoid being seen or hit by a stray bullet, he scuttled like a crab across several feet of ground, grabbed the icon, then stopped. A tortured, high-pitched wail lifted above the sounds of gunfire. Matt looked toward the top of the pyramid.

The Redeemer! The old man, in the center of the burning platform, twisted and screamed, robe on fire, hair ablaze, the flesh on his face like hot, running wax. Suddenly, a gunshot, its nearness like an air-filled paper bag exploding in Matt's ear, and the Redeemer disappeared into the flames.

Still on his knees, Matt whirled around. Two feet, spread wide apart, blocked his way. Matt's eyes traveled up the skirt of the robe and centered on the barrel of a chrome-finished pistol that he had already grown to recognize. "Damien!"

"I had to put him out of his misery, Mr. Berkeley.

T'was the only Christian thing to do."

Matt nodded. "Like you're gonna do for me?"

"Exactly."

Gunfire, the cries of wounded men and women, the threat to his own life, and again, Vietnam, only this time, it was not the ghosts of his past. It was the fear of dying and an overwhelming desire to live that goaded Matt into action.

Operating on automatic, Matt swung the icon, hit Damien's hand and knocked the pistol loose before it could be fired. Anticipating Damien's reaction, Matt whipped the icon around and rammed its bottom edge into the man's knees, causing him to grab for his knees and disabling him for the few precious seconds it took for Matt to get to his feet.

Refusing to relinquish his advantage, Matt swept upwards and smashed the icon's copper backing against Damien's face, sending him reeling and stumbling, back along the edge of the cliff. Suddenly, Damien was gone, tumbling through space toward the rocks and sea below.

"Too bad, Damien," Matt grunted, "but it was the only Christian thing I could do."

In the glow of the firelight, Matt saw Damien's chrome-finished pistol, a 45-caliber semiautomatic, and scooped it up. At the same time, more weapons fire, this time from the tree line on the far side of the clearing. Friend or foe, he didn't know, but he'd be damned if he'd allow himself to get caught in a crossfire between two forces, accidentally or otherwise, whoever they were.

With one hand holding the icon close to his body and the other gripping the pistol, Matt moved from behind the pyramid, away from the blast-furnace heat of the flames and red-hot embers of wood falling from the disintegrating platform. Keeping as low as he could and running away from the action, he was prepared to shoot if someone, anyone, tried to stop him. When he reached the trees and high bracken, the waist-high ferns slowed his progress, but offered near perfect cover as he kept the sound of gunfire to his right.

Matt stopped abruptly. In front of him lay the path to the village and the cutoff to the control center, its massive outline visible through the trees. He knelt at the edge of the path listening, watching. Except for the continuing stutter of automatic weapons and an occasional grenade exploding in the clearing on the cliff, he was alone. But not for long, of that he was certain.

Chapter 36

With both arms folded around the icon and holding it tight against his chest, its copper-bound weight already beginning to take its toll, Matt crossed the path and ran as fast as he could to the side of the control center. Breathing heavily, he sidestepped his way along the curve of the wall to a large, oversized steel door, more than likely a service entrance the size of a one-car garage door through which heavy pieces of equipment could be moved.

He leaned the icon against the wall, took a deep breath and, with Damien's pistol in one hand, swept the door's perimeters with the other hand. He quickly realized there were no hinges and no handle. Only a set of dimly lighted digital impressions flush with the surface of the door. An electronic lock! He could, however, feel tracks that ran along the top and bottom to allow the door to slide back into the wall when the correct digital combination was entered.

Matt stepped back and fired three shots directly into the block of numbers. The pistol's steel-jacketed bullets smashed through the numbered plastic faceplate, miniature circuit boards and metal backing. They ripped a hole large enough for him to stick a fist through. The door started to move, then just as quickly slammed back into its closed position.

"Okay, som'bitch," he growled, "let's do it again."

Two more shots, and a sharp burst of smoke and flame spurted from unseen electrical wiring somewhere in the opening. The door again jumped back an inch or two along its track, jerked spasmodically like a fly caught in a spider's web, and stopped.

"Damn it!" Growing more and more frustrated with his inability to open the door, Matt jammed the fingers of his right hand as far into the opening as they would go, planted his feet as best he could, then grunted and pulled. He felt it. A slight movement. Grunt and pull. With each attempt, more movement. Finally, the door grudgingly offered a little more than a foot of open space before it ground to a halt, refusing to go any farther.

Matt grabbed the icon, literally squeezed his way through the opening and found himself in an empty, well-lighted corridor that appeared to run the circumference of the fortress-like building. No guards, nothing to prohibit movement, but which way to go? Left or right?

Catching his breath, Matt placed the icon between his legs, popped the magazine from the pistol's grip and counted the remaining bullets. "Two," he said aloud, "plus one in the chamber." He shook his head and laughed. With that he was supposed to win the war and beat the bad guys?

Matt slapped the magazine back into the pistol, tucked the weapon beneath his belt, picked up the icon and turned right. Moving quickly from room to room, most with open doors, he saw each space was filled with desks, filing cabinets, computers and supplies, but no signs of life. Once around the full circumference of the building, only two doors had been closed, each of heavy steel and equipped with number-coded electronic locks like the door through which he'd entered moments earlier. One was the size of the large outside service door; the second the size of an average office door.

Common sense told him that behind these doors were the people, equipment and yes, the laser gun, its barrel more than likely still pointed toward the heavens.

It was back to the smaller door that he moved, searching each of the unlocked rooms as he went until he found what he was looking for: a supply room with wheeled dollies and motorized flatbeds for moving large pieces of equipment. Wanting to save the three rounds that remained in the pistol until and if he had to use them, he grabbed a tire iron from one of the flatbeds and continued until he again arrived at the smaller locked door.

Holding the icon against his body under one arm and, at this point, not caring how much noise he made in the deserted passageway, he smashed the face of the electronic key pad with the tire iron. Again, and again until sparks shot out and a spiral of smoke drifted upwards. The LED lighted keypad flickered and went dark. Using the flat end of the tool, he pried the door open enough to wedge his way through.

This time, something was different. Not a room, but an enclosed flight of metal steps, winding upwards along the curve of the wall and leading to an opening at least two stories above. Mechanical sounds drifted down the stairwell; a familiar voice shouted instructions. Cavendish!

Pushing the door closed behind him as tightly as he could, Matt moved up the stairway, two steps at a time. Once at the top, he emerged on a two-foot-wide metal catwalk which wound its way around and high above a room large enough to take up most of the building's ground floor. With a sharp intake of breath, he drew back against the wall to keep from being seen.

The room was like a NASA launch center. In the

middle, on a platform that had obviously risen from out of the floor, stood a massive tripod assembly supporting a device that resembled the star projector in a planetarium. A cannon-like laser rod extended from the device's highest point, directed upward through the opening in the roof.   Matt watched as the entire arrangement, from platform to rod, rotated clockwise on its axis, suddenly stopped, then reversed its direction as though in search of a target somewhere in space.

Cavendish flitted from one computer to the next. "Too slow," he admonished. "Hurry. The pyramid's fuel, it's almost gone. Find the problem, correct it, and fire!"

On the far side of the room were at least a dozen men and women dressed in white, all working feverishly at several banks of equipment studded with brightly lit electronic controls, computer displays and what appeared to be television monitors. In front of them, a screen that filled a quarter of the circular wall, as large if not larger than an IMAX theater screen. It provided a three-dimensional depiction of the northern sky.

Curved satellite trajectories, outlined in various colors, served as paths for small blips of light that glided across the display. Like a miniature galaxy, it was superimposed with the multi-sided image of a reflecting mirror at the screen's center. Far below, at the lower left-hand corner was a silhouetted likeness of the domed control center, its laser canon raised and pointed toward the mirror.

A low-pitched staccato sound suddenly erupted from one of the banks of equipment. A technician called, "It's ready, Doctor."

"Then fire."

"Not this time," Matt whispered under his breath.

Placing the icon flat on the metal grating, he took the pistol from beneath his belt, and lowered himself to one knee to allow greater stability and accuracy. With both hands gripping the weapon, he aimed toward the opening in the roof and fired. Three shots! The first was wide. The second struck the laser turret and penetrated the metal with a sudden flare of light and smoke. The third ricocheted off in a shower of sparks.

Screams and shouts immediately rose from the control center floor.

Matt watched Cavendish's head swivel in one direction, then another, desperately attempting to determine where the shots came from until, "Berkeley," the man cried, "you're supposed to be –"

"Shut it down, Cavendish," Matt ordered. Leaving the icon where it lay, Matt scrambled to his feet and half ran, half limped along the catwalk to a steeply inclined metal stairway leading down to the operating level. With the empty pistol pointed at Cavendish as he moved, he yelled, "There're troops out there killing your people, and you can bet your ass this is what they want. You've gotta destroy it."

"No! In our hands, this is the hope of the world, the power of the Redeemer."

"The Redeemer's dead, for God's sake," Matt shouted, quickly followed with, "Forget I said that," as he made his way awkwardly down a flight of metal steps. At the same time, he swung the pistol in a wide arc to cover everyone in the room. "Destroy it, damn it! Destroy the plans, everything, or they'll take it away from you."

As he reached the floor, an explosion rocked the room. The impact of sound and shock waves created showers of concrete dust from the rounded ceiling.

Acting on instinct, Matt dove for cover behind one of the equipment consoles.

As he did, the large steel service door on the far side of the room collapsed inward and four uniformed soldiers charged through the smoke. Orders were shouted in a language Matt didn't understand, but it was apparent those who rushed through the opening understood. A line of troops immediately took up positions around the control center. Again, the same voice, this time in English. "Do not move. You are safe unless you attempt escape."

A second voice, its accent a pronounced Russian Slavic, shouted, "Where is the man called Berkeley? I want him, and I want him now!"

Chapter 37

Peering from behind the console, Matt watched two men in battle fatigues, similar to the soldiers who first entered, walk across the room and stop before Cavendish and the huddled group of technicians. It was the smaller of the two – partially bald, a mustache, and wearing burgundy colored epaulets on his shoulders – who spoke first.

"I am General Ahmad al Kazemi, Iranian Revolutionary Guards, and you are?" Kazemi nodded to Cavendish who stood in front of the technicians.

Cavendish hesitated, then stammered, "Ca-Ca-Cavendish. Doctor George Cavendish, chief physicist for our... our little project."

Kazemi laughed. "We witnessed the demonstration of your *little* project when we came ashore."

"Berkeley! We know he is here. Where is he?" the second, much larger man with the Russian accent demanded.

Matt waited for Cavendish to speak telling them where he was, but it was unnecessary. The muzzle of an AK-47 assault rifle pressed hard against the base of his skull was enough to lift him to his feet and guide him from behind the console. Someone behind him snatched the pistol from his hand.

"Well, well, Mr. Berkeley, at last we meet," the Russian said.

"Let me guess. From what Cavendish told me, you must be the infamous Major Strizhenko of the KGB."

"Formerly of the KGB, Mr. Berkeley, but let me congratulate you. The Society is most pleased with your performance."

Matt laughed sourly. "I'm sure it is, and I'm sure Leila Howard, or whatever her name, is just as pleased."

"Hajir," Kazemi called.

Matt watched helplessly as Leila stumbled over the metal door, Hajir holding her by one arm and forcing her forward.

"I'm so sorry, Matthew," Leila said, her voice a half-whisper. "I didn't mean for it to happen this way."

"I'll bet you didn't," Matt answered, fighting back memories of a room in Paris and the heat of their passion. "And your friend there, good old scar face," he added, refusing Leila the opportunity for further explanation, "I haven't forgotten him, either."

"Enough," Strizhenko ordered, then to Hajir, "Berkeley is your responsibility." Turning back to Cavendish, he said, "You and your people will come with us. Bring what plans you can carry. Now!"

"Don't know who's fighting who, but from what I saw up on the hill," Matt said in an effort to needle Strizhenko, "getting out of here might be easier said than done."

"The General's men have set up a defense perimeter that will allow for our departure," Strizhenko fired back before shouting at Cavendish, "Hurry, Doctor. We do not have all night."

"Stay where you are, Cavendish."

The words, loud and forceful, echoed through the room. The voice from high on the catwalk was like a magnet. It drew every eye and every gun barrel in its direction. The voice's owner appeared to be armed only with the icon Matt had left on the catwalk and a portable

271

radio transceiver slung from his shoulder.

"The icon!" Cavendish cried. "You've got the icon." He might as well have been speaking to the wind. No one paid attention.

Strizhenko waved his hand for the Iranian soldiers to lower their weapons, before saying, "I know him."

To the man on the catwalk, he issued a rather pointed invitation. "Perhaps you would be good enough to join us, Mr. Hawkins of the Central Intelligence Agency."

"Not tonight," Hawkins answered. "You're at the end of the line, Strizhenko, and you, too, General Kazemi."

Ahmad Kazemi nodded, a smile of recognition on his face. "Good evening, Mr. Hawkins. Our last encounter, Beirut, Hezbollah, nineteen ninety-six, I believe. Shortly before the Israelis attempted to bomb our training camps. This time, however, the nose of the camel points in my direction."

"Don't think so, General," Hawkins countered, a sneer in his voice. "After what I'm gonna tell you, I think you'll find it's the other end of the camel you're lookin' at."

Matt saw Kazemi's eyes quickly narrow. A sudden loss of confidence spread across the man's face.

"It is a bluff, nothing more," Strizhenko shouted, raising a pistol in Hawkins' direction.

"Would I shit you, Strizhenko?" Hawkins asked with the sharp edge of sarcasm Matt had grown to recognize. "Would I shit the Leopard?"

Out of the corner of his eye, Matt watched as a full squad of six British Marines moved silently through the doorway, their weapons trained on Strizhenko and the Iranians. He automatically reached for Leila's arm and pulled her out of the potential line of fire.

"Tell him, Berkeley," Hawkins went on. "Tell him if he shoots, my guys'll turn his ass into so much dog meat."

Matt theatrically cleared his throat and nodded, causing both Strizhenko and Ahmad Kazemi to look back toward the door and the six Marines.

As Strizhenko's arm dropped to his side, Hawkins loosened the strap holding the portable transceiver across his shoulders and pulled it over his head. "I have here what's commonly known as a two-way radio. I'm gonna give this thing to the good General, and he's gonna talk to a British citizen of Iranian descent who calls himself Ali Rashadi. Mr. Rashadi borrowed a coastal steamer from his employer, Sheffield Transport Limited, and, to his great misfortune, wound up a mile or so off the Guernsey coast. Right now, both Rashadi and his ship are in the custody of the *HMS Avenger*, a British frigate, but don't take my word for it."

Hawkins leaned over the railing and lowered the radio by its strap to Matt. "Make yourself useful, Berkeley, and you, General, push the red button and identify yourself."

Kazemi took the radio from Matt and pushed the button. "This is General Ahmad al Kazemi. With whom do I speak?"

Matt could feel the tension in the room rising to crescendo level until, "Captain Ali Rashadi here," a voice crackled from the radio's tiny speaker. "I am deeply sorry, General. The British have captured my ship."

Without responding, the general thumbed the radio's power switch to OFF, then placed the set on the floor, his teeth set in anger, his eyes closed in defeat.

"How 'bout them apples, General?" Hawkins

chided. "Lemme give you the rest of the good news. The British Prime Minister's already talked with Tehran. Nobody wants a war over this, or even an international incident, so you were never here."

"How can that be?" Cavendish interrupted. "According to Berkeley, there are many dead, and –"

"I don't give a rat's ass what Berkeley said or how they explain it. Not my problem."

"And us?" Kazemi asked. "Are we to be eliminated to erase the evidence?"

"That's up to your own government," Hawkins answered from the catwalk. "So far as I'm concerned, you can round up what people you've got left and get the hell outta here."

"What about me?" Strizhenko asked. "What about Strizhenko?"

Hawkins laughed cruelly. "You come with me. I'm told your comrades in Moscow've got a room with your name on it in the Lubyanka, or is it the *Butyrka*, now?" To the Marines waiting at the control center's door, Hawkins nodded and said, "He's all yours."

"No," Strizhenko shouted, shrugging away from the Marines. "Anything you want to know, I will tell you. KGB, or the SVR, the new Russian Intelligence Service. Whatever you need for me –"

Strizhenko stopped, pointed at Leila, and added, "And Kazemi's plans for the Ahmadinejad woman."

"Ahmadinejad?" Matt blurted. "Leila?"

Hazir grabbed Strizhenko's arm. "What are you saying, Russian? What plans?"

Strizhenko ripped his arm from Hajir's grasp and bellowed, "To overthrow your president, you fool! Her brother, and perhaps even your Supreme Leader."

Hajir appeared momentarily stunned before

turning toward Leila and crying, "She devil!" He lunged for Leila's throat, but Matt's quickness caught him by surprise. Matt's fist against his jaw was enough to knock Hajir off balance and into the arms of two Marines who pushed him to his knees and held him against the floor.

"Political asylum!" Strizhenko shouted. "I demand political asylum!"

"Work it out with the Brits," Hawkins answered, waving to the Marines to take Strizhenko away. "Now get the hell outta my sight."

Matt pointed a finger in Hawkins' direction. "Leila stays. If she goes back now, she's as good as dead."

Hawkins held up the icon. "This is what you came for. Leave it at that, and like Cavendish and his people, she's not my fucking problem."

"Then I'll make it your problem!"

"No, please," Leila interrupted, taking Matt's hand and holding it momentarily against her cheek. "The time we had together was precious, but I must go back." Releasing Matt's hand, she added, "Truthfully, if they had tried to kill you, they would have had to kill us both."

"Leila, –"

"I won't forget you, ever," she said before turning to Ahmad Kazemi. "Shall we go, General?"

Suddenly, the platform supporting the turret and lasing rod began to turn, slowly at first, the low-level groan of internal belts and bearings increasing in pitch to a steady whine as the platform gained speed.

Matt whipped around, searching for Cavendish among the technicians. "What's happening?"

Cavendish's face was a mixture of surprise and wild delight. Clapping his hands like a child with a new toy, he cried, "It's the Redeemer!"

"Turn it off," Matt ordered.

"I can't," Cavendish cried. "It's the Redeemer, I tell you. It's the Night of the Angels!"

Console lights blinked while graphics reappeared on computer monitor screens, and suddenly, a steady burst of blue-green light emerged from the tip of the lasing rod and disappeared through the opening in the roof.

"Look!" Cavendish shouted, pointing at the far wall and the three-dimensional display of the northern sky. A line of bright green light erupted from the silhouette of the control center in the corner of the screen, streaked upward toward the satellite reflector, then backtracked just as quickly, following its original course, homeward bound.

"Oh, no! The pyramid! If the flame's gone out, the laser's going to –"

The words, coming from one of the technicians, were cut off by an explosion high in the rounded ceiling and the wrenching cry of concrete under tremendous stress.

Everything happened at once. Power surged, causing overhead lights to blink, on and off. Seams opened and stretched down the walls. Dust and falling plaster filled the air, dropping to a floor that shook and wobbled as though caught in an earthquake. Control consoles overloaded, some bursting into flame and smoke.

Panic erupted as technicians and Iranian soldiers, as well as several of the British Marines, sought safety against the walls beneath the catwalk.

As though an unseen hand had pushed a fast-forward button, every motion and every sound seemed to accelerate to double time, even triple time as Matt tried to shield Leila from the falling debris. The platform and the speed of its revolutions grew faster as it rotated counterclockwise back into the floor.

The cannon atop the laser turret, spewing a continuous shaft of blinding laser light, dipped steadily from the opening in the roof. A descending trail of scorched concrete and plaster followed the beam along its path, a line that angled lower and lower with each 360-degree revolution of the platform.

Screams and shouts filled the air from a shower of sparks as the beam cut through a section of the catwalk. Already loosened anchor bolts burst like gunfire from the wall as the metal grid tore away from the concrete and sagged downward, its skeletal structure crushing those huddled beneath its weight. One moment, Hawkins was visible, a stick figure riding a swaying serpent. The next moment, gone, lost in the smoke and dust that was rapidly building.

Matt pushed Leila to the floor as the laser swept steadily downward and around the circumference of the room. As the beam cut through the large, three-dimensional screen, hundreds of lights exploded in a starburst of fireworks that sent showers of sparks and glass through the air. Matt spotted Cavendish standing in the beam's path.

"Get down, Cavendish, get dow-w-w-wn!"

But Cavendish stood his ground. Oblivious to the beam, he shouted praise to the Redeemer as the rapidly circling "sword of the angels" cut deep into his right shoulder. A blast of yellowish steam followed the laser's searing course, down across his chest until it exited the body just above the left hip bone. With a face suddenly swollen with body fluids bubbling hot from every orifice, Cavendish folded like the flap of an envelope and toppled to the floor. A whirlwind of flames quickly engulfed what remained of the pathetic little man.

Distracted by Cavendish and the beam, Matt sensed rather than saw the movement, little more than a blur in the haze of smoke now filling the room. A pistol butt slammed against the side of his head and sent him to his knees as Leila's hand was torn from his. He saw her, fighting with Strizhenko, and then Hajir. Ignoring Leila's flailing arms and curses, Hajir dragged her through the doorway. Strizhenko, pistol in hand and close on their heels, laid down a wild barrage of covering fire as they fled.

"Leila-a-a!" Matt cried, pushing to his feet as the laser beam sliced into a bank of consoles. Almost simultaneously, a chain reaction of explosions hammered the walls. Still groggy from the blow, but lucid enough to know he was about to be cut to pieces by debris if he remained upright, Matt went flat against the floor as bits of jagged metal and glass shredded the air.

Suddenly, except for the crackle of flames and the groan of overhead concrete, the room was still; the laser, silent; the platform motionless; the air, dense with smoke; and then a moan.

Matt got to his feet, stumbled, shook the cobwebs from his head and started forward. Feeling more than seeing, he worked his way past overturned chairs, metal equipment bins, a body – whose, he didn't know nor did he care at that point – until he heard it again. The same moan, only this time connected to a hand streaked with blood and reaching through the smoke. Matt's eyes followed the hand and arm back to its source.

"Jesus!" At first Matt recoiled, then reached out to help. The face was raw hamburger, and the scalp torn and pealed. A jagged piece of metal protruded from the skull's longitudinal seam, while shards of glass, like miniature stalagmites, jutted from throat and chest. Ahmad Kazemi!

"Bājī Leila," he whispered. "She... she is my country's only hope. They will kill her. Please..." The face and body of a man already dead slipped back into the smoke, but Matt knew what Ahmad Kazemi wanted.

As a line of fire crept steadily across the room, Matt answered, "I'll try, General. I'll try."

"Berkeley, that you? Over here, goddamn it," a voice shouted above the ever-increasing roar of the fire and the intermittent groan of ceiling and walls.

"Hawkins! Where?" Matt called. "I can't see you. Talk to me."

"To your right. I'm trapped. I can't move."

Matt fought through the thickening smoke toward the voice, coughing and covering his face with his sleeve as best he could. Already his eyes had begun to water. His throat felt like he was swallowing acid.

"Over here, for chrissake, over here. My legs caught."

Finally, Matt saw him, barely visible through the smoke, propped against the wall. Part of the metal catwalk rested on Hawkins' blood-soaked right leg. Without a word, Matt unbuckled the belt from around Hawkins' waist and pulled it free. "Tie it around your thigh like a tourniquet while I try to lift the catwalk."

"What the hell for?"

"If you haven't noticed, your leg's bleeding like a stuck pig, so don't argue. Just do it, or neither of us is going make it out of here alive."

As Hawkins slipped the belt around his thigh, Matt took hold of the metal grating and tried to lift. No movement. Sweating heavily from the mounting heat, he wiped the moisture from his hands, took several deep breaths and tried again. This time, with muscles and tendons in his arms and neck standing out like cords of knotted rope, Matt felt the grating move, inch by agonizing inch. "Pull out," he grunted.

"I can't. It's still –"

"Pull out, goddamn it! I can't hold much longer."

Hawkins groaned as he tugged his leg from beneath the catwalk.

Matt dropped the metal grating, reached for Hawkins, then stopped.

"What the hell's wrong?" Hawkins cried.

"The icon," Matt shouted as the roof began to sag. "Gotta get the icon."

"Screw the fucking icon, for God's sake," Hawkins pleaded. "We gotta get outta here."

Moving low along the remains of the catwalk, trying to stay beneath the dense smog of smoke as best he could, Matt tossed aside debris until he saw the copper backing. "Got it!"

"C'mon," Hawkins shouted, "the fire's closin' in."

With his skin feeling as through it was already on fire from the blistering heat, Matt picked his way back to Hawkins. "Take it and climb on. You're going piggyback."

Hawkins pushed the icon away. "Not with that thing."

"No icon, no Hawkins." Matt shoved the icon into Hawkins' hands, then turned and squatted. "Either get on or burn."

Matt felt Hawkins' arm on his shoulder, then around his neck, the icon suddenly wedged against his back. His own knees buckled as Hawkins pulled himself up. He almost fainted when Hawkins' legs pressed against his midsection, pushing hard against the already cracked rib.

"We'll never make it," Hawkins hissed in his ear.

"You've waited too fucking long."

"Shut up," Matt snapped as he began to lift. The muscles in his calves and thighs screamed against the weight. The sutures in his thigh stretched and strained against skin and flesh, but there was no other way.

Stooped forward, his arms tight around Hawkins' legs, Matt grunted his way through the smoke and along the curved wall, skirting fires that blazed out of control. His eyes were awash with tears from the acrid fumes of burning circuit boards and wiring insulation. Dizzy with fatigue and nearly blind, he lurched, almost fell through an opening in the wall. The corridor!

Matt willed himself to keep his balance, to keep moving along the circular passageway until he found the outer door. With the sounds of more explosions and the grinding and cracking of concrete slabs urging him on, Matt squeezed Hawkins and himself through the doorway. He staggered forward to the footpath leading to the cliff, then dropped to his knees. He released his hold on Hawkins' legs and sucked in deep draughts of cool night air.

"We did it," Hawkins wheezed as he and the icon fell free of Matt's back. "We goddamn did it!"

Using the trunk of a tree for support, Matt pulled himself up. "Yeah, and now you're on your own."

"Whaddaya mean?"

"That gun of yours..." Matt jabbed a finger at a shoulder holster and the handle of a semiautomatic pistol that had shifted past the opening of Hawkins' jacket.

"What is it?"

Swatting Matt's hand away, Hawkins' answered, "Nine- millimeter Browning Hi-Power, single action. So what?"

"How many rounds?"

"Thirteen in the mag, one in the chamber. Why?"

With surprising speed, Matt grabbed Hawkins and flipped him on his stomach. Jamming a knee in the middle of the agent's back, Matt jerked the jacket halfway down the man's upper torso, effectively pinning his arms to his sides.

"Damn it, Berkeley," Hawkins screamed, struggling to get out from under Matt's weight. "Get your knee outta my back."

Pushing down even harder with his knee and pulling Hawkins's head back with one hand, Matt used the other hand to reach over Hawkins' shoulder, grab the pistol's handle and yank. The holster's Velcro safety strap *r-r-ripped* away as the pistol came free.

Once Matt pushed to his feet, Hawkins bellowed, "You dumb-ass sonofabitch, what the hell you think you're doin'?"

Shoving the pistol into his pants' pocket, Matt shouted over his shoulder as he started up the path toward the top of the hill, "If I'm not too late, I'm going to do my damndest to stop Strizhenko from killing Leila."

Chapter 38

Sporadic coughing gradually purged Matt's lungs of smoke as he moved into the clearing overlooking the sea. His legs and side, in fact, much of his body, ached with every step. He stopped for a moment to catch his breath.

Though flames from the base of the pyramid were all but extinguished, a patchwork of grass fires created by exploded grenades illuminated an open-air charnel house of robed bodies, bent and broken. He wondered which one was Jenny? Which her son? Others in combat fatigues lay scattered about the clearing, some wounded and being attended by Marine medics, some riddled into twisted, unrecognizable lumps.

Farther along where the cliff gave way to a steeply inclined hillside, three British Marines stood talking, two enlisted and, as best he could tell, an officer with a colonel's insignia on his jacket.

Matt called as he ran in their direction, "Two men and a woman trying to escape. Have you seen them?"

"Down there, whoever you are," the colonel answered, pointing toward the beach at the foot of the hill as Matt pulled to a stop, panting and holding his side.

"Names Berkeley, and why the hell didn't you stop them?"

The colonel stepped forward, a frown on his face. "I've heard of you. The troublemaker. There was an agreement. We had no choice but to let them pass."

"How long ago," Matt demanded. His eyes

searched the footpath that angled down the hillside and quickly disappeared into the darkness.

"Four, five minutes, perhaps more. I didn't –"

With an angry, "Damn!" Matt pushed past the colonel and his men, scattering rocks as he started down the path.

"Come back here!" the colonel barked, grabbing at Matt's arm. "You can't go down there!"

Matt swatted the hand away and plunged ahead.

* * *

With Leila's wrist grasped firmly in his hand, Strizhenko stopped, suddenly alert. Turning toward the sounds of the colonel's shouts and falling rocks, he growled, "Someone is following."

For a moment, Leila could see the outline of a man on the crest of the hill, silhouetted against the glow of the numerous grass fires, and then it blended into the darkness of the hill itself.

"Only Berkeley would be such a fool," Strizhenko whispered. "He must die, Hajir. Our failure, his responsibility. We will wait at the boat."

Pausing only long enough to promise, "I will stop him," Hajir pulled the knife from beneath his jacket and moved toward the footpath.

"Matthew," Leila shouted. Her voice carried past the ancient stone tower overlooking the beach and echoed up the hill and through the narrow valley. "Hajir is –"

Strizhenko's fist slammed against Leila's cheekbone, cutting off both words and vision. Her knees buckled. The softness of the sand reached up and offered its comfort, but hands yanked her forward and dragged her along the beach toward an outcrop of rocks hiding the inflatable boats.

* * *

From atop the stone tower, the ever-vigilant eye sensed presence of human prey in the lower right-hand quadrant of its zone of responsibility. Two images, movement erratic, the first charging forward, the second pulled along by the first, stumbling, falling, then struggling across the beach.

With its command module set on MANUAL FIRE MODE, the computerized "brain" instantly interpreted human movement and calculated the changing target angles, but could not issue an order to fire without input from its human master. The high-pitched buzz from its audio-alerting component cut the air like an electric drill.

Left for dead by Hajir, the man in the robe, cold and shivering, lay in a spread of blood that had seeped from the stab wound in his abdomen. Fighting the exquisite pain that shot through his body, he tried to rise, tried to move toward the "brain" and its command module. But his arms refused the effort, and he slipped back into that holding ground between life and death.

* * *

Leila heard Strizhenko's voice. It stabbed through the crust of her numbed resistance.

"Into the boat," Strizhenko ordered.

All at once, she felt his hands on her body, felt him lift and roll her across the air-filled pontoon and down onto the boat's fiberglass decking. Her head struck something hard, and for a moment, she drifted, no longer caring, no longer afraid.

285

* * *

Though alerted by Leila's cry and the word, "Hajir," Matt was still surprised by the sudden force of the blow. It knocked him sideways. His left arm caught the full thrust of a knife. Its razor-sharp blade sliced through shirt and flesh like a shark's fin through water.

"Die," Hajir hissed, his shadowed figure little more than a blur as Matt scrambled off the path and into the bracken. His arm burned from the cut, but he knew the pain, coursing rapidly past his elbow and into his shoulder, was only the beginning. He also knew there was no alternative. Either die without a fight, or take the initiative.

Holding his arm to staunch the flow of blood, Matt moved backwards, buying time and searching for a weakness in Hajir's attack, but a mixture of rocks and dirt crunched and slid beneath his feet, denying the foothold he so desperately needed. In the darkness, bracken fronds, like grasping fingers, wrapped about his legs and slowed his movement.

The pistol! He grabbed for it, but the adjustable rear sight snagged the inside of his pocket and he couldn't get
it out. "Damn it!"

Matt looked up just in time for Hajir's charge, catching the momentary glint of firelight from the top of the cliff on the knife's blade as it swept down toward his body. That split-second gleam gave him direction. This time, Matt's left hand shot forward. He grasped Hajir's arm at the wrist and dug his fingernails deep into the line of tendons and flesh. With Hajir's scream in his ears, he grabbed the open front of the man's jacket with his free hand and jerked forward, using his forehead as a battering ram against the nose. He immediately tried to bring his knee up into Hajir's crotch, but missed as the man pulled away.

Hajir's cry turned quickly into a deep-throated growl as Matt backed farther along the hillside, the bracken suddenly turning to solid rock beneath his feet.

From somewhere below, how far he couldn't tell, rose the sound of surf, carried on the wind that suddenly swept around him. He knew he had backed himself into a trap.

In front of him: Hajir and the knife. In his pocket, a semiautomatic, a weapon he'd been unable to tear free. To his rear, a rocky precipice and the midnight-black waters of the Gulf of St. Malo.

* * *

The robed man lay on the tower room floor, his mind wavering – on one hand the Redeemer, smiling and beckoning him toward paradise; on the other, Damien and a scowl of disapproval. His fear of Damien greater than
his trust in the Redeemer, the man knew he had to try.

Guided by the greenish glow of the target-data display screen and the "brain's" incessant alerting buzz, the man pulled himself through the sheen of his own blood. He groped for the command module and the button that read, SELF-FIRE MODE, but slipped and his fingers missed. In his mind, he heard Damien's curse, and he wept in desperation.

* * *

Suddenly, the distant roar of boat engines, and

then a spotlight. Its beam swept up the hill from somewhere on the water and centered first on Hajir, then Matt.

"Sonofabitch!" Matt cursed, but as Hajir closed, Matt used the light to his own advantage. Feinting to the left, then dipping below the slash of the now visible knife, Matt grabbed the belt around Hajir's waist and pulled him forward, at the same time falling backwards to the rock and using his legs to lift Hajir high in the air and over his head. A mistake, and he realized the error in judgment as the weight of Hajir's body created a rolling motion and carried them both over the edge of the narrow precipice.

The spot light and Hajir's cry followed him down until he felt the impact of the water against his back. His body whipped forward into a near fetal position as he sank beneath the surface. Almost immediately, he felt his lower back and hips dig into the bottom. Sand and gravel, it was shallow, no more than ten to twelve feet, judging from the lack of pressure against his ears. With the sting of salt water adding to the already increasing pain from the cut in his arm, he pushed off, knowing there was only one way he could go. Up!

Breaking surface, Matt spun around, once, twice, searching for Hajir. Was the man dead? Was he –

A cry filled the night as Hajir exploded from the water, his knife immediately stabbing and slashing in Matt's direction. Each slice of the air brought the blade closer and closer.

Matt knew he could tread water and backpedal, maybe even out-swim the man to the beach but it would only prolong the inevitable. He was already on the verge of total exhaustion. It was now or never.

With only a few feet separating the two men, Matt

took as deep a breath as possible, upended himself and dove. On the way down, he grabbed Hajir's ankle and pulled the struggling man along with him until he felt the bottom scrape against his shoulder.

Sensing panic in Hajir's frantic efforts to return to the surface and refusing him the opportunity to break free, Matt jerked downward and, rising up from behind, wrapped his arms around Hajir's waist and squeezed. The sharpness of his action was like a Heimlich maneuver, forcing the remaining air up and out of Hajir's chest in a single blast of bubbles. The sudden loss of buoyancy allowed both to momentarily sink back to the bottom.

Though the carbon dioxide buildup in his own respiratory system demanded an immediate injection of oxygen, Matt dug one hand into the sand and gravel to hold both Hajir and himself against the bottom. Not until he felt the man involuntarily fill his lungs with water did he release his hold and push upward.

As Matt's head broke surface, his body surged upward like the breaching of a whale. His mouth, already open and gasping for breath, filled the vacuum in his lungs. As the sound of boat engines rolled in from the sea, a spotlight swept the water. It blinded him for an instant, moved past, then back, bigger and brighter, cutting a rapidly diminishing path in his direction.

* * *

Leila pulled herself up as the inflatable gained speed, its engine noise tearing at her ears, the movement of the boat across the water throwing her from side to side. But it was Strizhenko at the throttle and the spotlight in his hand that forced her to look forward, past

Strizhenko   and   past   the   V-shaped   bow.
     At first, nothing.   Only the wind and spray whipping at her face and eyes. Together they created tears that streaked back into her hairline. And then she saw it, dead ahead, a face in the water. She knew and she screamed, "Matthew!"

Chapter 39

With the inflatable bearing down on the man who had become so important in her life, Leila threw herself at the wheel, ignoring the spotlight in Strizhenko hand as it swung in her direction. Its lens shattered against the side of her head, but not before one hand grabbed the wheel, sending the boat in a wild turn toward open water.

"Iranian whore!" Strizhenko shouted in the sudden darkness.

She felt him grab her shoulders, the crushing force of his hands lifting her to her feet, the side of the boat as he shoved, and the chill of the water as it closed over her head.

* * *

Matt swam as hard and fast as he could. He heard her scream and saw what he knew was Leila pushed from the boat, but in the darkness, could he find her? "Leila!" he called between strokes. "Leila!"

Her voice was barely audible above the growl of the boat's outboard motors now circling somewhere offshore. "Over here. I can't see you."

"That's okay. I hear you. Roll on your back. Work your arms and legs to stay afloat. Keep talking. I'm coming."

* * *

"I will find you!" Strizhenko shouted into the

wind, the death of Bājī Leila and Berkeley now an obsession. Snatching a flare gun from its mounting above the steering column, he pointed it toward the sky and fired. The tiny ball of light streaked upward, slowed as it reached the apex of its curve, and blossomed into a silvery white umbrella before dropping toward the sea.

He saw them. Quickly turning in their direction and increasing speed, Strizhenko forced another star shell into the open barrel of the gun, snapped it shut and pulled the trigger. Nothing! "Damn!" But he knew he was heading in the right direction.

* * *

With Leila treading water only an elbow's distance away, Matt tugged furiously at the pistol in his pocket, praying the damn thing wouldn't go off, torpedoing his manhood into oblivion. With a final determined jerk, the pocket tore away and the pistol came free.

As the bow of the inflatable loomed larger, Matt shouted, "When I say go, push away from me so he'll go between us."

"What are you going to do?" Leila pleaded, her voice raised above the sound of the oncoming boat.

Matt held up the pistol, barely visible in the darkness even to him. "If the bullet primers are sealed, we've got a chance. If it misfires, at least we tried."

* * *

With the angry face of Damien urging him on, the robed man lifted his weakened body from the stone floor and stretched forward once more. His only thought – the command module and the raised button that would allow the "brain" to assume control, the button labeled SELF-FIRE MODE. His trembling fingers searched Braille-like across the top of the keyboard. He found it and pressed downward. As the system's alerting signal went silent and the "brain" commenced operation independent of human instruction, the robed man fell away, knowing both Damien and the Redeemer would now be pleased.

The eye in the room at the top of the tower sensed multiple targets, three separate heat patterns: the largest, moving shoreward; the two smaller yet closer images, intermittent, at times disappearing altogether.

True to its programmed instructions, the "brain" designated the images according to distance and potential threat. Accompanying the three blips on the target data display screen were the instructions: TRACK AND DESTROY IN SEQUENCE. TARGET DESIGNATION: ALPHA, BRAVO, CHARLIE.

* * *

Unaware of his designation as Target ALPHA, Matt watched, treading water and holding his breath as the inflatable surged closer and closer. Timing! He knew, it was all in the timing. "Here he comes," he yelled, at the same time cocking the pistol hammer with his thumb.

"Go!"

"Matthew," Leila cried, "we can't –"

With only seconds to spare, Matt put his feet against Leila and shoved with all his strength. She disappeared from view as the inflatable sped past only inches from his face, Strizhenko's silhouette against the night sky.

Fighting the tremendous wash of the boat's wake,

Matt pulled the trigger, firing a series of rapid bursts, three rounds each, simultaneously twisting in the water as quickly as he could to maintain the inflatable in the pistol's sights until click!

"Damn it!" He snapped the hammer back, and again, click!

Over the sputtering of at least one of the boat's motors, Matt heard Leila call, "Did you hit him?"

"Don't know. An engine, maybe. You okay?"

"Yes, but –"

"Base of the cliff." Matt pointed. "Swim. It's our only chance before he comes back."

* * *

Even though he'd heard pistol shots, Strizhenko ignored the possibility that the inflatable might have been hit as he spun the wheel for another run at Matt and Leila. Not even the increasing stutter of one of the motors could interrupt his determination, until suddenly, with a loud *whump*, fire belched from the boat's starboard outboard motor. Simultaneously, Strizhenko realized the boat was not turning.

Closing rapidly on a collision course with the rock-strewn shore, starboard engine on fire, Strizhenko saw the stone tower. It loomed directly ahead. He whipped the wheel to starboard, then to port and back again, desperate to turn away from the beach and back toward the open sea, but the controls refused to respond.

* * *

The eye in the tower transmitted a sudden increase of thermal energy to the "brain," energy that overshadowed either Target ALPHA or Target BRAVO as the principal and closest threats.

Instructions flashed red in rapid succession on the target-data display screen: ABORT ALPHA, BRAVO. TRACKING CHARLIE. CALCULATING TARGET ANGLE. TARGET ANGLE DETERMINED. FIRE!

* * *

Visible for only seconds, then gone before the human eye could chart its path, a pencil-thin laser beam from one of the sentry ports near the top of the tower cut a slice out of the night. Almost instantly, the inflatable exploded in a ball of yellow-orange flame, mushrooming outwards, then curling toward the sky like a divine wind of fire and smoke.

* * *

Having reached the safety of a sheltering rock on the far side of the beach, Matt held Leila close as they watched the end of former KGB Major Viktor Mikhailovich Strizhenko.

"Praise Allah," Leila whispered, at the same time rubbing and blinking her eyes as though not sure what she'd seen. "But... was that..."

Trying to catch his breath, Matt nodded, "Part of it, I think. And hopefully, the last chapter in the Redeemer's so-called Night of the Angels."

* * *

From the room at the top of the ancient stone tower, the eye, cold and without feeling, resumed its programmed surveillance. The system's "brain," all-knowing of things that move in the night, of living creatures and the warmth of their bodies, waited patiently. Until instructed otherwise, it would protect the seaward approaches to St. Cyril de la Bot and what was once the earthly world of a man known as The Redeemer.

Chapter 40

LONDON

SOME WEEKS LATER

Visitors moved in and out of the bookshop near the entrance to Westminster Abbey, one of them a man with a walking cane, his right leg stiff, the outline of a brace visible beneath his trouser leg. Each step was a contest between willpower and pain.

He stopped and pulled a copy of *The Times* from the rack near the door, slapped a £2 coin on the counter and left. Making his way into the nave, he paused and read the headline sprawled across the top of the front page: IRANIAN TRIBUNAL CONDEMNS PRESIDENT'S SISTER

Beneath the headline, two pictures filled almost half the page: one of Leila Ahmadinejad, the other a passport photo likeness of Matt Berkeley. In the columns below, one paragraph caught his eye, a quote from the Iranian president himself.

"I will not tolerate those who plot to overthrow the sovereign Government of the Islamic Republic of Iran as did my sister and her accomplice, an American spy by the name of Matthew Berkeley. This man Berkeley is known to be an assassin for the Central Intelligence Agency as evidenced by the murder of General Ahmad al Kazemi, a true and loyal son of Iran. We will not rest until the Great Satan and this man pay for their crimes against the Iranian people."

Royce Hawkins closed the paper with a grunt and
tossed it onto one of the chairs bordering the South Aisle
as he hobbled forward on his cane, past the Choir and
Organ Loft. He stopped at the entrance to the South
Transept and Poets' Corner and scanned the sea of
tourists before him. He saw the man he knew would be
there, the one responsible for the pain he suffered in his
leg and for the humiliation he had endured at the hands
of Herb Samuelson.

Whispering to himself, Hawkins vowed, "If the
Iranians don't get you, Berkeley, someday I will, and
you'll pay for this..." He tapped the cane against the
brace on his leg, adding, "... and everything else." With
a final look in Matt's direction, he turned and shuffled
his way through the crowd and out of the Abbey.

* * *

Matt stood quietly behind the velveteen rope
barrier, ignoring the people and murmurs that moved
around him. Also unaware of the vengeful hate directed
at him by Royce Hawkins, his eyes were focused on the
icon inside the lighted, glass-enclosed case and the meld
of lines and colors that formed the *Transfiguration of
Christ the Savior*.

"Like poetry in color," he mused. "This really is
where it belongs, isn't it? Westminster Abbey and Poets'
Corner."

Lord Jeffrey Alanbrooke nodded. "Quite right.
Too bad, however, about Jenny and her son, but I
suppose it had to end one way or the other. Those things
usually do, but the other young lady?"

"Leila?" Matt asked, shaking his head sadly, the
memory of an afternoon in Paris flooding back from the

past.   "Went home hoping to do great things, but
unfortunately, according to *The Times*, she'll be executed
for trying to overthrow her brother. All she wanted to do
was free her people."

"And the Russian you called The Leopard?"

Matt laughed softly. "Except for his hand and the
boat's wheel it was fused to, not a trace. If he's dead,
end of tale, no pun intended. If not, he's licking his
wounds somewhere, and I hope that somewhere is far, far
away."

"But you," Lord Alanbrooke continued, "now that
the icon is returned, where do you go from here?"

"Had a friend in Paris I wanted to visit, but my
boss..." Matt smiled at the thought. "Actually, my ex-
boss since I'm retired. He has other ideas. Wants to keep
me busy to save me from myself and the past. Problem
is, the place he mentions? I've already been there.
Memories, both good and bad."

Pulling from his jacket pocket an e-mail he
received and printed in his hotel's business center, he
read aloud, "'Institute of Archeology, University of
Puerto Rico excavation on the island of St. Michael,
Lesser Antilles. Site plagued by theft of artifacts now
finding their way into the international black market.

"'Latest incident resulted in deaths of two
university students and loss of a priceless artifacts,
ancient Indian statuary called *Zemis*, representing spirit
gods brought to the island by the Arawak Indian when
they migrated from South America in the tenth century.
Contact team leader Dr. Carlos Pérez, Albert Town, St.
Michael, Country Code two-four-six, four-two-four,
zero-zero-nine-eight. Most urgent you join Pérez to
oversee security and assist St. Michael police.'"

"Ah yes, St. Michael. A former British possession

and still part of the Commonwealth," Lord Alanbrooke said, one eyebrow slightly uplifted as though he remembered the island and good times of his own. "The sunny Caribbean, palm trees, warm trade winds and even warmer women, or so I'm told." Alanbrooke gave a wink of his eye.

Matt chuckled. "Sounds to me like you speak from personal experience. But with my luck, our little Caribbean paradise will be one headache after another. I have to admit, however, if it's anything like this icon thing, it will sure as hell take my mind off the past."

"I do envy you, young man," Lord Alanbrooke said with a smile and a faraway look in his eyes. "The excitement in your life, like my days with good old Winnie during the big war. Only wish I was going with you."

"I can arrange it."

"Oh no, Mr. Berkeley. It's time I journey back to Chartwell and live with my memories, good memories, they be. But for you, my friend, as my old naval compatriots often say, 'Fair winds and following seas, and may God go with you.'"

THE END

ABOUT THE AUTHOR

WILLIAM KERR

William Kerr, whose naval career spanned 25 years of ship and shore commands, including liaison to the United States Congress on behalf of the Deputy Chief of Naval Operations (Logistics). Instrumental in the acquisition of the Navy's hospital ships, he retired at the rank of Captain before starting his writing career.

Kerr is the author of the best-selling series of action/suspense novels featuring Matt Berkeley, former Navy Special Warfare officer and security expert in the field of archeology. Originally from Mississippi and Florida, Kerr lives with his wife in Highlands Ranch, Colorado.

Made in the USA
Middletown, DE
17 May 2019